C0-AKF-837

Northern
Lights
Magic

PRESS
Box 115, Superior, WI 54880 (715) 394-9513

First Edition

Copyright 2004, Lori J. Glad

Cover design: Jillene Johnson

Cover Art: Dancing Aurora by Kathleen Conover N.W.S.
    Contact Kathleen Conover at: michstudio@aol.com

All rights reserved, including the right to reproduce this book or
portions thereof, in any form, except for brief quotations embodied in
articles and reviews, without written permission from the publisher.
This is a work of fiction. Any resemblance to real persons is purely
coincidental.

ISBN Number 1-886028-64-8

Library of Congress Catalog Card Number: 2004092666

Published by:

Savage Press
P.O. Box 115
Superior, WI 54880

Phone: 715-394-9513

E-mail: mail@savpress.com

Web Site: www.savpress.com

Printed in the USA

Northern Lights Magic

by
Lori J. Glad

Happy Mothers Day!

Lori J. Glad

5-04

Thanks

Mom and Dad

1

The highway abruptly split into four lanes, catching Kaycee by surprise. She tapped the brake and quickly scanned the green highway signs to find which exit would take her home. Her brow furrowed in concentration. She kept up with the swiftly moving traffic. The old familiarity of Duluth had become unrecognizable—the new freeway snaked past downtown while an arching overpass led traffic in three different directions.

Irritated that nothing could remain the same, not even the road to her family home, Kaycee pressed the accelerator. The sleek black Mustang surged forward up the ramp to Mesaba Avenue to take 2nd Street East. The car flew around the sharp curves past the Main Fire Hall, tires squealing in protest. She glanced at the speedometer and eased off the gas. But it was too late. There were red lights flashing in the rear view mirror.

"I can't believe this," she groaned. She maneuvered to the side of the road carefully obeying every rule of driving she could recall. "Don't the cops around here have anything better to do than harass drivers during rush hour?"

She felt foolish now that her plan had backfired. She had hurried out of work to miss the Minneapolis rush hour only to find herself smack in the middle of Duluth's rush hour and pulled over by the cops.

Kaycee looked in the mirror. Her eyes narrowed at seeing her own reflection. In her hurry to beat the Minneapolis traffic she still wore the heavy on-camera makeup and the last outfit she'd been modeling. She licked her lips, brushed her hair back with an expert flick of the wrist that sent the heavy gold bracelets she wore clicking against each other. With a deep breath she opened the car door.

With the fast-moving traffic, she cautiously stepped out

onto the black pavement. She straightened to her full height, which, in the spike heels she wore, was almost six feet. The black leather mini skirt clung to her hips as she gracefully turned to face the police officer approaching her.

Unfortunately, when Kaycee looked up, the officer still stood two inches above her. A pair of wire-rimmed reflective glasses showed a clear image of her face; and nothing of his. She felt as false as she looked. What was she doing? The thought of trying to con a police officer into not giving her a speeding ticket was tempting, but she knew she deserved the ticket.

The trooper silently watched her for a moment. His wide-rimmed hat was pulled low, shadowing his features. The only part of his face she could see was his lips stretched into a thin, disapproving frown.

"Officer, I..." Kaycee began before stumbling into silence, lowering her eyes.

She couldn't do it. Under his blank stare she felt naked, stripped of the detached air she used to protect herself. The professional model act that she put on at cocktail parties, business dinners, and walking down a runway surrounded by thousands of people. In front of this authority figure it disappeared. Right now, nothing remained of the detached Ice Princess, her unflattering nickname in the business world. Now she was just plain old Kaycee Swanson. A guilty Kaycee Swanson.

Kaycee felt the painful pricking of tears too long uncried behind her eyes. Here she was portraying every man's fantasy, from the tip of her professionally applied mascara to the black fishnet stockings and high heels. She was dressed to attract attention. She was trained so that every move attracted attention. At this moment all she wanted to do was shrivel up, crawl into her car, and have a good hard cry.

"Step back to your car, ma'am, and get into the vehicle."

Kaycee froze. "Excuse me?"

"Step back to your car and get inside," he repeated in a

clipped tone. "I will need to examine your driver's license, proof of insurance, and vehicle registration."

"Of course, officer," Kaycee said quickly. She turned, stumbled a step, and climbed into the seat. The trooper followed closely behind and stood slightly out of her line of vision.

Nervous by the abruptness of his manner, Kaycee realized she'd messed up and this guy was serious. She reached into the back seat for the well-worn denim backpack that served as her purse. She fumbled. Her hands shook. Completely miserable, she felt like a perfect fool. She found her wallet and handed her driver's license through the window. Then she leaned over and took out her registration and insurance cards from the glove box.

"There, officer," she said stiffly, angry that he succeeded in unnerving her so badly. She hid her irritation while staring out the windshield.

"About time," he said softly under his breath.

Kaycee turned an icy stare on him. Of all the nerve, she thought, wishing she could say that he was rude and obnoxious. Instead she chose to fume in silence and save herself from a more serious rebuke.

"That's the first sign of Kaycee Swanson I've seen so far," he murmured.

Kaycee's heart sank. He must have recognized her name.

I really, really don't need this right now, she thought. "When do I find out the charge, officer?" she asked briskly, anxious to get away.

The only reply was silence. The trooper bent down next to her window and handed back her documents.

"Pretty lousy picture of you on that license. I think I'd get it retaken," he said smoothly.

That was it. This time Kaycee turned to face him, her blue eyes blazing. "How dare you!" she cried. "You are the rudest—"

"Tell me, really, Kaycee," he interrupted her, "is that your real weight on your license? I don't know…140 pounds? Is that normal for a model?"

Kaycee's mouth fell open.

Then a slightly impish grin appeared at the corners of the trooper's mouth. He pulled the sunglasses down to the end of his nose and winked at her.

All of a sudden she found the right words to say. "Jimmy Zane." Her throat closed for an instant causing her to choke.

"It's been awhile, huh, Kaycee?" he said, grinning at her.

Kaycee felt color flood her cheeks as she stared at him. He looked so different, yet not different at all. The lopsided smile, those lips, and his eyes, brown liquid like malted milk.

She knew she had to say something. "How…How are you?" she finally stammered.

"I'm great. Been back in town for awhile now, but I haven't seen you around."

"No, I don't live here," she explained.

"I can tell by the way you're dressed," he said with a laugh.

Kaycee glanced dumbly down at her clothes.

"One look at you and I figured you were going to cause a traffic jam, or worse, if I didn't get you back in your car fast," he laughed again.

Kaycee watched him talk. He has the most attractive mouth, she thought. That was all she focused on.

He leaned closer. "By the way, there are no charges." His smile widened. White, even teeth shined in contrast to deeply tanned skin. "You weren't speeding… yet."

He was so close she could smell soap on his skin.

"Thanks Jimmy…Jim," she said, sounding dazed. "Is that a Duluth uniform you're wearing?"

"Minnesota State Trooper Jim Zane, my dear Kaycee, at your service," he tipped his hat with a chuckle.

Kaycee smiled. He talked the way he did in high school.

It was like the ten years since high school had never happened. They had not spoken since that awful night at the hockey tournament.

The radio attached to Jimmy's belt let out a shriek, startling them both.

He pressed the button on his shoulder mic and spoke into the receiver. He released the button and said, "Sorry I can't talk more, Kaycee, I have a call." He snapped his dark glasses back into place and replaced his hat. Instantly, he became a stranger again. Very formally he said, "I'm very sorry to hear about Grandma. She was a great lady. Maybe we'll have a chance to catch up at the funeral. Take care."

He gave her a nod and vanished back to his squad before he heard her utter a weak, "Good-bye." Seconds later the squad sped past her with a short blast from the horn.

Kaycee sat unmoving in the silent, insulated interior of her car. Slowly her body fell forward until her head rested against the steering wheel. She did not like to cry, ever. She looked terrible after she cried, and it was hard to repair the damage. Usually she swallowed her tears and continued on. It had become a habit. But there were always times like this when the frozen ball of feelings in the pit of her stomach melted.

Tears thick with salt burned her eyes, streamed down her cheeks. She was coming home for Grandma's funeral and staying composed was more difficult than she expected. And, of course, she never thought about Grandma without remembering Jimmy Zane.

2

Jimmy had been Kaycee's friend since fourth grade. During the summer before school, they met while exploring the ravine that the neighborhood creek ran through. The long, winding creek raged with rushing white water in the spring and sputtered merrily along the rocks during the summer. The area gave the pair plenty of fuel for adventure. It became everything from the Nile and the Amazon to Tarzan's home. They spent the entire summer together, and a fast and lasting friendship grew between them.

Kaycee, the impetuous half of the two, had an active mind. It raced with imagination and she created most of their games. Sometimes the games were fun, more times than not they took a dangerous turn and ended in disaster. Jimmy became adept at rescuing Kaycee from the situations she could not get out of.

One of the worst happened when Kaycee decided to swim out to a large granite rock at the mouth of the creek where it flowed into Lake Superior. They were ten-years-old and it was their first trip all the way down the creek to the lake. In many places very little water moved over the rocks, in others water with green sludge on top collected in pools. Each street had a bridge and at the water level there were long narrow tunnels made out of stone and brick to channel the water underneath. The tunnels were filled with damp, hanging moss and spider webs. By the time they reached the lake, Kaycee was hot, sweaty, and full of spider webs. To cool down and rinse off, she decided to swim ten yards out to a large exposed boulder.

Jimmy warned her that the spring run-off was freezing and that even a short swim was dangerous.

Kaycee ignored Jimmy and dove right in. Despite the shocking cold, Kaycee swam the rest of the way to the boulder and barely managed to drag herself out of the freezing water.

Watching, Jimmy knew he had to do something. He ran down the rocky shore and found a small dory hidden by a local fisherman. The dory was flat bottomed and light enough for Jimmy to drag into the water. He rowed in circles until he figured out how to use the oars. Frantic, he aimed the boat in the direction of Kaycee. He had no idea what to expect when he returned. For a second he did not see her. Kaycee had crawled into a shallow crevice of the black rock out of the wind. Her shaking body huddled in the narrow opening.

By the time they returned the dory and walked home via the streets instead of the creek bank, she was warm and her clothes had partially dried. Then her recklessness returned. She wheedled and cajoled Jimmy until he promised not to ever tell her parents. Jimmy agreed but only if she promised to listen to him next time.

Their friendship remained strong during the rest of junior high and did not change even as they started high school. They did their homework together after school and went to baseball games in the spring and soccer games in the summer. Jimmy was as familiar as her own family members.

The change in their relationship began in their junior year. The year Kaycee became caught up in high school and the new unexplored world of dating.

Ten years earlier Kaycee, at seventeen, was finally moving out of the awkward teen stage. She moved right into her first taste of the attention beauty brings. Suddenly, the boys that were completely unapproachable began to approach her. No longer did guys consider her a tomboy, this opened up an entirely new part of life.

That was when the problems with Jimmy first started.

3

K aycee turned down the cobblestone street lined with shade trees whose full branches blocked the sun. The leaves were starting to turn slightly. Traditional three-story houses stood back from the boulevard, decorated with masses of frost nipped wilting flowers. Kaycee's front tire sank into a pothole with a crunching sound. One drawback of the old section of town, the cobblestone streets were rutted and ancient. They buckled in some areas and rutted out in others making the street a hazard to a low-slung car like hers. The residents boisterously declared keeping the original cobblestone was worth it in maintaining the character of the area.

On the corner lot stood a tan three-story house with dark brown shutters and a large expanse of lawn. "Home," Kaycee sighed. She pulled over to the curb and parked the car. The street was empty. Kaycee frowned. "Why isn't anyone here?" She got out of the car and reached into the back for her bags. She tossed them over her shoulder and walked through the rusted, wrought iron gate and up the front walk. It was quiet, the only disruption an occasional call of a bird. Kaycee opened the front screen door and stepped into the cool hallway. The smell of lemon polish and baking bread hit her, followed by childish shrieks of laughter, loud voices talking, and pots and pans clanging together. Kaycee remained in the hall listening. She set her bags on the stairs. Seconds later, a small sturdy girl with flyaway blond hair tied in pigtails raced into view.

She stopped, took one look at Kaycee, and opened her mouth, letting out a wail. "Aughhh, Granma." The sound pierced Kaycee's ears. The toddler turned on her chubby bare feet and scrambled from the room.

Kaycee followed behind her niece, not surprised by Trixie's reaction.

Ellyn Swanson hurried from the kitchen wiping her hands on a towel as she bent over to listen to the youngster's cries. She looked up to exclaim, "Oh, Kaycee, it's you! I couldn't understand a word Trixie was saying."

"Hi, mom. Trixie didn't recognize me in this get up," Kaycee explained with a quick smile. She stepped forward to kiss her mother's cheek. "It's so good to be home."

"You're late, did you have trouble?"

"Not really, just a lot of delays. I left the studio without changing, but it didn't help. I can't believe how bad the traffic downtown has gotten. And what's with that horrible expressway?"

"That's been done all summer. It does help with the traffic heading up the shore, but it's an eyesore." Her mother paused and looked at her, "You're not wearing that tonight are you?"

"Mother, I would never."

"Thank goodness," Ellyn shook her head. "How am I supposed to know your taste hasn't changed. You're surrounded by this kind of thing all the time." She frowned. "I don't know, Kaycee, these outfits, they seem to get more suggestive... I know you're an adult, but please don't let Kathie see it. I'll never hear the end of it. And for heavens sake don't allow her to put it on. Your father will have a stroke."

"Your hair looks great."

Ellyn reached up and patted her bangs, "Thanks. I just had it done."

Trixie remained hiding behind Ellyn Swanson's legs peeking shyly at the stranger. Kaycee smiled at the toddler who immediately popped a fat thumb in her mouth before ducking back behind Ellyn's legs.

"Trixie, you stop treating your Auntie Kaycee like this," Ellyn gently scolded her. Trixie eyed Kaycee suspiciously and beat a hasty retreat to the kitchen.

Ellyn sighed, "I'll find her hiding under the sink. I always find her hiding there. I finally moved everything out. I was afraid she might poison herself."

Kaycee laughed. "She sounds just like her mother. I'm going upstairs to wash all this junk off my face and change. Maybe then she won't be afraid. Right now, to a two-year-old, I probably look like the wicked witch of the west."

Ellyn turned back toward the kitchen. "I think that's a good idea, honey. A shower always makes you feel more alert. I have a sink full of potatoes to peel."

Kaycee took hold of her arm before Ellyn could escape. "Will you stand still for just one minute?" she said with a frustrated laugh. "Is everything working? You're not doing too much are you?"

Ellyn, barely five-foot-three inches tall, leaned briefly against her oldest daughter and gave her a hug. "I feel like Trixie hugging you. How tall are you in those heels?"

"I don't know, tall enough I guess, and you didn't answer my questions."

"I'm all right, considering." Her words caught in her throat, then, she recovered. "People have been so kind. Mother would be amazed at how many will miss her. She always said how she outlived everyone she knew, but in her simple way she touched so many lives. It's funny how a person's funeral brings all of the people together except for the one who is being remembered. That just goes to show how a funeral is for the living."

Ellyn looked closer at Kaycee's blouse, touching the material. "What are those spots on that expensive material? Oh what a shame, but I'm sure I can get them out. Don't you bother taking this to the cleaner."

Kaycee leaned down to kiss her mother's petal smooth cheek. She said, "The company cleans it. The outfit doesn't belong to me."

"That's nice, but I know I can do it. Do you know what the stain is? That would help me get rid of it. I'll save them the money."

Kaycee shook her head. "No, mom, I'm returning it to the studio. They can clean it."

"Fine. Have it your way. You're rooming with the girls. Your sister Cyndy and Tony are supposed to arrive tonight sometime, so they will be in your old room."

Kaycee nodded. "Wow, I haven't seen Cyndy in a long time."

"No, it's been awhile since they've visited, but then it's been a while since you've been home, too. I know why Cyndy hasn't been here. She lives in Boston."

Kaycee knew her mother was waiting for an explanation. She did not have one. She looked away and said, "I'll hurry and get ready so I can help you down here before everyone arrives."

"I do expect some kind of explanation, Kaycee," Ellyn called after her.

Kaycee scooped up her bags and hurried to the second floor. A quick knock on the first bedroom door at the top of the stairs received no response, so Kaycee let herself in. She opened the door into a large room with two single beds. One side of the room was a complete shambles, clothes strewn over the bed and littered across the floor. Makeup and fingernail polishes cluttered the vanity; a sizeable pile of dirty tissues lying on the floor.

The other side of the room was a complete contrast to the chaos. Every item was in its place. A white lace bedspread without a wrinkle was home to a well-worn stuffed horse and doll. Kaycee remembered Karyn's joy on Christmas morning when she found the doll under the tree.

"Some things don't change," Kaycee thought, laughter bubbled in her throat.

Kathie, her seventeen-year-old blond bombshell sister, had always been unconcerned with menial cleaning and so she remained a slob. While Kaycee's youngest sister, Karyn, a shy fifteen-year-old, with dark brown hair and warm brown eyes had always meticulously maintained her dolls, their clothes, and accessories.

Kaycee set her suitcase on the floor and walked across the room placing her makeup case on the dresser. She saw a section had been cleared off for her and knew it was Karyn who had taken the time to provide a welcome. There was an empty drawer in the dresser left half opened to show it was available for use.

Kaycee quickly emptied her suitcase. Suddenly, she felt a twinge of anxiety about facing her sisters. What if they had gone and grown up while she was away?

Nine months had passed since her last visit. If dashing in on Christmas morning and then dashing back out the day after was considered a visit. The previous Christmas she barely saw or spoke to any of her sisters let alone Kathie and Karyn. The holidays were a busy time in the modeling industry.

The relationship Kaycee kept with her younger sisters was important to her. She felt they remained close even though she was gone so much. They wrote letters. Kaycee sent them phone cards in the mail. They called often. Karyn usually ended by begging Kaycee to come home. Kaycee remembered one conversation quite clearly. Karyn specifically said, "Granny's not doing well, and Mother wants to see you. Please try to make it home this weekend."

Then Kathie's letter arrived. "Everything around here is so dull. With Granny not feeling well, mom and dad don't want to leave her alone in the house. We have to spend all summer vacation stuck at home. Please let me come down and stay with you."

Kaycee's conscience pricked her hard. "What a fool I am to not have listened," she said out loud.

4

K aycee was just out of the shower when the bedroom door flew open banging against the wall.

"Kaycee!" Kathie shouted loudly as she flew through the door. She dropped her backpack and jumped at her older sister. Just as quickly she jumped back and exclaimed, "Aaah, you're still wet!"

Kaycee, startled by Kathie's exuberant welcome, grabbed her sister and kissed the top of her head. "You afraid of a little water?"

Kathie moved away. "Your hair is like sopping wet." She walked over to look in the closet after noticing the empty suitcase on the floor. "How long you been home?" she asked with her head inside the closet.

"About an hour." Kaycee quickly slipped into her shirt and was buttoning it when Karyn knocked and came through the open door.

"Kaycee!" she cried in delight. "I thought it was you."

She stepped into her older sister's arms and burst into tears. Astonished, Kaycee tightened her arms on the trembling shoulders of the girl and pulled her close. Kaycee met Kathie's eyes. Kathie shrugged. She did not seem surprised at her sister's behavior. Then she returned to investigating the clothes Kaycee put in the closet.

The tears lasted only a few minutes. Karyn pulled away with a shaky laugh. "I'm sorry, Kaycee, I didn't plan on doing that, but I'm so glad you're here. Mom has wanted you home." Karyn brushed tears from her eyes, sniffed loudly, and took a deep breath to compose herself.

Kaycee, with a heavy heart, studied Karyn silently. She didn't know her sister any longer. This person showing the beginnings of womanhood was a complete stranger. Not an intelligent word of comfort came into Kaycee's head.

"You soaked her shirt with tears," Kathie said.

"What?" Karyn asked.

"You didn't have to soak her with your crying the minute she finally does come home," Kathie scoffed.

Kaycee glared at Kathie. "Be quiet."

"I'm sorry, Kaycee," Karyn's face flushed a deeper shade of red. "I didn't plan on it. It just happened."

"Don't listen to Kathie," Kaycee said quickly. "She just wishes her face looked as good after she cries, especially when there's a funeral tomorrow."

"Look who's talking, Kaycee," Kathie retorted. "You can't hide you've been crying, even hours after it happened," she paused, smirking at Kaycee.

Kaycee stared in astonishment. "How did you know?"

Kathie shrugged, "Lucky guess. Why wouldn't you be crying? Everyone else around here is."

Karyn nodded in agreement. "Mom keeps busy, but she cries the whole time."

"This is the first family funeral I can remember," Kaycee murmured, "and when a person as special as Gran dies, it's doubly hard. Tell me what's been going on around here."

Kathie flopped onto her stomach across her bed and reached underneath to pull out a box of chocolates. After studying the piece of chocolate for a second, she took a bite out of the candy and slowly chewed it. "Absolutely nothing. This place is so boring."

Kaycee and Karyn just stared at her.

"What?" Kathie cried. "Do you want a piece?"

"Do you buy boxes of chocolates for yourself?" Kaycee asked with a chuckle.

"No," Kathie made a face at her and took another bite. "A boy bought these for me."

Kaycee frowned. "Who?"

"Tom MacIntyre," Karyn chimed in. "He calls twenty times a day. It's really annoying."

Kathie rolled onto her back and stretched like a lithe young cat. "Only because the phone is never for you," she said.

"Karyn...phone!" Ellyn called up the stairs.

Kaycee and Karyn started to laugh at the irony. After a moment, Kathie caught on to the joke and joined in.

Karyn flew out the door without another word. Kaycee sat down on the corner of Kathie's bed to pull on her blue jeans.

"Seriously, how is Karyn doing?" she asked Kathie. "Karyn's always been extra close to Gran."

Kathie shoved the candy back under her bed.

Kaycee teased, "What else do you have lurking under there with the dust bunnies?"

Kathie sat up and crossed her legs. She said in a hushed voice, "Karyn was the only one home that day when Granny," she paused, looking at the floor uncomfortably, "you know…when it happened."

Kaycee shook her head. "When Gran died? I had no idea. Poor Karyn. How awful for her. Why was she alone?"

"Gran went into a coma for three days."

"Mom never told me that," Kaycee complained as she pulled on her socks.

"The last day, mom decided to leave for awhile and run some errands she'd been putting off. She thought it would be okay. And besides, Karyn was here. It just happened. Right after mom left…Karyn was real calm. She called dad, and he came right home."

Kaycee clenched her eyes tightly. She remembered Gran, always busy fixing something for someone else, a smile on her face and singing Italian ditties as she baked endless batches of cookies. When she lived in her own house, she hid foil-wrapped chocolate balls for the grandchildren to find. Every one of the grandchildren, when they reminisced about Grandma's house, remembered that. Kaycee knew Granny had lived a full life, but still found it hard to let her go.

"You know what Karyn said about it? She said Gran got a glow on her face that looked real peaceful and that was it."

The two sat in silence.

"I miss her, Kaycee," Kathie said softly, her voice heavy with tears. "You haven't been around much since Gran moved in. It's been great. The cookie jar was always full. She ate her popcorn with tons of butter on it. It tasted so good that way, and there was always somebody around who would listen to you talk even if you didn't have anything much to say."

"Sounds wonderful," Kaycee said with a slight laugh. "Popcorn with tons of butter." She stood, careful to keep her back to Kathie to keep her sister from seeing how upset she was. She reached for the hairbrush and began to pull it through her thick hair.

"Sometimes when Gran baked, she'd forget some of the ingredients, so the cookies looked really funny and were hard as rocks."

Kaycee laughed again. "I bet mom made dad eat them like she used to do when we would bake for him? Poor dad."

Kathie laughed. "No way. She didn't want to hurt Gran's feelings, so she'd throw them away when Gran wasn't looking. He would've broken a tooth on one."

Both of them burst out laughing.

Karyn returned, watching them laughing with a bemused look on her face. "What's with you two?"

"You have to sleep on the floor," Kathie changed the subject.

"If that's okay with you, Karyn?" Kaycee asked her sister. "Or you can bunk with Kathie, but I don't think anyone would want to do that."

"Kaycee's afraid to have you sleep with her," Kathie explained. "She doesn't want to mistake you for one of her boyfriends."

"Hey!" Kaycee interrupted sharply. "That's enough, Kathie. You've gone too far and it isn't funny."

Kathie showed no remorse as she made a face at her sister. "I was just teasing."

Kaycee shook her head. "Guess what, that kind of teasing isn't funny."

"I knew she was teasing, Kaycee," Karyn said primly. "I'll sleep on the floor on my side of the room just in case Kathie has bugs under her bed."

"You'll probably be safe except something may carry you under Kathie's bed. Who knows what's living under there eating her box of chocolates."

"You're just jealous because you can't have candy," Kathie said becoming sulky.

Kaycee laughed. "Me? I eat what I want. Chocolate's something that doesn't appeal to me often."

Kathie eagerly sat forward. "Did you bring an outfit from work? Can I see it, Kaycee? Please?"

Kaycee knew she would regret it but nodded yes. "Just be sure you remember to rehang everything when you're done."

Kathie looked offended as she jumped off the bed. "Of course I will."

With a wary look at the clothes thrown everywhere in the room, she murmured, "Right, look at your mess. I don't want to waste my time at home ironing."

"Not with mom here you won't," Kathie laughed. "She won't let anyone touch her iron. 'I can do it much faster, dear, you run along.' " Kathie mimicked their mother so closely Kaycee couldn't help laughing at her. "I'm going down to help mom," she announced.

Kathie glanced at her. "Really, oh...well, I'll be down in a little bit to help."

"Remember, Kathie," Kaycee instructed in her best mom voice, "nothing low cut. Dad won't go for it."

"You're such a party pooper," Kathie stuck her tongue out.

5

Kaycee gave her younger sister a hard look. With her blond hair tousled in an appealing way, her bright blue eyes and contagious smile, she saw the face that could easily be her replacement in the modeling business. As Kathie pulled clothes off the hangers, Kaycee turned to Karyn who was showing signs of joining Kathie in trying on the dress clothes Kaycee had brought for the funeral. "Karyn, you go ahead and try on whatever you like, but please make sure everything is hung up when you've finished."

Karyn clapped her hands and darted forward, her face glowing. "Of course, thanks so much, Kaycee."

Kaycee quietly closed the door on the giggling girls and shook her head with a smile. Her own looks had matured to where the demand for her face in photo shoots was beginning to slow. Her modeling job for the department store, and its many nationwide chains, had been securely locked up in a contract that expired at the end of the season. It did not include the summer style shows. After that, she had to face the fact that the department store would not negotiate a new contract. She was probably going to be unemployed. One choice for the future was to take a chance with freelance modeling. Freelancing was risky and though, for a time, money would not be a problem, Kaycee felt incompetent to market herself.

Kaycee paused at the top of the main staircase to listen to the activity below. The sound of voices hummed. This was not unusual for her parent's house, which always seemed to be filled with people and noise. At holiday time it became almost chaotic with her two married sisters, Maris and Cyndy, and their families. Kathie and Karyn's friends stopped by uninvited just as Kaycee's high school friends had been inclined to do. There always seemed to be fresh cookies and cocoa available in the Swanson home. After the quiet of her apartment, the activity was a shock, but the shock wore off quickly.

Today, Kaycee welcomed noise and activity. It kept at bay her guilt about not seeing Gran before she died. She ran down the stairs. The thought of answering personal questions did not discourage her. Taking a deep breath, she opened the swinging kitchen door. Immediately the smell of food and the heat of too many bodies in one place struck Kaycee. In the thick of things, Ellyn stood at the refrigerator handing out bowls of salad to be brought into the dining room. This looked just like one of the family holidays.

"Kaycee, darling!" Aunt Florence squealed with delight. "Come here and let me take a look at you. I page through those magazines you work for and cannot find one picture of you." She smiled, the extra flesh on her face separating into deep folds. Aunt Florence was not really Kaycee's aunt. She was Gran's cousin but always insisted on being called Aunt. Flo was from Ellyn's side of the family, so she was short but much stockier. Her hair was rinsed bright blue over the gray. Nobody in the family knew if her hair was real or a wig. "Tell me, Kaycee, are you still in the modeling business or have you found something else?"

Kaycee placed a bright smile on her face when she accepted her aunt's peck on the cheek. She pulled away to say, "No, Aunt Flo, I haven't found anything else. I'm mostly modeling for catalogs now, not magazines."

"Have you found a young man yet? I hear successful women intimidate men. Is that why you haven't had any luck?"

Kaycee nodded, smiled and said, "I'm still single."

Aunt Flo frowned. Her small mouth became lost in the wrinkles around it. "Oh dear, that's so sad. At your age, too. If you want to meet some down to earth men, my JoAnn knows all kinds. She works at Jacoubi Enterprises downtown. She tells me there's so many eligible bachelors working there. I guess they move from the Twin Cities to work up here. Really it's no problem. I'll ask her tonight."

Kaycee edged away, hastily cutting her off. "Thank JoAnn for me, but right now I'm too busy for any kind of relationship."

She spun around and intercepted Ellyn carrying a tray of sandwiches. Ellyn gratefully handed it to her. "Kaycee, please set this on the table."

Kaycee turned to hold the tray in front of Aunt Flo's face. "Here, Aunt Flo, you best eat something before we have to leave. Who knows when the wake will end." Aunt Flo proved to be easily diverted and helped herself to a sandwich.

Kaycee delivered the tray, setting it on the family dining room table that might have groaned with the weight of the many full plates covering every square inch. The elegant dining room was filling with visitors. Kaycee glanced around the dining room and saw a few familiar elderly faces among the many guests in the room. As she moved between the dining room and kitchen to replace refreshments, she overheard many wispy voices telling fond stories of Gran.

A stream of people continued to walk through the front door. Some carried food; others brought coolers filled with cans of pop and beer. In some ways it did not seem like anything but a big family reunion, certainly not a gathering for the death of a loved one. Kaycee greeted aunts, uncles, and cousins she had only seen a few times in her life. The time for the visitation crept up, and soon the house began to empty as people left for the funeral home.

Kaycee was in the kitchen filling the dishwasher with dirty dishes when her father, Stewart Swanson, walked through the back door from the garage. He caught sight of her immediately and gave her a tired smile.

"Kaycee, you made it." He held his arms open. Kaycee stepped into the warmth of his embrace and hid her face in the collar of his coat. He tightened his arms around her shoulders and gave her a deep, heartening squeeze. Never did she feel as safe as when her father held her like this. After a moment he released her and patted her shoulder.

"The drive home went okay?"

Kaycee nodded. "You look tired, dad. Are you all right?"

"Thank you for asking. I'm fine," he replied. "Your mother isn't sleeping well. I guess it affects me, too."

Kaycee opened the oven and took out her father's plate of hot food. Her mother never failed to fix him a plate and put it to warm in the oven when he was going to be late coming home.

"I'll just take this upstairs with me," he said, brightening slightly at the appetizing aroma of his roast beef dinner. "It's late, almost time for the wake. I need a shower before then. Is there any coffee, honey?"

She saw the coffee machine was on and the pot empty.

Kaycee kissed his cheek. "I'll bring you a cup of fresh coffee when it's ready."

He touched her cheek. "That will hit the spot. Maybe then I can stay awake."

Kaycee was still smiling when her father shuffled up the maid's staircase. He, too, had not changed much since she last saw him. It was comforting to find her parents still the same despite what was happening. She made coffee then filled the sink with soapy water to wash some of the pots and serving dishes. She wondered where her younger sisters were.

She washed dishes until the coffee was ready when Ellyn walked in from the dining room carrying more. "Whew! It's certainly warm for this time of year," Ellyn commented as she piled them in the sink.

"Where are Karyn and Kathie?" Kaycee asked. She poured a cup of coffee and put the cup in her mother's hand. "This is for dad," she explained.

"He's home? I was beginning to wonder if he would make it at all." Ellyn paused, deep in thought. "Last I saw Karyn was outside saying good-bye to some friends, and Kathie I haven't seen at all." Ellyn moved toward the back stairs. "When did your dad sneak in?"

"About twenty minutes ago."

"You better get moving. Leave the rest of this until we get back. When you see Kathie please light a fire under her. If she makes us late tonight, I don't know what I'll do to her," Ellyn instructed as she walked up the back stairway.

Kaycee followed her mother, went into the girl's bedroom, and looked around to be sure nothing of hers was lying on the floor. Her clothes seemed to have been replaced in the right order, so she dressed, touched up her makeup, and went downstairs.

Her dad was standing at the foot of the main stairs. "Karyn's ready, so we'll take her with us," he said.

"Will you wait for Kathie?" Ellyn asked Kaycee, straightening her coat. "I cannot begin to imagine what takes that girl so long to get ready. She is always behind."

"Sure. I'll wait," Kaycee agreed, but fretted once her parents were gone.

"Darn it, Kathie," she muttered, pacing back and forth in the hallway. She looked at her watch.

"Ready and waiting in the front hall," she yelled up the stairs.

No reply.

"Promptness is a virtue," she yelled a few seconds later.

Kaycee impatiently checked her watch. "We are now officially late," she called, exasperated. "I do not believe I am late for Grandma's visitation. Kathie, this is it."

"What?" Kathie asked, walking down the stairs as she clasped a bracelet around her slim wrist. "Gee, Kaycee, get a grip. It isn't like we're going to be missed for awhile anyway."

6

Kaycee glared at her and slowly appraised her outfit remembering what her mother warned her about Kathie's taste in clothes. The skirt was above the knees a decent length and the pale blue sweater she carried looked suitable. With a glance down at her own plain dark blue top and skirt with white piping down the collar, she felt like the older sister. As she spun on her heel and walked out the front door, she muttered under her breath, "I guess I better get used to feeling old."

Kathie, her pace unhurried, followed. She slipped her bare arms through the sleeves of the sweater exclaiming when she saw Kaycee's car, "Wow, Kaycee, this is a great car! A convertible. When did you get it?"

"I bought it in June. Put your seatbelt on," Kaycee said calmly as she started the engine.

Kathie scrambled to get inside caressing the dashboard before she reached over to begin pressing knobs on the radio. "A CD player and everything. Let's put the top down. It's such a beautiful night, probably the last we'll have. Come on, Kaycee, please?"

The car eased away from the curb. Kaycee hit the brake, letting out a grieved sigh. "You are such a pest." She pointed to a clip on the interior of the car next to the front windshield. "Pull that."

Kathie squealed with delight. "All right! You're the best."

Kaycee pulled the clasp on her side and then hit the control for the roof. A whine sounded and the top slowly began to collapse behind them. She drove away.

"Come on, Kaycee, give it some speed," Kathie pleaded. "Sports cars are supposed to squeal around corners."

"Really, and where did you hear this revelation?"

"Billy, this guy from school, sometimes gets his father's

sports car. Geez, I hope some of my friends see me in this car," Kathie said, watching the traffic closely.

"I thought Tom was buying you chocolates, now this Billy. You're a busy girl."

"They're both just friends. Don't start parenting me," Kathie said.

Kaycee glanced at her. Kathie had just echoed something she, herself, had thrown at Jimmy Zane in high school. She winced at the unpleasant memory but could replay it sentence for sentence. "You're jealous of Tod Mathisen, Jimmy Zane," Kaycee had taunted him. "You wish the girls at school flocked around you like they do Tod. He has everything, a great sports car, he's popular. He can do anything he wants."

Jimmy shook his head. He said soberly, "You're dead wrong, Kaycee. Tod is nothing more than a troublemaker. Getting involved with him is putting you right smack in the middle of a bad group. You're too smart for that. I just hope you don't get hurt before it sinks into that thick skull of yours."

"Will you quit trying to be my parent? I can take care of myself."

"Like I warned you before, Kaycee, be careful. Tod's ideas of fun are a lot wilder than anything you've ever done."

Kathie interrupted her reminiscence. "Kaycee, we should have turned back there. Don't you remember your way around Duluth?"

"Of course I do. I wasn't paying attention, that's all," Kaycee defended herself.

"Right!" Kathie scoffed, giggling as Kaycee pulled an illegal u-turn and sped back to the funeral home.

7

The parking lot of Daughtery's Funeral Home had one of the best views of Lake Superior, and Kaycee took her time putting the top up. Kathie had already disappeared into the funeral home.

The autumn color in the leaves of the trees across the lake was just beginning to show. They speckled the deep green horizon against the dark blue water. An ache filled Kaycee's chest, a feeling that only returned when she came home and then battled with her looming departure.

The beauty of the Duluth area, the stillness of the coming night, the gentle rush of leaves in the wind, all of this was the feeling of being home—truly home. Until now, she had not been able to put her finger on what was bothering her. She was homesick. That was why she kept putting off visits here. She was homesick and did not want to admit it, not even to herself. After ten years away, she wanted to come home. She missed the people who were important parts of her life. She missed the daily interaction with them and mostly she missed being taken care of.

Maybe she was finally growing up. Jimmy Zane immediately came to mind again. He'd been born mature. Although, Kaycee was not the only one who escaped from Duluth right after high school graduation, Jimmy had done his own disappearing act. Where had he been? What had he been doing?

Kaycee walked down the hallway of the funeral home. She wrinkled her nose at the strange smell and did not want to think about what caused it. The doors were all shut until she reached the back of the building. She recognized the people standing in the hallway talking in loud whispers. There was no reason to whisper, yet she knew she would do the same. Something about the place forced you into using a quiet voice. The first person Kaycee saw standing inside the long carpeted room lined with folding chairs was her sister Maris, who was holding Trixie.

Maris was a slightly softer version of Kathie, only with Ellyn's brown eyes. In looks, Kathie, Karyn, and Maris favored their mother's Italian side. Kaycee and Cyndy were the two with black hair and strong features of the Swanson side of the family.

Maris hurried over to Kaycee carrying Trixie on one hip. "Kaycee! Finally! I thought I was never going to see you," Maris cried and threw her free arm around Kaycee's shoulder. "You look absolutely wonderful. We all thought you'd be pulling your hair out because of Kathie. Nobody moves slower than that girl." Maris rolled her eyes in the direction of Kathie.

Kaycee shook her head. "She wasn't too bad."

"I heard my little Trixie threw a fit with you this afternoon. I'm sorry about that. Two-year-olds have minds of their own. It takes a little getting used to. Wait a minute. I'm going to give her to Will. I have to talk to you."

"Where is Will?"

Maris frowned and searched the room. "Oh, I see him he's over there with dad. It looks like they're talking to the priest. It must be time for the service. Don't you take one step away from here, Kaycee, I'll be right back."

Kaycee nervously played with the strap of her purse. Slowly, she looked around the room. There was the casket, and it was open. In front of the casket, a small portable kneeler was set up and someone was kneeling on it. Kaycee was surprised to see it was Kathie. Slowly, Kathie stood and walked over to where Ellyn and several other people were standing by a poster board filled with a collage of pictures.

"There," Maris returned out of breath. "It's amazing how heavy that little girl gets after awhile. She's so tired right now I don't think she could stand if I put her down."

Kaycee looked at her younger sister and asked suddenly,

"How do you do it?"

"Do what?"

"Deal with a small child while all of this is going on? I feel so worthless, Maris. I never once came home to see Gran, and now I don't think I can even make it over to her casket to say a prayer. I can't believe you can deal with Gran's death, a two-year-old, and a husband."

Maris slipped her arm around Kaycee's waist. "The great part about being family is that you don't have to do anything, Kaycee. Nobody knows what to do or how to act. The best we can do is to be here to help mom and dad. If you can't go up to the casket, nobody's going to say a word…although, for your peace of mind, you better make an effort. The way you're feeling about not seeing Gran, it might be best if you say good-bye now when you have the chance."

Kaycee looked aghast. "I don't know if I can. I've never seen anyone in a casket before."

"Kaycee, you really have nothing to feel guilty about, if you don't want to go up there then don't. Come on, let's go find out what's going on." Maris pointed across to the front corner of the large room at Ellyn, Kathie, and Karyn.

People were coming into the room. Many chairs were already occupied. Kaycee wondered if finding a seat later was going to be a problem.

Walking across the room, Maris and Kaycee were joined by dad and Will who carried the now sleeping Trixie over his shoulder. "Hi, Kaycee," Will said quietly.

Kaycee leaned over to press a kiss against the baby fine skin of Trixie's rosy cheek. "Hi, Will, you must have the magic touch to get her to sleep so fast."

Will shook his head. "Didn't you hear her fussing? I finally had to take her outside, that's where she fell asleep."

Maris moved closer to her husband to whisper, "Who cares where she fell asleep, just be quiet so she doesn't wake up until the service is over."

Father Mike signaled for the people standing around in groups to find a seat. The funeral director ushered the family out into the hall. Kaycee found herself pressed to the back of the room by the large windows facing out onto Third Street. Bright light from the setting sun danced on the lacey curtains. Kaycee did not see Maris anywhere, but Stewart was right across from her. Kathie stood next to him.

"What's going on?" Kathie whispered.

"We have to wait out here for a moment," Stewart told her. He reached over to tap Karyn on the shoulder. He said softly, "Karyn come over here with me and Kathie." He looked around the room and saw Kaycee. Kaycee and Stewart were both taller than most of the people in the little room. They could see each other without much difficulty; Stewart's blue eyes were so like her own. He smiled at her and asked in a stage whisper, "Are you all right?"

Kaycee nodded, yes. Just to have her family close by gave her a feeling of warmth inside.

Stewart said, "I haven't seen Cyndy and Tony, have you? Otherwise, I take it they haven't come into town yet. Have you heard anything?"

Kaycee shook her head and said, "I didn't bring my cell phone."

The director came back and told them it was time to return to the main room. Everyone moved forward, filing in to sit in the first rows. Kaycee glanced at the people seated and recognized several of them from earlier at the house. She sat down in the first vacant seat she saw and looked up to see the casket was directly across from her and still open. A small, metal crucifix hung from the inside lid right above Gran's head. Kaycee looked away. She was seated in the very place that made her most uncomfortable. A hand reached out and clasped her hand. It was Ellyn. Kaycee grabbed on and held tight. Aunt Katrina, Ellyn's younger sister, sat on her other side. Both Ellyn and Katrina had thought to bring tissues.

When Father Mike began speaking, they both began to dab at their eyes. Kaycee fiercely concentrated on the priest and not on Gran.

When the short prayer service ended, Kaycee attempted to slip away but she was penned in by the surge of people who wished to speak to Ellyn and Aunt Kat. Kaycee, unable to do anything but be patient, could only wait. The need to escape burned within. Just as she was about to rush away, a hand on her arm stopped her. It was her mother. Kaycee looked down into Ellyn's tear-filled eyes.

Ellyn whispered in a soft voice, "Please, will you come with me and say good-bye?"

Kaycee's heart jumped into her throat. The words, "No, please, please don't make me do this, mommy. I don't want to see Granny dead," came to mind. Numbly Kaycee allowed her mother to lead her. Once there, Ellyn pulled her down onto the kneeler. Kaycee looked and saw a perfect replica of her grandmother. A feeling of relief washed over her. It wasn't Gran. Not the Gran she knew. The beautiful spirit of the warm caring woman who filled so much of her childhood with joy had flown. The spirit was gone and all that was left was not frightening. Kaycee folded her hands and bowed her head in prayer, not for Gran, but for the whole family. It was going to take time to adjust to life without her.

8

K aycee stood outside the house in the warm darkness listening to the sound of dogs barking. Her father's station wagon pulled up and parked behind her Mustang. Kaycee walked over to the passenger door and opened it. Ellyn stood up with a shallow sigh. "I'm glad to be home, finally we have a moment to ourselves." Once inside the house, they remained quiet. Even as Kathie and Karyn helped to clean up the mess left by the pre-visitation relatives, the two girls acted unusually subdued.

Karyn gave a huge yawn as she closed the curtains in the kitchen.

Stewart said to Karyn, "Go to bed kiddo, Kaycee and I will help mom. We need to be up early with everybody having to shower."

"I'll be last," Kathie piped in.

Stewart laughed, "That's a first from you, my girl. You two get to bed."

Kaycee walked into the kitchen carrying dirty glasses. "Where am I sleeping? What's going on with Cyndy's plane, has anyone heard?"

Stewart walked over to the refrigerator and opened it to look over the contents. He said over his shoulder, "Cyndy called on Maris's cell phone while we were at the funeral home. They won't be coming in until tomorrow morning. There's some hold-up with their flight. The airline sent them home, said they couldn't take off tonight. Boston has become extra strict with regulations. It slows everything down."

"That's awful," Ellyn cried. "Did Cyndy think they'd find a flight tomorrow? The funeral is at nine o'clock in the morning. They'll have to leave in the middle of the night to make it on time."

Closing the fridge door, he said, "Worrying won't change

anything. They'll do the best they can." He shrugged. "Kaycee, you get your old room, at least for tonight."

Kaycee yawned. "Karyn won't have to sleep on the floor. Dad be sure to tell her when you go upstairs."

"How did you know that's where I'm heading right now?" He walked over to give Kaycee a kiss on the top of her head.

"I'm a mind reader. See you in the morning."

Stewart walked slowly up the back stairs.

Ellyn silently began to fill the dishwasher. "I'm shocked at how tired I am. I don't know if it's the stress or the people."

Kaycee's head throbbed and the last thing she wanted to do was wash dirty pans. "Mom, go upstairs. I can finish down here. It won't take me very long."

"Don't be silly, honey. It will go twice as fast with the two of us. I want to talk to you anyway. What did Jimmy Zane have to say? It was so good of him to come tonight. Especially since so many years have gone by since he saw Mother." She glanced at Kaycee. "I thought his special effort might have been for your benefit."

Kaycee gave her a blank look. "I never saw him."

"What? He arrived right after we did. How could you have missed seeing him?"

Kaycee frowned and said impatiently, "Because I wasn't there. Kathie made me at least a half an hour late. He must've left before I even got there."

Ellyn smiled, "Don't get so upset, he promised me he was coming to the funeral tomorrow. I think he said he was going to be there with his dad. I'm surprised Derek is in town. He travels so much with his job." Ellyn slammed the dishwasher shut and reached over to pat Kaycee's arm. "You'll be able to talk to Jimmy tomorrow. Tonight was rather difficult to face, but I think because of it, we're all a little better prepared. I'm glad Jimmy's living in town again. I always thought it was such a shame you two drifted apart. He was a good influence on you. I didn't worry as much when Jimmy was with you."

"He pulled me over when I was coming into town today."

"He's been back in Duluth for two years," Ellyn said.

"You never told me that. Why?"

"I didn't? How odd. I'm not sure when I found out or who told me. It was probably Maris. Will knows Jimmy from high school. I think they played football together. Did he give you a ticket? I can imagine how surprised he was to see you."

"No, he didn't give me a ticket. I wasn't speeding. He knew it was me before he stopped me. All he wanted to do was say hi. I wouldn't have known he lived here again if he hadn't told me."

"I'm sorry, honey. It wasn't like it was a big secret."

Kaycee shrugged. "I only wondered if you did it because of the bad memories."

"Why would there be any bad memories where he's concerned? He was your best friend for longer than anyone else. I'd think you'd be delighted he moved back to Duluth. It's the best place to raise children. Maybe Jimmy has found someone he wants to marry and settle down with."

Kaycee glared at her and hastily demanded, "Well, has he?"

Ellyn laughed. "Not that I know of. I was just guessing. I told you tonight I talked to him for about fifteen minutes. He never mentioned a fiancée, and he was definitely alone." She covered her mouth, yawning. "I'm going to bed or tomorrow will be impossible. Don't stay up too late." She turned to Kaycee and kissed her on the cheek.

"Good night, mom. I'll be upstairs in a few minutes."

"I'm so glad you're here with us. It's such a shame about Cyndy and Tony. Your dad already locked up so you don't have to worry about doing that."

Kaycee watched Ellyn disappear up the back stairs before she turned to the sink. With a sigh, she pushed up her sleeves. Her body was tired, but her mind raced. She filled the sink with hot water and soap and began scrubbing pans.

So Jimmy Zane had come to the funeral home and she missed him. The deep feeling of disappointment surprised her. After ten years, why was she fretting about not seeing him? How ridiculous.

When she finished the pans and wiped down the counter, she took two aspirin. Her head hurt worse than before. What she needed was sleep. To maintain any semblance of control tomorrow, sleep was absolutely necessary.

9

After spending the night tossing and turning, Kaycee gave up on sleep. Whether the unfamiliar mattress or her jumbled feelings were keeping her awake, she did not know. When there was enough morning light for her to see, she left the bed and got dressed.

The rest of the family remained sleeping, so Kaycee let herself out the front door into the brisk morning. She walked down the silent street for several blocks before turning back. When she walked up the front porch, she could see the curtains were still shut. Kaycee glanced at her watch thinking, "How odd that mom's still sleeping."

She opened the door and walked into the kitchen, opening the curtains first before she did anything else. Sunlight streamed in the three big beautiful windows dad had installed. "What a beautiful day," she thought, looking out onto the deck. She watched the chickadees and sparrows flit between the two empty bird feeders searching for food. Kaycee debated whether she should fill the feeders first, but decided right now, coffee was more important. She started the coffee brewing in the percolator. Her father preferred coffee perked to coffee made in a coffee machine, so they still used a traditional percolator. In the refrigerator was a bowl of muffin batter. It was just like when Kaycee lived at home. Her mother made a triple batch of muffin batter on Monday so they could have fresh muffins before school. Ellyn still carried on the tradition. Kaycee reached in and took the bowl out to begin spooning the batter into the muffin pan and then she added a small handful of fresh blueberries. Her actions were slow and messy. Her proficiency in the kitchen had disappeared since she moved away. She rarely cooked. The only time she baked was when she was home. Baking was never as easy as it looked when her mother did it. She placed the full pan in the warm oven to bake. Then she undertook the task of cleaning up the mess she had made.

The telephone on the wall rang. Kaycee ignored it, hoping somebody upstairs would answer. Finally, she walked over muttering, "Obviously, nobody else in the house wants to answer it." Lifting the receiver she said, "Hello?" The timer for the muffins went off. "Hi, Maris, hold on," Kaycee said. She balanced the phone under her chin and opened the oven to reach in to pull out the pan. "Ouch!" she cried when her wrist touched the hot top rack. The phone crashed to the floor. "Wait a minute, Maris, don't talk," she cried, chasing the phone as it skittered across the floor. "Sorry about that. I dropped you. What? What did you say?" She held the phone with one hand and the oven mitt with the other while fishing in the oven for the pan. "Trixie did what? Do you think she has the flu?"

With a sigh, Kaycee set the pan on the stovetop. "I don't know, Maris. Trixie wouldn't go near me. I didn't give her the flu. Let me call mom to the phone." Kaycee covered the receiver and yelled up the stairs, "Mother, phone."

She was beyond caring if anyone in the house was still asleep. They had no right sleeping so peacefully when she was in the kitchen surrounded by chaos. Kaycee fixed another pan of muffins and tidied up the kitchen.

Several minutes later, Ellyn walked down the stairs to say in a cheerful voice, "It certainly smells wonderful down here. Fresh muffins, just what your father was asking for, Kaycee. You *are* a mind reader."

Kaycee looked up at her mother. Digging at the muffins with a spoon, she cried, "Look at this mess, I forgot to grease the pan."

"They look fine, dear, and I'm sure they taste delicious."

"Did you answer the phone?" Kaycee asked.

"Your father is talking to your sister. She always finds a crisis of some kind in the morning."

Kaycee put the spoon down and sucked on her burn. Again, the phone rang. "I am not answering that thing," she declared. "The last time, I burned myself."

"Poor thing," Ellyn said as she stacked a plate with the muffins and set it on a tray with two cups of coffee and a plate with butter. "Your father and I will be downstairs as soon as we're ready for the funeral. Please keep the phone at bay if you can, dear, unless of course it's Cyndy or Tony."

Kaycee frowned. "I don't—"

"I knew you would. Thank you, sweetie."

Kaycee stood watching her mother disappear up the stair-well as the timer went off for the second pan of muffins. The phone began to ring again and she threw her hands in the air before rushing to the oven. She answered six calls from people wanting to know when the funeral began. She cleaned the second mess she'd made and stacked the muffins on the counter. She left the room, running upstairs before the phone rang again.

"Shower's open," she heard Karyn yell, followed by a door slamming.

Kaycee dashed to the bathroom and took a cool shower. Her clothes were still in the girls' room so, wrapped in a huge blue terry cloth towel, she went to the girls' door and, knocking first, she opened it. The bedroom looked even messier than before. "What's going on?" she exclaimed.

Karyn emerged from the walk-in closet and said, "Hurri-cane Kathie hit. She's trying to find an outfit for the funeral, and watch out, she still hasn't found anything."

Kaycee hurried over to the closet and declared, "She's not wearing my dress, and this time I'm not waiting for her. If she's late, she can walk to the church."

"I'm dressed so I'll see you downstairs," Karyn said. She picked up a half eaten, slightly overdone muffin off the dresser and bit off a big bite, then stepped over the mess on Kathie's side of the floor and left the room without a backward look.

Kaycee gave a sigh and reached into the closet to take out her black dress. One tip she learned from being a professional model that she truly appreciated, and from Kaycee's point of view there were few, she could dress, fix her hair, and apply her makeup in twenty minutes flat. Of course when she was working on the set, makeup and hair professionals redid everything. Kaycee had learned enough to do an adequate job herself. When she was finished getting ready, she left the room without looking back just as Karyn had done.

10

A t the Cathedral, the somber tones from the huge pipe organ in the music loft filled the vaulted ceiling. Walking down the aisle with her family, Kaycee kept her eyes lowered. The beautiful voice of the soloist who sang her grandmother's favorite song from mass, along with the organ music, was stirring. Kaycee kept her eyes focused on the floor while trying to block out the ache in her heart. For the first time in her life she had seen her mother cry. Not just tears, but helpless sobs that burst out from deep inside. Ellyn clung to Stewart looking like she had no strength left to help herself. They followed directly behind the casket, moving down the long aisle and out of the church. Kaycee looked away, unable to keep her own tears under control while watching the helplessness of her mother.

Kaycee walked slowly down the aisle with Kathie and Karyn on either side. Her tears had dried, but the two younger girls were sobbing and hung their heads, hiding their faces behind their long hair. Kaycee wished there was something of comfort she could say, but her mind remained blank. She glanced behind and saw Maris carrying Trixie, who was fast asleep. The little girl lying on her mother's shoulder looked like an angel. For a moment, the sight of the peaceful sleeping child blocked out her sadness and Kaycee smiled. "The old die, but the new are born," words from an Alan Jackson song, went through her mind.

At that moment, Kaycee saw Jimmy Zane. He stood tall, almost military style, and he looked so handsome, so familiar, she felt a thrill of excitement and her smile widened. He had shown up. He was here. Now she could talk to him. For some reason, Kaycee felt it was important to talk to Jimmy today.

His expression was odd. He looked puzzled. Kaycee wondered what was wrong. Their eyes met briefly, and she wanted to immediately stop and talk to him but she was swept along as the family processed out. Karyn began sobbing uncontrollably and Kaycee put her arm around her suffering sister. Kathie took Karyn's hand, and the three girls hurried across the windy parking lot. But, in her mind, Kaycee wanted to be talking to Jimmy.

Back at the church after the burial, while food was being served, Kaycee went in search of Jimmy. She saw him sitting at a table crowded with people and tried to get across the room to talk to him. Every three steps in his direction another person would stop her and insist on telling her their memories of Gran. She tried to find him again as the crowd thinned out, but he was already gone.

11

Kaycee sped home along Sixth Street, fuming with irritation because Jimmy left without talking to her. Kathie and Karyn were in the car with her, so she controlled the emotion. She thought she had learned to hide her feelings, but at this moment she struggled to conceal her exasperation from her sisters. Nothing went right today, she thought, and it's all Jimmy Zane's fault.

Thinking back, she thought about where the whole problem started. It was at the cemetery. He had stood close enough to the family to hear the priest but next to the road. The wind ruffed his thick brown hair as he stood with his hands behind his back staring at the ground, his lean face grim. She had fought against a rush of longing to be near him. What was it about him that brought out this feeling? Was it the safety of the past? Jimmy represented a carefree time in her life, with no deaths. If she recaptured the past, there would be no pink casket to deal with now. Oh, how badly she wished to bring back those untroubled times to hide in. Listening to the sniffling and sobs of her family, she could not leave them and rush over to Jimmy, not now while the final blessing was being said. Slowly, the feeling of desperation faded and all she felt was empty.

Then at the church, Ellyn had walked by and Kaycee asked, "Mom, did Jimmy say good-bye to you yet?"

"You missed him again? How strange. It's almost like the two of you are actually avoiding each other."

It had never occurred to her that Jimmy might be avoiding her, and that caused the annoyance she now felt.

Back in the present, Karyn interrupted her thoughts, asking from the back seat, "Kaycee, did you see that tall, good-looking guy at the church? He looked about your age. Was he a friend of yours?"

The comment was so out of character, both Kathie and Kaycee turned to stare at her in surprise.

"The guy with brown hair who was standing like a soldier? Do you know him, Kaycee?" Kathie repeated with a laugh. "Of course she knows him, that's Jimmy Zane."

Kaycee glanced at Kathie and demanded, "How come you sound so smug? What do you know about Jimmy Zane?"

Kathie shook her head at her sister. "Oh really, Kaycee, did you think because you dumped him none of us ever saw him again. He only avoided coming to the house when you were home."

Kaycee stared out the windshield, then mumbled, "I never dumped him."

Kathie smirked. "That's not what Maris told me, but who cares? That's ancient history. Why were you avoiding him today?"

Kaycee snapped back, "Me avoiding him? Are you kidding? I tried all day to talk to him. I think he was avoiding me. And after he made such an issue about stopping me on the road just to say hi, what is with him?"

Startled, Kathie burst out, "He stopped you, when he was working? Did you get a ticket?" She laughed.

Kaycee shot her a dark glare. "No!"

"Who is he? An old boyfriend?" Karyn interrupted.

"Goodness, no! He's an old friend, that's all. When we were kids, we had some great times together. But during high school, we found different friends and drifted a part. I haven't seen him since high school."

Kathie shrugged, inspecting her fingernails. "He's been working as a trooper around here since I was a sophomore, so it must be two years. Karyn you *have* to remember him. He was always hanging around the house."

Karyn shrugged. "No, I don't remember."

Kaycee asked Kathie, "Do you know where he went to school?"

Kathie paused, enjoying the limelight. "Let me think. First, tell me why you're so interested in what happened to a guy you couldn't stand, or at least that's what Maris told me you said. And why don't you ask Jimmy yourself? It's allowed. Girls can call guys in the modern age."

"Don't believe everything Maris tells you. No way am I calling him. It's been almost ten years since I've seen him. I just want to know what he did once he left Duluth. Spit it out."

"You're going to have to let me borrow your car tonight, or I won't tell," Kathie bargained.

"No way! Keep your information to yourself. I'll just ask Maris."

"Maris? Okay, okay, I'll tell you," Kathie said. She rushed on, "Will talks to Jimmy once in awhile. Jimmy went into the Army and flew helicopters. Then he was a cop down south somewhere."

"South where? Southern Minnesota?"

Kathie shook her head. "No," she declared impatiently. "South, south. Like New Mexico or Arizona. No wait, Texas. I think it was Texas."

Kaycee had not expected that.

"After the Army, he flew helicopters fighting forest fires in California and then moved back here," Kathie finished.

Kaycee was silent. Police work in Texas was especially dangerous. And firefighting? None of this sounded like the levelheaded, sensible Jimmy she remembered.

12

Monday morning in the Swanson household brought a semblance of order back into the life of the family. Kathie and Karyn returned to school, Stewart went to work, but Kaycee remained home with Ellyn. She did not have to return to the Twin Cities until Tuesday. The mail carrier had delivered another stack of letters and sympathy cards. They sat in the living room while Ellyn read the sentiments out loud to Kaycee.

In the middle of one long letter, the front door opened and Karyn came in, dropping her book bag on the wooden floor in the front hall. "Hello," she called. Ellyn paused to return the greeting. "Hello, honey, how was your day?"

Kaycee turned toward the door. "Hey, Karyn, how was it to be back at the old grind? Did the dear old East teachers dump a load of homework on you?"

"Yes, it was awful. Look at my backpack. I could barely carry it up the hill."

The telephone rang and Karyn leaped at it. "I'll get it," she cried unnecessarily.

Kaycee turned back. "Go on, mom."

"Kaycee, phone," Karyn called.

Kaycee looked at her mother, who looked up from the sheet of paper with a smile. "I'll wait to finish the letter. I'm going to check on the supper." Ellyn slowly unfolded herself from the comfortable position in the overstuffed chair. She stood, stretching her petite frame. "I'm finally feeling a bit normal today. I must be on the road to recovery."

Kaycee jumped off the couch and gave her a hug. "I'm so glad, mom. This has been so miserable."

Ellyn smiled even as fresh tears filled her eyes. "You're right, it has been miserable, but I'm glad we could all be miserable together."

"Hey, Kaycee, are you going to get the phone?"

Kaycee reluctantly stepped away from Ellyn. "It's probably the department store's booking agent with my next assignment. I'm going to take it upstairs. Karyn, hang up when I yell down," Kaycee said as she ran past Karyn and up the steps two at a time.

Kaycee picked up the receiver in her bedroom, slightly out of breath. "Hello, Kaycee Swanson here," she said and caught sight of her reflection in the mirror. She made a face at the pale and disheveled woman looking back at her. There was absolutely no resemblance between her and the model. When she heard from the receiver, "Hello, Kaycee. Jim Zane here," the hand holding the receiver began to shake. It was him. He sounded like he was standing in the room with her. Her befuddled mind refused to put two words together.

"Are you there? Kaycee, are you there?" he asked. His voice became faint. "She hung up. I can't believe it. She hung up on me."

"Jimmy," Kaycee found her voice and said quickly into the phone. "Jimmy!" she called louder. "I'm here. I didn't hang up."

There was a scuffling sound and then Jimmy's voice came across the line. "Oh, sorry, Kaycee, we must have had a bad connection."

"I saw you at the funeral service," she said. "Thank you for coming. It meant a lot to my family and to me."

"I wouldn't have missed it. I'm just sorry I didn't find a chance to talk to everybody." He paused. "How are your parents doing?"

Kaycee nervously wrapped the telephone cord into a knot. "They're fine, considering. The girls went back to school today so everything felt a little more normal."

"Except that you're still here."

Kaycee frowned. "What?"

"You're mom's probably happy you could stay when everyone else left."

"I think she is—I hope she is."

"Listen, Kaycee, I know this is short notice, but I was kind of hoping we could get together while you're home. Are you busy tonight?"

Kaycee did not answer. This is what she had wanted to happen, but now that Jimmy was taking the initiative, doubts caused her to hesitate.

Jimmy went on, his voice sounded cheerful. "I thought we might go some place and catch up. Have a little dinner. It's been awhile since we talked, and I'm sure one of us has something interesting to share."

Kaycee looked up and caught the mirror reflection again. The paleness that had been in her face vanished and was replaced by a distinct red blush. She took a deep breath. If she said yes, it meant she would have to let him back into her life. Almost automatically she blurted out, "Any idea where you'd like to go?"

13

Fifteen minutes before dialing her parents' number, Jimmy grabbed the phone and saw the whiteness of his knuckles as he gripped the receiver. He hadn't been this nervous since his first parachute jump. "I must be crazy to do this. Why am I putting myself at her mercy again? I'm a fool."

All during the funeral and then afterward, Jimmy had watched Kaycee. She was perfect and absolutely beautiful. He couldn't take his eyes off her. The way she moved. The sleekness of her pulled back hair revealed the ivory smoothness of her skin. The tilt of her chin and the length of her exquisite neck—oh she was a beauty, always had been.

Even when he pulled her over before the funeral, Jimmy knew she would be more beautiful than the pretty girl from high school. And he was right. Her beauty was warmer and softer than when she was young. As for how her personality matured during her years of fame, he had no idea. So far, he hadn't seen any sign of the emotional girl he had known a lifetime ago. The Kaycee he knew then took pleasure in living and enjoyed life with such a passionate joy it was infectious. The Kaycee Swanson he watched at the funeral was supposed to be grieving the death of a much-beloved grandmother, yet she moved through each part of the farewell and funeral with a composed detachment that left him feeling she had become a robot for the Hollywood scene.

Now she was perfect, and beautiful yes, but back then she was a brat. She had instantly fascinated him when they met in fourth grade. She was scrawny, all bony arms and legs and those mischievous big blue eyes. They were alike; Jimmy, too, was painfully skinny, but he was taller than anyone his age. He was quiet to the point of shyness.

Kaycee on tiptoe barely reached his waist. In any situation, she had a penchant toward belligerent outspokenness. When she lost her temper with him, which happened often, she came flying at him like she was actually capable of physically doing him harm. He always laughed at her because it was like some yappy little terrier carrying out a challenge it couldn't possibly survive or win. Kaycee never considered if the odds were favorable or not, she just jumped in head first, facing consequences later.

Now, as he was considering calling her and inviting her back into his life, he saw what a complete mix-up their relationship was even then, at the tender age of ten. In the beginning, Kaycee treated him like a big brother. Then he took on the role of her friend and rescuer. It took Jimmy many years to recognize that how he felt about her was not the same as what she felt for him. He was crazy about her and constantly had to fight his jealousy while watching her date other guys. He never wanted her to guess his true feelings. He recognized the flaw in their relationship, but it wasn't until high school that he finally had to accept she would never see him as anything but a friend. If he had it his way, this time would be different.

So why was it so hard to dial the phone? Over the past ten years, he'd kept himself busy in other parts of the country doing dangerous jobs. After awhile he realized he was lying to himself. He still lived with the hope that Kaycee was going to be a part in his future, an important part. He had to come back and prove there was or was not a chance for him with Kaycee. He needed to find out if he meant nothing to her. He had to find out which it was going to be.

And it all came down to this moment. He dialed the number and thought all his fears had come true when it appeared as if she'd hung up on him without so much as a kind word. Relief flooded through him when he heard her voice.

"Jimmy." Kaycee's voice surprised him. His name spoken so familiarly was the same voice from the past, the one that called to him in his dreams.

"I'm here. I didn't hang up. Any idea where you'd like to go?"

"Where would you like to go?"

"How should I know? I don't know anything about Duluth nightlife any more."

He thought about the laughter in her voice. Suddenly, the cultured, precise accent made her sound like a stranger.

Jimmy took a deep breath and said tensely, "So, give me a clue about what you like to do. Everything in Duluth is pretty much the same. Some of the businesses have changed names but that doesn't mean the food or the atmosphere has changed. Duluth is Duluth, take it or leave it."

Kaycee laughed again. "I'll take it, but you're wrong. Every time I come home something is different. Like the highway coming into town. I don't even recognize it as Duluth any more."

"Uh, Kaycee, that's been like that for a long time, maybe seven, eight months."

Kaycee retorted, "So my mother reminded me. Great, I guess neither of us is going to make a decision. Should I ask Kathie? She seems to know a lot about everything around here."

"Don't tell me Kathie's already dating."

"I don't think with anyone steady, not that I've heard anyway. But that girl is full of information."

Jimmy fell silent.

Kaycee asked, "Well, what do you think? Should I brave the ridicule of asking my seventeen-year-old sister's advice or do we take a chance and just get together and go with the flow?"

Jimmy chuckled. "Don't ask Kathie. I know a place."

"Then I need to know time and what I should wear," Kaycee pressed him.

"Seven-thirty and remember this is Duluth, dress casual."

"Does that mean I have to leave my tiara at home?"

"Yeah, along with your mink coat." He heard her laughter and he smiled. Maybe she hadn't changed as much as he thought.

"Oh, you're too cruel. I thought you'd want to take me to the hot spots and show me off."

"Not a chance. I can't keep up with the competition."

"You can't? That's not what I hear."

"Really? Don't believe everything Kathie says. That girl talks too much, I'll have to put the fear of the law into her soon."

"I think it would take jail to knock the spunk out of her. Oops, I think she's just come in, so I've gotta go. Thanks so much for calling, Jimmy. I can't wait to see you again, and this time I'll have you all to myself. See you soon."

Jimmy slowly hung the receiver back on the cradle, his heart pounding fast. "Steady," he warned himself out loud. "This isn't the Kaycee Swanson you once knew. Better not take what she says too seriously, not until you get to know her again." He felt a rush of adrenaline, heady as whiskey, flow through him. Only she made him feel this way.

14

A fter the family finished eating supper, and as Karyn and Kathie brought the dessert of fresh blueberry pie to the table, Kaycee broke the news that she was going out for the evening with an old friend.

Ellyn gave her a studied look. "But, honey, you've been with me all day and you've only had one phone call. Did you call one of your high school friends?"

"No, he called here."

"He?" Kathie squeaked. "A guy? Who was it?"

Karyn piped up. "I answered the phone! You said it was your agent! The only other guy you've talked about is that guy from the funeral."

"Jimmy? Jimmy Zane called and asked you out on a date?" Kathie demanded.

"No, he didn't ask me for a date."

Stewart cut a piece of pie, put it on a plate, and handed it down the table. "I'm assuming you barely touched your food because of this?"

Kaycee handed the pie to Ellyn. "I don't remember if he said we were eating or not."

Kathie started to laugh. "Whoa, you must've been really nervous. Where is he taking you?"

"I don't know."

Kathie said excitedly, "I bet it's that new country-western bar."

Kaycee laughed. "You can't be serious, not in Duluth?"

Kathie looked worldly once more. "Of course in Duluth. As a matter of fact, they play a lot of country at the high school dances now. Anyway, I heard he likes country. Remember, he lived down in Texas and that's all they listen to there. He's never been to New York City. At least I don't think he ever had a reason to visit New York. Did he, Kaycee?"

Kaycee didn't bother to look at her sister. "What are you talking about?"

Kathie shot her an impish look. "Well, you and Jimmy have both been gone for a long time and now he moved back to Duluth two years ago and that's about the same time you moved to Minneapolis. Funny," she looked at the ceiling, "you only live a couple of hundred miles away from each other. There are a lot of coincidences between the two of you."

"Only to a teenager with an overactive imagination," Kaycee squashed her sister's assumptions coldly.

"I guess, maybe."

Stewart interrupted them in a clipped tone. "That's enough out of you, Kathie. Hold your tongue. Kaycee's business does not include you."

Kathie sullenly fell silent and began to eat her pie.

Kaycee pushed her chair away from the kitchen table and stood. "I'm going to get ready. I'm sorry I can't help with the dishes, mom."

Ellyn waved aside her apology. "Go and enjoy yourself. You never go out when you come home."

"That's because I hate leaving any of you while I'm here. I see so little of the family, I haven't wanted to go out."

"Now that Jimmy is back in town this may be the opportunity to get reacquainted with old friends. Won't that be fun?" Ellyn added.

Kaycee dressed quickly in blue jeans and a pale blue angora sweater that did amazing things for her eyes. With one last critical look in the mirror, she grabbed her jacket and ran down the stairs.

Stewart waited at the bottom holding a leather binder. Kaycee stopped and kissed his cheek. "You look like you're waiting for me."

"I am," Stewart said with a grin.

"I hope you're not planning on giving me the lecture about curfew and proper behavior on a date?"

"Do you need it?"

"Not anymore. I've learned how to fight my own battles." She glanced at her watch.

"Good girl, you've always been a fighter. I just wanted to remind you we haven't gone over your financial portfolio since last Christmas."

Kaycee frowned. "It's been that long? How is it doing?"

"I couldn't possibly tell you that in the five minutes you'll be standing here."

"I'm sorry, dad. I completely forgot about it."

"I don't care as long as you're not getting anxious to make any changes. You don't have to look at it until tax time if you don't want to."

Kaycee sighed with relief. "Great, we'll do it then. Thanks so much for taking care of this for me." She glanced at her watch again. "Have to go. He's probably waiting outside already. Please leave the door unlocked, I have no idea where my key is."

Stewart nodded. "I'm sure you'll be bombarded tomorrow for details about tonight so be prepared."

"I'll just tell the girls to mind their own business. I don't have to tell them anything."

Stewart chuckled. "I meant from your mother."

"Oh no. I just don't understand what is with this family and Jimmy Zane, especially since we have never been anything more than friends," she yelled back over her shoulder before she slammed the heavy front door closed.

15

The sharp chill in the late September night caught her by surprise. As she waited on the front porch, Kaycee hastily pulled her jacket on. The smell of fall was unmistakable—wood smoke, damp leaves, and pine needles mingled in the air. A beat-up Blazer pulled up in front of the house, and she hurried down the sidewalk. The door opened and Jimmy stepped out of the truck as she reached it. The gathering dusk hid their faces.

"Kaycee, I didn't expect you to wait outside."

"Hi, Jimmy. I know that. I wanted to come out. It's so beautiful. Fall evenings in Duluth remind me of football games at Public School Stadium and apple picking."

"And keggers at Brighton Beach," Jimmy added.

"I was never too fond of those. There's too much poison ivy in the woods around there."

Jimmy followed her to the passenger side and opened the door.

Kaycee climbed in and settled herself, locking her seatbelt into place while Jimmy walked around the truck.

As Jimmy buckled up, Kaycee asked, "I've never asked you, how is your father doing? My mom told me he was at the funeral, too."

"Yeah, he was home for it. He's doing great," Jimmy said, starting the truck and pulling away from the curb. "He still works way too many hours. He's never home, but he doesn't seem ready to slow down. He loves his job."

"Are you living at home?" she asked. "Not in some swinging bachelor's pad?"

He grinned. "Yeah, sounds corny, but we both like having the company."

"It doesn't sound corny to me. I live alone and it's...well, it's lonely."

Jimmy glanced at her. "Are you hungry?"

"Are you?"

"No, not really. I'm asking because there's a club on Jean Duluth Road, where some of the people we went to school with hang out. I thought we might stop in there. They serve great burgers and fries but don't have a very big menu. If you wanted to eat something other than that we'd have to go someplace else. How do you feel about live music?"

"It's okay. Usually loud."

"They have live music but the band doesn't start until later. What do you think?"

"Yeah, sure, it sounds fun."

They pulled into the parking lot of a long one-story building. The sign on the side of the building didn't mention country music, so Kathie had been wrong.

When they walked inside, the interior was brightly lit and the air clean. Rough wood paneling lined the walls and pillars. Flagstone floors were covered with peanut shells.

"What in the world?" Kaycee exclaimed. "Don't they have a cleaning service here?"

Jimmy smiled, took her arm. "It's part of the look. Eat peanuts and throw the shells on the floor."

Kaycee looked around. The bar was already lined with people and some of the tables were full. "This must be a popular place."

Jimmy nodded as he moved through the room searching for a place to sit.

Kaycee cried, "Look, isn't that an empty table?" She pointed into the room at the back of the building.

"That's the pool room. Are you sure you want to sit back there?" he asked.

"Why not, maybe I'll even challenge you to a game."

"So you like pool?"

"Sure I do. Doesn't everybody?"

He shrugged his broad shoulders.

"We don't have to play if we sit back there, do we?"

"No, of course not," he said, leading the way to the back room.

They sat down and a waitress wearing a white tee shirt and a short black skirt walked over. Before the waitress opened her mouth, Jimmy asked Kaycee, "What would you like to drink?"

"Lite beer sounds good."

"That's fine for me, too."

The waitress nodded, snapped the gum in her mouth and walked away.

"I suppose this place is pretty lame compared to the places you have to choose from in the Twin Cities," Jimmy said.

"I wouldn't know," Kaycee said, as she looked over the crowd. "I don't go out very often at night unless I'm told to attend some function."

"Told by who?"

"The company that's sponsoring the event I'm modeling for. Right now I'm working for a department store in Minneapolis. They don't sponsor special events like the big clothing companies do, so once I'm done working I usually go to my apartment." She smiled at him.

Two glasses and two bottles of light beer were set unceremoniously on the table in front of them.

"Could you start a tab for me?" Jimmy asked the waitress.

"Sure will," she said and gave him a cheeky smile that set Kaycee's teeth on edge. Kaycee picked up the beer bottle and took a quick gulp and immediately, she choked.

"You okay?" Jimmy asked.

"Yes," she wheezed, trying to catch her breath.

"You should drink more slowly if you're not used to alcohol," he warned.

"What do you mean by that?" she demanded, though still gasping.

"I don't know. After the description you just gave of your social life, I assumed that drinking wasn't allowed either. How is life in the convent?"

"That's so funny."

Jimmy shrugged. "This is a new angle for modeling. The puritan life of a model. Sounds like a best-selling novel. If you market this right, you could make a fortune."

Kaycee laughed. "I didn't make it sound that bad."

Jimmy raised his eyebrows. "I thought it sounded very pathetic, and I almost felt sorry for you. The fame, the money, nice clothes, and makeup, it sounds like everything women enjoy. Let's not forget the shopping. You work in a department store, how convenient."

"Maybe at first, but even paradise can turn into a drudge."

"Like I said, I almost feel sorry for you. Why don't you quit if you don't like it anymore?"

Kaycee sighed. "You make it sound so easy, but nothing is that easy, even if you don't like it anymore. What about you? Do you still like being a trooper?"

He grinned, leaning back in the wooden chair. "I've only been working here for a couple of years, hardly enough time to get sick of a job."

"Well, then, the job you had before this."

His smile widened. "Tricky. If you want to know what I've been doing, why don't you ask?"

"I would, but I didn't want to be rude…at least not yet."

"So you're going to be rude later, how nice. After I left Duluth, I worked as a Texas Ranger for four years."

Kaycee stared at him. "That's much more dangerous than I imagined. What made you become a Texas Ranger?"

"A friend of mine. We were in the Army together and after we decided not to re-enlist, he told me his uncle worked as a Ranger before he retired. It sounded like a challenging job, so we both applied and, consequently, were hired."

"What made you leave? I can just imagine the romantic

image a Texas Ranger has for every available woman." Kaycee paused to take a good look at him. He looked the same—serious, but there were laugh lines at the corner of his mouth, and his eyes were clear like he had no hidden secrets. Jimmy's most attractive feature was his honesty. In high school, Kaycee had not felt this way when his honest remarks were directed at her, but now after living in a beleaguered world filled with smooth talking con men, honesty was important. She couldn't keep her eyes off his mouth—a strong jaw, with a ruggedness in his looks and actions she did not remember, and his lips. Kaycee glanced away. She certainly did not want him to notice her fascination with his mouth. "Yes, I can see you as a Texas Ranger. You'd look very handsome in the white ten gallon hat and cowboy boots."

Jimmy gave a sarcastic laugh. "There is no ten gallon hat."

"But the cowboy boots?"

He held out his foot to show her the scuffed cowboy boot he wore. "I like cowboy boots. They're practical."

"But none of it was enough to keep you in Texas? I must say I'm intrigued. What could possibly make you leave all that and return to good old Duluth?"

"Like you said, even paradise can become a drudge."

"Why do I find that hard to believe?"

"Just like it's hard to believe you're tired of modeling."

Kaycee lowered her voice and muttered, "More like the modeling business is tired of me."

Jimmy leaned forward and asked, "What was that?"

Kaycee shook her head and sighed. "Nothing."

Jimmy, on impulse placed his hand over hers. "It has been a long time, Kaycee. Over the years, I've thought about you."

Kaycee looked at his long fingers and blinked rapidly to dispel the sudden tears in her eyes. She surprised even herself when she wrapped her hand around his and clung to him. "How long has it been? Too long. We're complete strangers now. It's like our friendship didn't exist. I hate that. I've never had a friendship like the one we shared." She glanced at his face. He wore a strained expression along with something else, was it impatience? She'd gone too fast dumping her heart and loneliness in his lap. The first time they have a conversation and she makes him uncomfortable. Hastily, she withdrew her hand and nervously moved to pick up her glass, sipping the cold, bitter brew.

Jimmy frowned. "A lot has happened to both of us since then. We couldn't go back to the way it was."

"We can't go back, but could we still be friends?" she asked softly, a touch of hope in her voice.

"Friends? Kaycee I don't…"

"Jimmy!" At the abrupt interruption, both Kaycee and Jimmy jumped. They looked up in unison. Jimmy stood. "Paul," he reached out to shake the man's hand. "Stella," he nodded at the woman. "What are you doing out tonight?"

"It's our anniversary," Paul laughed, slapping Jimmy on the back. He looked down at Kaycee with obvious curiosity.

"Kaycee Swanson, this is Paul Denali and his wife Stella," Jimmy said. "Paul's a Duluth police officer."

Paul was medium height, slimly built, and had recently clipped brown hair. He had an easy smile that he didn't hesitate to show. "Jimmy's too polite to say that I'm just a measly city cop while he works for the entire state of Minnesota," Paul joked with a laugh. "It's nice to meet you." He held out his hand to Kaycee.

Kaycee smiled back and shook his work-roughened hand.

Paul put his arm around the woman next to him. "This is my wife, Stella."

Kaycee smiled at the petite woman with baby doll blond curls surrounding her small face. She gave Kaycee a quick look, and then stopped to give her a second look that lasted longer than the first. With a look of concentration, Stella turned away.

Kaycee knew that look. It was recognition.

16

The crack of a pool break resounded loudly and all at the table turned to look behind them. Paul said to Jimmy, "You aren't playing?"

"Nope, not tonight."

Paul glanced at Kaycee and nodded with a knowing smile. "Right, not with the ladies."

Kaycee jumped up and with a look at Stella said, "That can't possibly be meant as a challenge, but I think we should take it as one. How do you feel about a game of doubles?"

Paul and Stella declined. Stella turned to press a hand against her husband's chest. "Honey, where is that waitress with our drinks? After you find her and my wine, you can play your old pool game. I'm completely hopeless at it."

Paul grinned at Jimmy. "I'll play the winner between you two," he said.

Kaycee walked around the one vacant table and pulled out the plastic pool rack. "If you find a decent cue, I'll rack."

Jimmy shrugged out of his jacket. The cue caddie was down at the other end of the room. By the time Jimmy returned, Kaycee had the balls arranged and was back talking with Paul and Stella.

"You breakin', Jim?" Paul called with a smirk.

Kaycee looked at Paul and then over at Jimmy. She asked with suspicion, "Why do I get the feeling I'm being set-up?"

Stella eagerly supplied her with the reason. "Because Jimmy is really good at pool. Both of the guys volunteer for the Boys and Girls Club of Duluth, and they sponsor pool tournaments every three months. Jimmy's been teaching the kids down there how to shoot, and they're thrilled to finally be good enough to beat him."

Jimmy walked away to break. A striped ball fell into the corner pocket. Kaycee crossed her arms with a sigh and asked

Paul, "Will I even get the chance at a shot?"

They watched as Jimmy sank four more balls before he missed. Handing the cue to Kaycee, he grinned and said, "You've got solids."

Kaycee took the cue and looked over at the table. Two striped balls remained and seven solids. She slipped her arms out of her jacket and draped it over the dividing wall. The cue stick was warped, but she made a decent showing by getting three solids.

"Who doesn't spend any time shooting pool in bars?" Jimmy teased as he walked around the table to take the cue.

Kaycee laughed, shaking her head. "Not me. There's a pool table in my apartment building."

Jimmy countered, "You're just too cheap to pay for your pool games."

"What about you, taking advantage of a non-profit organization just to get free pool games?"

"Touché," Jimmy chuckled. He took his time clearing the table.

Kaycee conceded to Stella, "You're right, Jimmy's a really good player. Now the guys can play." She slid into the chair across the table from Stella.

"I'm a real fan of fashion," Stella finally said after silently studying Kaycee's profile. "Paul complains that I spend a fortune on fashion magazine subscriptions, but it's my only entertainment, except for special occasions like tonight."

Kaycee knew where the conversation was heading and wanted to avoid the subject. She said, "Your anniversary! What a wonderful event to be celebrating."

"After six of them, I guess this is the kind of thing you end up doing," Stella replied with a slight shrug.

Kaycee leaned her chin on her upraised hands and briefly studied the woman across the table from her. Stella looked too young to have been married six years.

"Six years, that's a milestone. Isn't it said the first three are the hardest?"

Stella set her wine glass down. "Yes and no," she replied. "I don't know about other couples, but Paul and I dated for about a year before we married. Before that, I still lived at home with my parents. It took me awhile to get used to being away from home and being married. I don't know which one was a bigger adjustment."

Kaycee was surprised by Stella's frankness.

"Is modeling as difficult as they say?" Stella asked.

"Not if you learn to be disciplined. It's a matter of training yourself and then following the program," Kaycee answered. "Not too many people recognize a model unless they are high exposure. I haven't worked for any of the big companies for a few years. How do you know I'm a model?"

"I've seen you a couple times in our newspaper. Once when you modeled in Paris and then when you started to work down in the Twin Cities. I think it's great that a local girl made it into the international modeling market."

"That's really nice of you," Kaycee said, "but in my opinion, six years of marriage is a lot more important."

As the guys returned from the pool table, Kaycee stood and asked, "Who won?"

"Paul," Jimmy said.

"Hey, wait a minute," Paul cried. "You mean we're not playing again?"

"Naw," Jimmy said, taking a swig of beer. He turned and reached for Kaycee's hand. "You feel like dancing?"

Kaycee, puzzled by the unexpected question, looked around the crowded area, "There's no music and no dance floor. What are you talking about?"

Stella jumped up. "The dance floor is upstairs, but the music hasn't started yet."

Jimmy tugged on Kaycee's arm and led her across the room.

Stella started to follow, but Paul put a hand on her shoulder and stopped her saying, "Shush, woman. Can't you see Jimmy wants to be alone with her? He doesn't need a dance floor."

Stella gave Paul a narrow look. "How come you don't feel the same way about me?" she asked tartly.

Paul looked at his wife and smiled. "I do, honey. It's just that we have a house we can disappear to any time you're ready."

Stella sighed and snuggled against his side. "Are you sure Jimmy is after her, or is it her money?" she asked slyly.

Paul glanced down at her and frowned. "What does that mean?"

"You didn't recognize her?"

He shook his head no. "Should I?"

"Of course! She's a big time supermodel from New York City!"

Paul laughed. "No way, not her. She looks too normal."

Stella nodded knowingly. "Well, she is. She's been featured in catalogs for the big department store chains. She says she isn't high exposure, but I see her face in my magazines quite a bit. I think she's in here trying to hide out from the media."

"This would be the last place anybody would think of looking," Paul admitted in a low voice. "Bet she's never been in the swimsuit issue."

Stella pushed against his ribcage. "That is not what makes a supermodel, Paul," she declared scornfully.

"Depends," he murmured, wiggling his eyebrows.

Stella giggled pressing a warm kiss against his neck.

17

"Did you leave anything at the table?" Jimmy shouted to be heard over the jukebox and the people talking as they threaded through the crowded room, dodging people and waitress trays.

"No," she shouted back. "I don't carry a purse and I've got my jacket. Why?"

Jimmy did not pause as he pushed open the front door, and they escaped hand-in-hand into the cool night.

"It didn't look like we were going to get much talking done with them there."

"Stella recognized me from the magazines she reads."

Jimmy slowed his steps. The ground was uneven and covered with coarsely ground gravel. "We better slow down or you might turn your ankle. What's wrong with being recognized? Isn't that why people become celebrities, so the general public can recognize them? I've never understood why stars get so ticked off when their public shows up and wants a picture or an autograph."

Kaycee said indignantly, "I am not a snob like that. I don't have a fan club, and I don't want one. It's just odd that Stella knew me. It doesn't happen often, and I never know when it happens whether they'll hate me or love me. I've found it's healthier to skip out before I do."

"Like we just did?" he asked.

Kaycee frowned, then laughed. "Exactly! They seemed like a nice couple. Do you socialize with them?"

He unlocked the passenger door and opened it for her. "I see Paul once a week at the Boys Club. It isn't often Stella comes around. What do we do next? Want to go for something to eat?"

Kaycee glanced at her watch. "No, I can't. It's almost ten o'clock."

"Ten o'clock, so what?" he said, leaning against the door. Kaycee hesitated then said, "That's my curfew."

"Curfew…oh right!" he said as he slammed the door shut.

Inside the blazer, she shivered. The air was cold enough to mist her breath. When he got in, she said, "I certainly won't apologize. It would be impossible for me to maintain the craziness involved in modeling if I hadn't learned to fix my schedule and stick to it every single day."

Jimmy shrugged. "I'd get sick of that fast."

"No, it's just an adjustment."

"Yeah, I'll bet it was."

Kaycee gave him a suspicious glance. "You believe me, right?"

"Of course, why wouldn't I?"

Kaycee looked out the side window to softly say, "I just wanted to be sure. You were right, Duluth hasn't changed much."

"Why did you expect it to?"

"From what Kathie was telling me, I thought maybe some radical group had come in and corrupted the entertainment scene."

"With beatniks and rap music?"

"I don't know what with, but I'm relieved it hasn't."

"There are a lot of coffee shops appearing everywhere. I suppose that's pretty radical for the Northland."

"So the New York influence is here, too?"

"More like the Mini Apple. So I'm to head for your parents' house?"

"Yes, I'm a boring date who has the curfew of a tenth grader. Welcome to the real world. I guess you can get used to anything if it's important enough."

"You're right, if it's important enough. I take it your work is important enough?" he asked.

"Well, yes, I think it is."

Silence fell in the car as they drove along the dark streets.

With very little traffic, they made good time. Jimmy pulled the car in front of her parents' house. The front light was on and so was the living room light.

"Now that's a familiar picture," Jimmy said.

Kaycee leaned forward to look at the house and smiled. "Yes, it is," she remarked as she moved to unlock her door.

"Kaycee, before you go there's something I have to tell you." Gone was the teasing banter in his voice. He sounded grim. "This is something that happened recently," Jimmy cleared his throat, "well, last year."

"Oh," Kaycee murmured.

"You remember Tod Mathisen from high school?"

Unprepared by the mention of Tod's name, her anger jumped to the surface, "Why are you bringing up Tod? After all these years, you certainly don't need the satisfaction of gloating about what kind of person he was," she said. "Really, Jimmy, I always gave you more credit than being that petty and after ten years...don't you think Tod Mathisen caused enough trouble between the two of us? But I'll admit it out loud just this once, and then I never want to think about him or what happened again. Everything, everything you told me about him was true. He's a classy jerk, and he used me." Kaycee looked away. She couldn't face Jimmy, but her anger kept the words tumbling out of her mouth. "He was very smooth, very well-prepared, and I thought the most romantic man in the world. Like a dummy, I fell for him. All his lies and promises. Do you believe that guy actually tried to take advantage of me? What a complete jerk. Then he dumped me cold. As a matter of fact, he did dump me. He left me out in the country. I walked three miles to get home at two o'clock in the morning. There, is that enough of the details? I'm sure you and everybody else heard about it all at school. You were right. I was the fool. How many times I wished I'd been smart enough to listen to you and left well enough alone."

A hush permeated the hollowness of the vehicle. Jimmy

cleared his throat before he spoke, "I'm sorry, Kaycee. I had no idea."

Jimmy's hand wavered above her shoulder, undecided whether she would allow him to comfort her. Lightly, he set it down. "Kaycee, please believe me when I tell you, I didn't know Tod was that bad. But I knew he had a string of girl-friends."

She stared out the front windshield. "I've moved on and forgotten about it. So help me, if I meet a guy like him snooping around one of my sisters...I really don't know what I'd do. I just can't bear the thought of one of them—" Kaycee reached for the door handle and flung the door open. She turned to face him. "Why did you bring up Tod in the first place?"

She saw him hesitate when he said, "Tod's dead."

Kaycee covered her mouth with her hand, "Dead?"

"A car accident."

"He never grew up."

"No, he never did."

Kaycee sighed and shook her head. "Was he married or have any children?"

"No, he was still single."

Kaycee remained silent. She stepped on the running board, sliding from the bench seat of the Blazer. Her composure back to normal she said, "I'm going back to Minneapolis tomor-row, so I'll say good-bye now."

"You don't stick around Duluth too long, do you?"

"My time isn't my own. The calendar on modeling runs about a year ahead of the rest of the world. And I'm a slave to that."

Jimmy tightened his grip on the steering wheel. "You should think about coming around more, now that Gran is gone. Think of how much easier it would be for your mother to adjust to what's happened."

Kaycee said coldly, "Thank you for your concern. I'll remember your advice about my parents and what you think is right for all of us. Good-bye, Jimmy."

Jimmy sat and watched Kaycee run up the sidewalk and into the house without a backward glance.

Seconds later, the porch light went off.

He was angry with himself for bringing Tod out of the past. Bitterly, he slammed the gears and let out the clutch. Old habits die hard, he thought. Like me sticking my nose in Kaycee's business. His tires protested as they squealed on the gravel.

Jimmy had not told her the whole story about Tod's accident. Tod had been killed by a drunk driver...himself. One rainy night at 3 a.m., he passed out at the wheel of his sports car and ran off the Twenty-first Avenue West ramp. Nobody else was involved.

Tod's accident certainly wasn't Jimmy's first D.O.A., but the image of Tod's lifeless body haunted him. He'd seen countless automobile deaths and many a lot worse. The entangled heap of steel that had been Tod's car impaled on a steel pylon of the underpass was unrecognizable. But what really bothered him was when he had to tell Tod's parents about the accident. The elderly couple's total devastation as they heard of their only child's death was tormenting. Jimmy didn't like Tod, but that had nothing to do with witnessing his parents clinging to each other. Their entire life's work was lying broken and lifeless on a slab at the morgue.

Now the memory blurred with his anger at what Kaycee had told him. Tod had hurt her and so had he. He hurt her and that was the last thing he ever wanted to do.

* * * * *

Kaycee thought back to her foolishness. Leaning on the door, she realized just when the hope of renewing their friendship seemed possible, she started a meaningless argument about the past. Kaycee locked the front door and ran up the stairs. At least she was going back to Minneapolis tomorrow and once back in her own world she could forget. She could forget Jimmy and the feelings he brought to life in her. She could forget that for a brief moment when with him tonight that she wanted to touch him, touch his skin and hold him. She actually had wanted to ask him why they had never fallen in love with each other. He was the kind of man any woman wanted in her life.

18

The old windows of the big house let in the icy fingers of the January cold. The heavy draperies were closed to keep out as much of the draft as possible, yet they stirred with the force of the wind shrieking outside. The shrill ring of the telephone brought Ellyn out of a sound sleep. Reluctantly, she stuck her head out of the warm covers and listened. The phone rang again. Shivering, she pulled the quilt tighter around her shoulders and nudged Stewart's broad back. The phone rang again, and slowly Stewart sat up and she heard him pick up the receiver. Squinting, Ellyn turned the clock to face her. Two o'clock in the morning! Oh no! No news at two o'clock could be good. Fully awake now, and more concerned about the safety of her family than the cold, Ellyn sat up and switched on the light. She listened closely to Stewart's half of the conversation.

"Kaycee, yes love. Is everything all right?"

He murmured to Ellyn, "She's fine."

Back into the phone, he asked, "What was that? Great, great, honey, I can't believe it happened so fast. Some people go years without having something like this happen in their career. Yes, of course...I understand," he yawned. "We're absolutely thrilled for you. Call us back in the morning with all the details. Goodnight. I love you too."

Stewart fumbled with the phone until it rested in the cradle.

"It's two o'clock," Ellyn stated. "What was that about?"

Stewart yawned again, "She was excited."

"What about?"

"Oh, you know, that movie deal she was auditioning for. She told us about it at Christmas. She just signed the contract tonight."

Ellyn slowly lay back on her pillow without responding and stared at the ceiling searching her mind for any memory of Kaycee and a movie. She was certain she had never heard of it before this moment. "At Christmas, Kaycee told me she was taking acting lessons at the Art Institute in downtown St. Paul. I don't remember hearing anything about a movie audition. You knew that Kaycee was trying out for a movie and didn't check to make sure I knew about it?" Ellyn pulled the covers off of Stewart's prone body. "I can't believe you. She's worked so hard taking those acting lessons at night, paying all that money for the school. I cannot believe you didn't tell me she was auditioning for a part," her voice rising as she spoke.

Stewart reached for the covers and tried unsuccessfully to get them back.

Ellyn kept a tight grip on the blankets, "I want some answers."

With a sigh, he reluctantly pulled himself into a sitting position. "It must not have been Christmas then. I'm sorry, I don't know when she told me, but I thought you already knew or I would have told you," he attempted to soothe her. "With all that's been on your mind, you've been so busy dealing with your mother's estate and cleaning her things out of the attic. Then, Maris and Will announced about the new baby…I just forgot."

Ellyn sat up and, surrounded by blankets, crossed her arms over her chest and stared silent and angry into the room. "Thank you for your concern," she said in a tight voice. "But I will find it very difficult to forgive you if you ever just forget and keep something about my children from me again. That is, unless I'm busy burying you at the time."

Stewart pulled the blankets up over his chilled body and chuckled. "That's a deal I think I can keep, my dear. Now can we go back to sleep?"

"One more thing, Stewart. You realize Kaycee thinks of you as her knight in shining armor. If she hears that you forgot about this how do you think she'll take it?"

Stewart lay still and then said hoarsely, "I don't know, but I do know our eldest daughter has a tendency to hold a grudge."

"I'm sure she wouldn't with you. Especially now when she'll be so occupied with this movie. My goodness, an actress. I can't believe she's an actress."

Stewart sighed. "I'll have to tell her in the morning. She's calling back then to explain everything about the movie."

"Are you certain that's what you want to do?"

"It's the only thing I can do if I ever want to face her again without feeling like a complete heel."

Ellyn snuggled back under the covers with a smile of contentment. She said softly, "I believe you're right, dear. That's probably the best way to handle it."

Stewart glanced at the lump in the covers his wife's figure made. She was completely hidden under the layers of comforters, and once settled she didn't move. Obviously her conscience was not disturbed, but his was. Without any attempt to settle under the warm covers, he remained sitting up. He stared at nothing, but his mind raced. The grandfather clock down the hall first chimed three and then chimed four times. Only then was he satisfied with what he would say to Kaycee on the telephone tomorrow and he slipped into a dreamless sleep.

The Swanson house was in an uproar after the news of Kaycee's upcoming movie debut was spread throughout the family. Not only was Kaycee cast in a small but pivotal sequence, it was to be shot on the North Shore's Palisade Head right outside of Silver Bay. Kaycee was still in Minneapolis, but this weekend she was going to move home for the six weeks the film company was shooting there.

Kathie and Karyn especially were thrilled to bask in the excitement of their sister becoming an actress and being involved with a movie crew in Duluth. They were not thrilled with the extra work Ellyn gave them to do in preparation for

Kaycee's arrival that afternoon. Ellyn had them cleaning out Kaycee's old room. Kathie was sent to bring clean sheets from the laundry room so the bed could be made. Kathie brought the sheets from the basement but stopped to secretly pick up the telephone and dial it. She spoke softly into the receiver, "Lindsay, Kaycee is coming home today in a little while, so I'll ask her about the other actors in the movie. What do you think if they ask for extras, do you want to do it? Kaycee will know everything before it can be advertised so we'd be picked for sure. I'm so excited! What if Freddy Prinze, Jr. is in it? I would die to meet him!"

Ellyn's voice from the top of the stairs interrupted, "Kathie, where are those sheets?"

Kathie covered the mouthpiece and called back, "In a second, mom, the phone rang." She whispered fiercely into the receiver, "No, they're not from Hollywood. Kaycee told me the film crew is from the Twin Cities. Okay, forget it. You're right. There are no film crews in the Cities. You know everything because you read movie magazines. Talk to you later. Bye." Kathie replaced the receiver with a bang.

"I hope that wasn't Kaycee," Stewart said, walking into the front hallway from the kitchen. He set his briefcase on the entry table and opened the closet to hang his coat.

"Why would Kaycee call?" Kathie exclaimed as she tried to disentangle herself from the telephone cord.

"I don't know, but if she needs to get a hold of us, I'd like the line to be open."

Kathie picked up the pile of bed sheets from the chair, and started up the stairs. "I am so sick of everybody being a know-it-all about movies. You'd think all of my friends have a sister starring in a movie that's being filmed here."

Ellyn waited impatiently for Kathie at the top of the stairs. "Don't hand the sheets to me, my dear, you're the one who is making the bed. Karyn has done enough, and I have to start supper. You better get busy if you plan on making your basketball game tonight."

Kathie wailed, "Not all by myself. Mom, that isn't fair. I can't, it's impossible for one person to make a queen-size bed. And I have basketball in an hour. There's no way it can be done by then."

Ellyn shook her head. "Don't even bother complaining, Kathie, just do it."

"Fine!" Kathie stormed down the hall muttering under her breath.

In the dimness of the January twilight Kaycee pulled up in front of the house. Her parent's house looked sad with remnants of Christmas garland and lights hanging in clumps. The wreath was gone from the place of honor on the door and left on the porch for the trash bin. The narrow front sidewalk was covered with ice. Kaycee opened the trunk of her car and lifted the heavy suitcase. She was not looking forward to carrying this over that ice. She slammed the trunk and stepped over the knee-high pile of snow at the curb and trudged up the walk. Several times her feet slipped but she regained her balance. When she opened the front door out of breath, she called, "Hello, anybody home?" She dropped the suitcase and flexed her back.

For a second, the house was silent. Then the kitchen door opened and Ellyn came rushing out. "Kaycee, you're here. I'm so glad! I have a huge favor to ask. Your father and I are going out for supper, could you please pick Kathie up at East at about eight? Her game should be over by then."

Kaycee grinned. "No problem, mom. How is everyone?"

Ellyn reached up to brush a kiss on Kaycee's cheek. "We're all wonderful, just a bit rushed tonight. I suppose Stewart could have let Kathie use the car, but that girl isn't a careful driver and all this ice—it's just too dangerous."

"No, I wouldn't have given Kathie the car either."

"How are you, dear? The driving on the freeway wasn't a problem?"

"Completely clear. Am I in my old room while I'm home?"

"The girls and I cleaned and vacuumed this afternoon, and the sheets on the bed are freshly washed. It's ready for you to move in."

Stewart walked into the room pulling at his tie. "Ellie, are you sure a tie is necessary?"

"Yes," Ellyn said. "Kaycee's here. I'll be right down, Stewart." Ellyn patted Kaycee's arm and hurried up the stairs.

"Hi, honey. This place is a mad house as usual."

"I didn't expect anything less," Kaycee said with a smile as she walked over to kiss her father.

"You'll be the only one home for awhile. Karyn's babysitting for Maris, Kathie—"

"Kathie will be waiting for me to pick her up," Kaycee interrupted.

"Your mother filled you in. She's a fast talker. Welcome home, dear. You're mother's been in heaven ever since we found out you'll be here six weeks."

"It's good to be home, dad."

19

One week later, Kaycee pounded on the bathroom door and demanded, "Kathie, let me in. I've got a review meeting downtown in thirty minutes."

The door flung open and a blanket of steam hit Kaycee in the face. Kathie, clad in a towel, pushed past her. "It's not my fault I woke up first. If you want the shower to yourself, you'll just have to get up earlier."

"How early? Five o'clock in the morning? Forget it," Kaycee shouted back, slamming the bathroom door.

Sitting at the kitchen table drinking their coffee, Ellyn and Stewart looked at each other.

Ellyn shrugged. "It doesn't take long for them to renew their screaming technique."

Stewart sipped his coffee before remarking in a dry tone, "Kaycee always did have a good scream, but I think Kathie's pretty loud herself."

"Do you think Kaycee's regretting giving up the hotel suite the film company offered her?"

"I think that happened probably on Tuesday. Today is Friday, so she's beyond regret by now."

Ellyn smiled. "Hopefully the room has been occupied by someone else and she's stuck with us for another five weeks, if we're lucky."

The sound of several doors being slammed on the second floor made them both chuckle.

"Think of the money she'll save in the future."

Ellyn winced as a door was slammed repeatedly, then laughed. "What are you talking about now?"

"She won't have to pay a cent for therapy. All that door slamming has to be relieving a lot of tension."

Traffic heading to downtown from the East end of Duluth was a mess at eight o'clock in the morning. Kaycee was already a bundle of nerves. Today the director was going to start working on the first of her scenes, and here she is stuck in traffic on Twenty-first Avenue. Kaycee edged the Mustang around the stopped cars and into the parking lane where she passed the stalled traffic to turn onto Third Street. Now at least she could get moving. The traffic along Third Street remained heavy, but in less than fifteen minutes Kaycee was turning into the parking ramp of the Holiday Center. She grabbed her satchel and ran inside the lobby. With a quick look at the closed elevator door, she dodged to the stairwell. It was two flights down to the main level where the filming crew had a reserved conference room. It was here, for the past week, the crew members and the other staff had been meeting. Kaycee paused in the hallway to catch her breath. She ran her hands through her hair trying to put it in order.

"Hey, Kaycee," Joe said as he walked past her toward the conference room.

"Joe," Kaycee rushed after him. "I'm late. Did anyone notice?"

Joe shrugged. "I don't know I just got here."

Kaycee felt her fear lift. She wasn't the only late one. She followed Joe into the bright, white room. Everything inside the room was white—the walls, the carpet, the light fixtures, and the furniture. It was blinding when all the overhead lights were turned on. After the gray of outside, Kaycee blinked as her eyes adjusted.

Joe slipped his sunglasses from his pocket and placed them on his nose. "Geez, Lance, can't they tone the room down a bit? It gives me a headache every time I walk in here."

"That's tough, Joe. If it keeps you awake, then it's served its purpose. Ms. Swanson, you will be on the floor today for the rehearsal of your first scene. Please go to wardrobe to be fitted and then to makeup. We're getting close to going on-site for filming, people. Let's finish up in the next few days, and we can move on to Palisade Head."

When Kaycee walked past Joe she heard him mutter, "Do not pass go, and do not collect two hundred dollars."

Kaycee looked at no one but softly giggled at Joe's joke. Once in the hallway, she took a sharp left to find the wardrobe department. It promised to be an extremely difficult day. She was going to be under scrutiny all day long. Vigorously, she rubbed her forehead. What she needed to do right now was pretend this was the runway of a fashion opening and treat it with the same detachment she used when faced by thousands of people staring at her like she was a piece of meat. Maybe then she would find it bearable.

Two days later, Kaycee had finished the last studio rehearsal and was ready for the on-site shoot. She sat at one of the dazzling white tables while, Joe, the floor manager, stage manager, and site manager stood in the front of the group. He looked unusually serious with the clipboard in front of his nose as he read the day's agenda. "Listen up, people, we've just been hit with a four-day cold spell. The weather service let us know that the bitter cold is now leaving the atmosphere and some milder weather is on the way. Either way, we have to begin filming on location. We're in danger of going over budget if we don't keep on schedule, so we'll begin today traveling to Palisade Head and filming as much of each sequence as we possibly can. Kaycee, you're the lady of the hour. The cliff scene is top of the agenda. If the lake effect wind hasn't drastically altered the cloud cover, we will film, hopefully, the entire clip.

"The studio company has hired some local law enforcement to help us with safety at the site. They will be available to help with the cliff scene just in case the lake proves to be smarter than our technicians."

There was laughter from several of the technicians.

"The law will also be helping with traffic control and keeping civilians off the set. Everyone is required to wear your identification tags outside of your coats at all times to be recognized. If you don't, you're on your own with the local cops. Okay, folks, that's it. All technical crew and cameramen get on the first bus going up the shore."

People scattered as soon as Joe stopped talking.

Kaycee moved more slowly. She gathered together her script and her position diagrams and slipped them into her canvas satchel before she put on her winter gear.

"Ms. Swanson," Lance Paine, the director, said as he walked past her, "I was watching the film of the rehearsal. In the action sequence on the cliff face there is a definite problem. It's something you're doing. I can't pick it out right now but until I do, I want you to understand the opportunities to film at Palisade are going to rely a lot on chance. We need to nail the scenes and right away. Do you understand?"

Kaycee nervously swallowed. "Yes, I believe I do."

"Good, I'll see you at the cliff."

Kaycee angrily watched Lance walk out of the conference room. She pulled her hat on her head and then slipped her arm into a sleeve. How dare he put that kind of pressure on me, she thought.

Joe suddenly appeared at her side. "How are you doing? Are you all right with this?"

Kaycee shrugged. "I'm okay, it's just that he's so…bossy. He doesn't like me because this is my first acting job. So he says that I'm totally responsible for getting this shot the first time. That's a complete contradiction, and I can't be responsible."

"He's the boss. It's his job," Joe said simply. His tone voiced neither approval nor disapproval. "It also gives him somebody to blame if it doesn't go right."

"I know, but he just plain annoys me."

"Get used to it, most directors are just like him, or worse."

"Thanks, Joe, that makes it a whole lot easier," she said.

"Is that it? Anything else bothering you?"

"No, should there be?" she said, when she should have

told him the truth. She should have said, "Joe I'm afraid of heights. How can I dangle off the front of a cliff attached by thin wires to a crane when I'm scared of heights?" She couldn't do it. To admit her fear might stop her from controlling it when she needed to. She wasn't going to lose her role because of a silly childhood fear.

"That's good…good," Joe said. He flipped open his clipboard. "You are first on my agenda today, Miss Kaycee. Can you make the first bus?"

"Yes," Kaycee said, struggling with her clothing.

"Great! I'll go save you a seat. Once we're on location, I'll have time while the crew sets up to give you the lay-down of what's going to happen. Of course, you'll have to go for makeup and wardrobe." He glanced at her. "This won't be the actual fall anyway. We can't shoot that scene until Richard Dawes is on the set. You'll just be lowered down the side of the cliff. You okay?" he said, looking at her closely. "You just got kind of pale for a second."

Kaycee shook her head. "I'm fine. Thanks for your help."

Joe left, and Kaycee finished tying her boots then threw her bag over her shoulder. She trudged up the stairs and outside. The people were waiting next to the first bus.

Kaycee moved to the door. Somebody yelled, "Hey, it's already full. You'll have to wait for the next bus." The bus door opened and Joe stuck his head out. "Hurry up, Kaycee, we're ready." As she sidestepped around them, Kaycee heard somebody say, "Don't you know she's the actress doing the stunt today. She has to be on the first bus."

"Who is she? I've never seen her before."

"Some model turned actress."

"Oh, great. Somebody with all the looks and no brains. We're gonna be out on that frozen rock all day."

Kaycee shuddered at the callous voice as she climbed aboard the luxurious bus and dropped into the first empty seat. She set her bag down and leaned her head back to close her eyes. This was only the beginning of her nightmare.

On the highway ride to Palisade Head it looked as cold as it felt outside. The wind whipped the frozen trees back and forth. There was very little snow on the ground, making what was left look dirty, but the lack of snow was common for January. It usually began to snow again in February. The gray skies with dark, black clouds woven through them, warned there might be a break from the cold. Kaycee stared out the window of the bus at the expanse of water that stretched to the horizon. Even with the overcast sky, the rising sun sent bright clouds of orange and pink to mix with the dark clouds. The sunrise was spectacular.

Worried about what was in store for her at the cliff, Kaycee pulled her notes out of the bag and began going through them. She wanted to memorize as much of the directions as possible. Joe had gone over it with her in detail many times. Just the image terrified her. The only speaking part in the upcoming scene was one long, suspended scream. She closed her eyes and swallowed hard.

The Palisade Head area where the shoot was going to take place was not unfamiliar to Kaycee. It might explain why she felt so nervous about it. The Swanson family had often driven up the shoreline of Lake Superior on Sunday afternoons to picnic. The cliff was too dangerous to picnic with young children. There was no protective fencing between the rocks and the three-hundred-and-fifty-foot drop into the lake. She remembered looking down from the peak of the cliff into the water pounding against the base of the rock. She watched the screeching gulls wheel overhead in groups. Now all she felt when faced with the memory of that height was a healthy dose of fear.

The bus groaned and the gears protesting as it began the ascent up the road leading to Palisade Head. Kaycee found it hard to believe they'd arrived so quickly. Usually, the drive felt like it took forever.

20

The bus emptied out quickly, but Kaycee remained in her seat. When she was the last passenger, she stood and walked down the narrow aisle tightening her scarf and pulling on her mittens.

"Kaycee! We've gotta get going," Joe called. He was waiting at the front of the bus. The cold seeping through the open door turned into steam in the overly warm bus. Kaycee walked toward him. Joe was a medium kind of a guy. He was not tall or short. His hair was not long or short. He was not handsome or homely.

When he introduced himself to the staff he did so by saying, "I'm a medium kind of guy." Of course his reference was not to his appearance. On the first day he told them, "I'm not overly picky about rules except where safety is concerned. I don't yell a lot, but if I do yell you'll know I'm really mad. I usually am a middle of the road guy."

Kaycee liked him. He was direct but used humor to lighten the tension the director seemed to infuse into the group. She trusted him. Trust was not something Kaycee gave easily, even on minor matters. Today, Joe literally had her life in his hands, so to meet someone who, in a few short weeks, had earned her trust was a big deal.

Joe stepped off the bus and rubbed his hands together. "Whew, this is cold. I'm going to show you the trailer where you'll go for makeup and wardrobe. You'll be using the same trailer the entire time we're here. Then I'm going to check the setup at the cliff. We might not be able to film, but I want you completely ready either way, okay?"

Kaycee nodded following him across the packed icy snow.

"Lance called and said the sky, right now, is perfect. That nasty wind has died off so the helicopter can hover in front of the cliff face. There's your makeup trailer." He pointed across the lot at a row of small camper trailers.

Kaycee looked at the white camper with ruffled curtains visible in the windows. She veered away from Joe and started toward the door.

Suddenly, the sleeve of her jacket was grabbed from behind. Kaycee spun around and faced a red-faced Joe. He was holding a cell phone.

"Sorry, but Ralph just phoned. They want you at the crane to be fitted for the harness. Then you can go to makeup and wardrobe."

"Ralph? Who's Ralph?"

"He's the head cameraman. Don't you know the head cameraman is the law on the site? Even Lance has to listen to what Ralph says."

"Oh!" Kaycee said and hurried to keep up with Joe's quick strides.

When they reached the edge of the lot and passed through the brush and piled snow around the rim of the parking area, the long arm of the crane came into view. It was painted black and gray. Kaycee wondered if the paint scheme would blend in with the clouds.

"You do realize that the actual fall can't take place until Richard Dawes arrives? He has to push you off the cliff."

Kaycee grimaced. "Yes, I do know. How friendly of him, and I don't even know the man. You told me that before."

Joe shot her a sidelong glance. "You will. Right now, we'll be working on the scene where the girl tries to save herself by climbing up the cliff. Of course, we both know that doesn't happen."

She nodded silently.

"Today, if the conditions are right, we're only going to need a small segment of your climb up the cliff face. They'll lower you 25 feet. You start climbing up and the 'copter camera will roll film."

The waivers and warnings about the filming of this scene had been a list taking up two sheets of computer paper, single-spaced. There were so many she couldn't finish reading it because of the images it brought to mind. She already decided when she first read the script, "I'm going through with this no matter how dangerous the scene turns out to be."

The Palisade Head area seen by tourists and locals throughout the summer months was usually blocked off during the winter. The Department of Natural Resources set out large cement roadblocks to keep vehicles off the steep road leading to the top. The area they were walking through right now did not resemble anything Kaycee remembered as a child. The snow on the parking area had been piled over the trees and brush bordering it. Camper trailers lined one side of the clearing and heavy gray canvas tents lined the cliff side. The tents were set up for different purposes. One was used to house props that weren't in use. The largest was the mess tent, and the other was the communications and weather tent, which meant there was a two-way radio inside. One large camper was set off from the others and Joe pointed it out. "That's Richard Dawes's dressing room."

Other smaller camper trailers near the parking lot were for the filming crew. The boom of the crane was suddenly right in front of them and looked immense, stretching out into the sky. Diesel smoke and a loud rumbling engine sound came from the crane. There was a group of men standing around the machine.

Joe pointed to a big, red bearded man standing in the middle of the group. He was talking and pointing at the sky. "That's Ralph. He's the head cameraman, and several of those others are his camera crew. Some of them are prop men. Wait here, I'll be right back," Joe said and walked carefully over the frozen ground. The sight of the cliff's edge caused people to use cautious movements.

Kaycee turned her back on the panoramic view hindered

by the low cloud mass blending the lake and the horizon together. She pulled her scarf up to cover more of her face and then slipped her hands into her pockets.

"Ms. Swanson," a polite voice said behind her.

Kaycee turned to see a prop guy bundled in a furred hood and parka with a layer of fleece covering most of his face. "Would you follow me, please?"

Kaycee turned her mind from the fear that ate the pit of her stomach as she followed the man closer to the cliff's edge. In situations like this, she kept repeating, "Act, don't think!"

Men soon surrounded Kaycee. They were bundled the same in fleece and parkas. She could only see their eyes. One held a leather harness in his gloved hand. His instructions came out muffled. "Please lift your arms. Straighten your spine. Not like that. There, that's good. Now with your shoulders back, keep your spine straight." The group finally stepped back when the harness was secure. "There, let's give it a try. Just stand still. The crane is going to lift you off the ground to see how this is going to work."

The engine of the crane grew louder. Diesel smoke shot out into the cold making perfect puffy black clouds.

Kaycee tried to prepare herself as she felt the slack go from the wire, but she still jumped as the harness tightened over her chest. The pressure built on her lungs as her feet left the ground. Panicking, she violently waved her hands in the air. The crane stopped. Slowly, she was lowered. The suffocating stopped as her toes touched the ground. When enough slack allowed her movement, she doubled over to catch her breath.

One of the prop man stepped forward. "What's the problem?" he asked, pulling the harness back to its original position.

"I can't breath. The harness is pressing right against my lungs. Hanging from the crane, I won't be able to breathe."

The man frowned. He looked her over. Pulled at the harness over her chest and then at the hook attachments on the back. "You don't have enough padding," he said, then turned to Joe. "This harness must be designed for someone with more muscle."

"Or more fat," Joe interrupted.

"Whatever. She can't use it the way it is now. She's too thin."

"Then think of something else," Joe said impatiently. He motioned for the men to help her out of the harness. "It's freezing out here. Come on, Kaycee, let's go."

"We're probably going to lose the sky. Paine won't like that."

"That wind might kick up again," another member of the prop crew pointed out.

"Too bad, that's your problem. My actress isn't going to suffocate because you guys can't figure out a harness for a woman. Call me when you come up with something that's going to do what it's supposed to," Joe said. Then he turned his back on the men and took Kaycee's arm. He led her unresisting away from the cliff toward the trailers. "We're going to have to figure some way to pad the harness. You go to the trailer and let them start on your makeup. I'll call when it's ready."

"Okay Joe, stay warm," she said through her scarf as she trudged off toward the trailer.

21

The small white camper had been set in the battered bushes surrounding the cleared area. Prickly sticks stuck out from under the base and through the slats of the metal steps. Kaycee hesitated at the bottom and looked at the small window on the door crusted over with ice. Then she stepped up and knocked. After a few seconds the door flung open. Kaycee was face to face with a woman about thirty with frizzy light brown hair and black plastic rimmed glasses. The woman stared at her and then pushed up her glasses.

"Michelle?"

"It is you!" Michelle said with a laugh. She pressed her hands together and looked toward the sky. "Thank you, God." Michelle stepped aside and with a flamboyant wave beckoned her in. "Come on, come on, it's freezing."

Kaycee stepped inside and asked, "What was that all about?"

"I've been sitting in here making myself sick because I knew I was going to meet you today. The thought of some uppity model pushing me around for five weeks scared me to death."

Kaycee pulled off her hat and smiled. "Wait a minute. Nobody pushed around the Michelle I knew in New York. What happened? Did you suddenly get soft?"

"Are you crazy? Of course I did. This is a plush job compared to working the fashion shows. I have a few clients for a couple of months and my own private office. That is so much better than the shows where forty skitterish women a day were pushed through my chair. This is the life."

She reached for Kaycee's hat. "Hurry up and get this stuff off. We have to get to work on your facial."

"Are you going to fill me in on what you've been up to and how you ended up in Duluth, Minnesota, of all places?"

"You know me better than that," Michelle said with mock horror. "Would I bore my clients with stories about my life when I could be hearing exciting tales of models and actresses?"

"Don't look to this actress for excitement. So far the only exciting thing that's happened to me is getting this part. After that it's been one technical lecture after another."

Michelle sighed as she shook open the plastic sheet and patted the seat of her adjustable chair. "Will you get over here? Okay, you talked me into telling you what I've been doing. If it puts you to sleep, don't blame me."

Kaycee settled into the chair and waited patiently while Michelle wrapped the sheet around her and then fiddled with the chair until she was satisfied. Then Michelle firmly guided her head back against the cushion and began to spread a cold, smooth cream on her cheeks. She asked, "Would you like me to explain what I'm doing?"

"I don't think that's necessary."

"Oh good, I have a terrible time remembering to stay on the subject when somebody wants me to tell them each and every step. I've been doing this so long a lot of it has become habit. Then I have a complete mental block when I'm supposed to be explaining something. It doesn't go over real well with the picky types. Don't answer me now. The cream has to set for a minute while I find the colors you'll need. Your winter coloring is really white."

"Thanks!"

"I said not to talk. Just relax this is supposed to be relaxing."

"I'll try and remember."

"Don't talk!"

There was a knock on the door almost an hour later. It was a messenger from Joe. "They're ready for you, Ms. Swanson."

Kaycee was outfitted. Not only was she clothed in the

newest technology of winter survival clothing to combat the cold. She was dressed in an expensive cross country ski outfit of baby blue with bands of yellow and red around the wrists and ankles and across her chest. Her hat and ski gloves matched the bright colored stripes. At any cross-country ski resort, she would make an attractive addition.

Kaycee had just reread the script trying to put herself into character. She hoped it would stop the butterflies in her stomach. If she pretended she didn't know about the cliff and the fall, maybe it would become the surprise it was supposed to be.

"You look fabulous, now go break a leg," Michelle said. Kaycee frowned.

"That's supposed to mean good luck."

"I know that."

"Good luck."

"Thanks." As Kaycee left the camper and walked alone across the clearing, she saw Joe hurrying toward her from the communications tent.

"Kaycee, you look great. The wind is holding off, for now at least, so we can test the harness and maybe even get some footage shot."

"That's good news," Kaycee replied, raising her voice as the noise of the crane became louder.

When they reached the cliff, Joe paused to give her a final inspection. He needed to be certain she was dressed in the right outfit with the right accessories and to make sure her makeup fit the situation. Her thick black hair was trapped under the stylish, but unattractive, hat, and she looked pale. A few strands of her hair blew across her face, and two red spots on her cheeks stood out with the cold. Her beauty held a touch of tragedy in it. The audience was sure to get the same feeling.

When they walked to the crane it was the same crowd of men standing there.

"If this works, then the crane will place you down the side of the rock face," Joe explained, in a shout.

Kaycee nodded. She leaned closer to him to hear above the roar of the motor.

"Just like they taught you at the indoor rock wall, handholds and footholds have been cut out and reinforced with rubber. I'm going to keep repeating these instructions to you," he said. "Then I know for sure you've heard them." Joe flipped through the papers on his clipboard. "You did pretty good at rock climbing. This will be easy for you," he finished with an abrupt, impersonal tone.

He paused and covered his mouth with his hand to warm his lips up. "It's cold, but I think not as cold as when we arrived."

Kaycee's face was covered with fleece to keep her makeup from freezing, and she was not feeling the cold yet. "I'm fine," she shouted back to him.

"You will have to climb the rock face even though the crane is holding you. If you only let the crane pull you up, you could hurt yourself. You need to move along and stop yourself from banging against the rock. It isn't very far, you can do it." He patted her shoulder.

He moved aside as the crew came over with the padded harness and re-fit it under Kaycee's jacket. With the extra padding, she felt as stuffed as a teddy bear and probably looked just as attractive. The prop man again hastily explained the signals to her. "Do you understand?" he yelled in her face.

Kaycee gave a thumbs up.

The prop man motioned to the crane, and it immediately roared to full power. The slack in the line tightened, lifting Kaycee onto her tiptoes. The harness didn't bother her this time, so she gave another thumbs up signal. Joe moved forward and took the fleece off her face. He straightened her hat and scarf. Kaycee looked up and saw Ralph watching. He wore a hat but no scarf. His cheeks above his beard were bright red, and his eyes looked dark underneath bushy eyebrows. He nodded to Joe. Joe patted Kaycee's arm again and then stepped away from her. The engine roared and all eyes watched her reaction. The motor became deafening as the engine revved into a higher gear.

"Has the helicopter checked in?" Ralph asked one of the men who never left his side.

The man gave the thumbs up and Ralph nodded, watching Kaycee dangling over the cliff and then he looked to the sky for the helicopter.

Kaycee went over the edge of the cliff. The instant she became airborne, she inhaled so fast she froze her lungs. She shut her mouth. Kaycee tightened her lips and closed her eyes. When her back slammed against the rock wall, her eyes flew open. The first thing she saw was angry gray-black water white-capped and frothing piled against rocks below her. White-capped waves engulfed sharp ice-covered rocks where a body could be smashed to pieces. A terrible roar from behind the cliff surprised her. Suddenly, the wires holding her began to swing. A helicopter flew into view and the force of the wind caused by the helicopter blades set her into motion. Horrified, Kaycee watched the rock face covered with frozen water spray as the wind forced her into the rocks. With a shriek drowned by the helicopter's roar, Kaycee held out her legs and pushed herself safely away for the moment.

"Kaycee," a voice from the helicopter called, "do not swing the cables." A high-pitched whine from a speaker followed the voice.

"Kaycee, smash your face against a rock wall," she mimicked and reached out to grab at an outcropping of rock to hold onto. "I don't think that was written in my contract," she cried out ruefully.

"Kaycee quit talking to yourself. We'll catch it on the film," the voice directed.

Kaycee grimaced then kept her face still as she gingerly

positioned herself on the cliff like she practiced in the simu-lator. Once she felt her position was secure, she turned to glare at the entire crew in the helicopter. She gasped at how big it was and how close it flew to the rocks.

"Okay, that's fine. Now remember why you're hanging out here. It's getting cold so if we're going to get this on film we need to get moving," the director said through the speaker on the helicopter. "You have just been pushed off. You've managed to grab a chunk of rock and in a last ditch effort to safe yourself you need to climb up or you'll freeze to death. Ready on three, the camera will be rolling...one, two, three...roll 'em."

The rock felt cold as she slowly scrambled along, finding the handholds before moving her body up. The cold was un-relenting, and her fingers began to numb as she moved from one hold to the next. She felt satisfied. I must be making good progress, she thought.

"Cut, Kaycee, stop!" the voice boomed behind her.

She held on, pressing herself against the rock, and imme-diately felt the cold begin to seep through her clothes.

"We need you to look down, Kaycee," Lance said. "The helicopter is going to drop so the camera is below you, then we'll begin shooting again."

Kaycee nodded her head slightly. She wiggled her toes and her fingers to keep the circulation moving.

"Kaycee, on three we'll shoot...one, two, three...action."

Kaycee leaned her body slightly away from the cliff to look down at the gaping area between her and the water. The treacherous height did not scare her like it should. "How odd, when I was so scared before. I don't feel anything right now," she thought. A wave crashed below. Still she felt nothing. Her hat slipped from her head to float rather elegantly down-ward, the bright colors stark against the gloom below. It landed in the brown foam of the waves and moved back and forth with the tide until the material sank beneath the waves. Kaycee pressed her cheek against her ski glove and closed her eyes. "It's so cold. Why do I suddenly feel so cold?"

"Kaycee!" a sharp voice snapped, causing the speaker to shriek. "Kaycee, you okay?"

She did not move. Her skin burned. She tried to reach up and touch her face but her fingers and toes had no feeling in them. She hid her face in her arm to protect it.

"Kaycee, we're going pull you in," a commanding voice said.

It sounded different than before, almost comforting. "My brain must be fuzzy. That mole of a director could never sound comforting."

"Are you capable of keeping the wires steady so you won't hit the cliff face?" Someone yelled at her. It sounded far away.

"Kaycee!" the speaker shrieked.

Slowly she shook her head no. She didn't think she could move at all. A panicky feeling swept over her. "I'm freezing to death."

The helicopter roared to life behind her. It lifted into the sky above her head. The numbness was spreading except for a sudden trembling in her muscles. If she continued to shiver like this she might lose her grip and fall. "Oh God," she whispered, "please don't let me fall." Kaycee wanted to scream but couldn't. "They left me! I'm alone hanging off a cliff exposed to the elements. They know something's wrong. They have to. They wouldn't just leave me here to freeze? My fingers will freeze first. Then, I'll lose my grip and fall into the lake. The fall will kill me, but if not, the cold lake water will. Why do I always hear freezing is a peaceful way to die? It's horrible, and it's happening to me!"

Desperately, she pressed herself against the rock. Something snaked down the cliff past her head. Slowly, she turned to stare at the thin black wire. "I hope I don't have to reach for it," she thought as she waited for the voice to tell her what to do. "I can't remember if I'm supposed to be doing something. What is it?"

The line moved by itself, whipping against the rock. Kaycee turned her face away and buried it into the curve of her arm. The wind was blocked, her cheek warmed. When she looked around again, boot-covered feet were hanging next to her head.

"Kaycee," a voice above her said, "you're going to be all right. I'm here to make sure of it." He shifted his weight, moving closer to her.

Kaycee felt safe. "The voice isn't going to let me die out here all alone. The voice is going to get me back."

"I'm going to climb over you."

Kaycee whimpered as he pressed her hard into the freezing rocks. It cut into her torso and legs.

He eased his weight back away from the cliff to give her more space. The weight of his body blocked the wind and secured her from the emptiness behind. Immediately, she felt hopeful.

"I won't let you fall," he said into her ear, "but you have to help me by climbing as much as you can."

He shook the safety lines attached to her and made sure they were still tight. "On three, Kaycee…one, two, three…move," he barked loudly into her ear.

Kaycee moved. She didn't know how, but her arms and legs were moving up the side of the cliff slowly but steadily. Against her back, Kaycee could feel the deep thumping heartbeat of the man supporting her weight as they climbed the cliff face. Of course, her rescuer was doing most of the work, hauling her along. Suddenly, the top of the ledge appeared, and she was shoved over onto flat ground and into waiting hands. The safety harness was stripped off her and replaced by a heated blanket. It was wrapped tightly around her violently shaking body.

22

Several men carried her across the slippery ground to her trailer. Waiting inside was a nurse practitioner. She took over as soon as Kaycee was brought into the camper.

The journey from the ridge to the trailer only took a matter of seconds. The entire episode only lasted about twenty minutes.

After Kaycee was taken away from the cliff, a solid, muscled figure in an army green insulated jumpsuit was helped off the cliff face. He peeled off the protective facemask and stared after the little group hurrying her away. Another blanket was offered to him. He took it with a grateful smile and shrugged it over his shoulders, shivering slightly.

"Great job," one of the prop men said as he unbuckled Jimmy's safety harness. "We got the whole thing on film. You had some awesome moves out there, man."

Jimmy shrugged. "It was nothing one of your stuntmen couldn't do and probably with a lot more style."

They laughed. "We'll let you know when the film's ready. You'll want to see it."

"Sure, thanks," Jimmy said absently. As he walked away from the cliff, he rolled the insulated line and hook in a neat loop. "I'll have to return this," he thought. "Lucky break, I decided not to pilot today."

It was Kaycee's debut out on the cliff, and he wanted to watch her instead. Once she got into trouble, there was no way he could have been able to concentrate on flying. "That girl makes me crazy, and she doesn't even know it."

He kept the blanket wrapped around him as he walked over to the trailer he'd been told Kaycee had disappeared into. A woman, unrecognizable under her bulky coat, hurried down the steps.

"Is she going to be okay?" he asked.

The woman stopped and smiled at him. She had been at the cliff edge with the crew to watch the rescue. She recognized the man responsible for bringing the actress to the top of the cliff. She had noticed then the height and build of this local while he was struggling into the harness. They certainly grow them nice up here in the cold, she thought.

"The nurse is with her now. They're concerned about exposure."

"They should be, frostbite is serious."

"You come back in a little while. We'll know the details then," she said. She smiled once more at him before she disappeared in the direction of the mess tent.

Jimmy stood next to the trailer for a second. Then he turned and walked toward the communications tent. He felt like a truck just ran over him, not because of the cold or the physical strain of the rescue, but the mental strain of worrying about that girl.

Jimmy pushed open the flap letting a blast of cold air into the heated tent. Peter Kent was the meteorologist sitting behind the table that held the short wave radio. Through it weather reports came directly from the national weather service.

"Hey, Jimmy," Pete said.

"Hey, Pete," Jimmy said, securing the flaps that kept out the wind. He stepped over to the table where the computer weather printouts were strewn. "What's the wind chill factor?" he asked. He picked up one of the sheets looking over the information printed there.

"Twenty below zero," Pete answered. "It dropped fifteen degrees in less than an hour."

Jimmy frowned. "I thought it was something like that," he murmured more to himself. "It felt awful cold out there."

"Too cold to be hanging off that cliff," Pete agreed. "Heard what happened out there. Tough on that actress, is she okay?"

Jimmy nodded. "Yeah I guess so. The winds picked up. No more helicopter today." He set the report back on the pile of papers.

"Looks like you have an easy time for the rest of the day. You'll need it after what happened."

Jimmy shrugged. "I'm not done yet," he said, and knew Joe was soon going to introduce him to Kaycee as the local security involved with the site. He was also hired to help keep civilians from bothering the actors or actresses. Since Kaycee was the only actress on the site right now and because of the dangerous scenes her character was involved in, the film company felt she was a safety risk. So much for why he was hired, now he wished he could figure out why he had applied for the position. Kaycee did not want a caretaker or a father figure. She made that plain enough during their last meeting. After what Jimmy saw her go through today, he trusted nobody but himself to watch out for her. There was real danger involved, and he was ready for it.

"Hey, Pete," he said suddenly, "do you think I could get a copy of the script for this movie?"

Pete slipped the headphones off his ears and scratched his head. "I'm not sure," he said. "Try Joe, the skinny guy who carries the neon clipboard. If he doesn't have one, I bet he'll know where to get one."

"I know, Joe. I bet you're right. Thanks."

"Sure, no problem."

Jimmy left the tent. The heater inside made it almost too hot in the insulated suit he wore. He needed to change. The protective suit kept him warm, but it was nothing to look at. He certainly didn't want to meet up with Kaycee while he was still in it. The bitter wind outside had lowered the temperature further, and the crew was busy securing everything against the cold night. The filming was going to have to wait until the cold let up.

* * * * *

"Are you sure this is allowed?" Kaycee asked Michelle. She turned in front of the mirror and watched her reflection with pleasure. "It truly is beautiful but—"

"Don't you worry, Kaycee," Michelle said. "After what happened to you today, you deserve to stay warm. Just bring it back when you're done filming in this forsaken place, and I'll return it to wardrobe for you."

Kaycee brushed her hands across the softness.

"It has to be getting colder. I can't see out the windows at all anymore," Michelle warned.

Then Kaycee opened the trailer door.

"How can it get any colder? What is this? The North Pole?" Michelle wailed in disbelief.

Kaycee slammed the door shut. The wind caught at her, almost pushing her against the outside of the trailer. She pulled the luxurious fur coat tighter at her neck and tucked the scarf closer to her skin. A white fox fur coat with an ermine collar, she felt wickedly decadent wearing such a thing. It was like wearing a huge diamond tiara for everyone to see. Her thoughts briefly on the animal activists and what they would say or, worse, do, didn't last long when the wind whipped around her and she barely felt it. The cold couldn't penetrate the fur coat that draped down past her knees. If she had a fur hat and muff to wear with it, then nothing on her body except her face could get cold.

While hanging on the cliff face today, she thought this kind of warmth was not possible. She wasted her time wearing all that high tech clothing to fight the cold when all she needed was what she was wearing now. "The designer of what little critters wear is the master designer of all," she thought with approval. "Joe, I have to find Joe."

Jimmy saw her come out of the trailer and hurried away from the mess tent to fall into step beside her.

"Hey," he said cheerfully. "You look pretty toasty."

Kaycee stopped abruptly and turned to look at him. Once

again he showed up out of nowhere and helped to save her life.

"Are you feeling okay?" he searched her face slowly. The flesh looked slightly red but showed no white areas of frostbite.

Kaycee held out her gloved hands and wiggled her fingers. "If you need to see my toes, then I'll insist we go indoors," she teased.

Jimmy chuckled. "That won't be necessary. But it sounds tempting. You look fit enough."

"Thank you." She paused to look at him out of the corner of her eye. "I found out you know."

"Found out?" Jimmy repeated.

"Did you think I wouldn't?"

Jimmy took her hand and slipped her arm through his, and they began to walk again.

"It's too cold to stand still for long. We might turn into living ice sculptures."

She giggled. "They told me the name of the local officer who was flying the helicopter."

She paused to smile at him with a look on her face that stopped him in his tracks. He felt an overwhelming desire to take her in his arms and kiss her right here, right now. "What a nice way to warm up," he said softly.

"What did you say?" she asked.

"Nothing," he replied. Gratitude is nice, he decided, grinning at her. When she acted like this, all warm and welcoming, he liked it.

"Why didn't you tell me you were working up here?" Kaycee asked. "I was looking for Joe to find out if it was true."

Kaycee must think I was hired to fly the helicopter. Jimmy could tell by the way she was acting that she must not know about the actress security part of the job.

"I'd rather have had you tell me that you'd been hired,"

she accused him.

"Sorry, but I didn't have the chance."

"Oh, I have to find Joe anyway," she told Jimmy, walking again. "He sent me the strangest note. He's probably worried that I'm traumatized from what happened on the cliff." She sighed. "I guess I won't know for sure until we have to shoot the scene again."

"That won't be today," Jimmy supplied helpfully.

Kaycee glanced at him with tears in her eyes from the wind, or at least he thought they were from the wind.

"I was in the radio tent when the weather report came through. The helicopter's been grounded."

"Oh, too bad for you," she said as they reached the tent. Jimmy held the flap open for her to duck inside. The tent almost sweltered to those who came in from the bitter cold. The number of bodies congregated in here gave off enough heat to raise the temperature. Jimmy took off his parka and laid it across a table. He had changed into a flannel lumberjack shirt of blue and black.

Kaycee unbuttoned her fur coat but kept it on.

The confined area was full of men. Joe was not one of them.

The outside flap blew open, and Joe stumbled in. He reached for the flap and re-covered it.

"Kaycee," Joe said. "You look warm in that get-up."

"I am. Even that wind can't get to me," she said, as she rubbed her cheek against the collar.

He looked down at his clipboard. "Any permanent damage from what happened?" he asked. He kept his eyes on the page of notes.

"No, not physical."

"You didn't suffer any ill effects from it?" He looked up with a piercing stare at her face. "You aren't afraid now, are you?"

Kaycee didn't flinch. She merely shook her head no.

"This kind of unexpected stuff happens all the time, even to the experienced actors and actresses. Just don't let it bother you." He gave her a lopsided grin. "Anyway, you'll have some time to recover. We won't be re-shooting that scene for a few days. This wind is going to stay. Aren't we the lucky ones?" he added sarcastically. He paused to cross out several lines from his paper.

Kaycee opened her mouth to ask a question when he spoke up again.

"Oh, you met Jimmy Zane?" he asked. "He must be in here somewhere. Zane, you in here?" Joe called out.

Jimmy walked away from the group carrying a coffee cup and waved to Joe.

"He was the one out there on the cliff with you," Joe explained, "in case you hadn't found that out yet. I'm sure he didn't find the time for proper introductions at the time."

Jimmy walked up to stand next to her.

Joe nodded to him. "Jimmy's been hired to act as security, Kaycee," Joe said abruptly. "You can tell by his performance this afternoon that he's well-qualified for the job."

He looked at Jimmy, then motioned to Kaycee. "This is Miss Kaycee Swanson, Jimmy. Now I'll let you two get acquainted." Joe moved away from them without noticing Kaycee's stunned silence.

For a moment, Kaycee neither spoke nor moved. Her eyes flew to Jimmy's face. "This has to be a mistake," she said, but he refused to look at her.

"Joe," she cried, chasing after him. She barely gave Jimmy another look.

Joe paused, but only to pick up a Styrofoam cup and fill it with steaming coffee.

"I thought what happened was routine. Why do I need a security guard? Are you expecting something else to happen? Something worse than being frozen onto the face of a cliff?"

Joe sipped the coffee, not meeting her eyes. "Of course not, but this is a high risk area. With the cold and the wind and the dangers of the cliff, you are the only liability so far because you're the only cast member of the movie on the site. For the time being, the security is at your disposal. Get used to it."

Kaycee turned to look at Jimmy who stood watching her. His expression unreadable.

"The first bus is loading," came the announcement from the entryway. Kaycee was the first one out the tent flap without a thought about the bitter cold.

23

Back home in the warmth of Ellyn's kitchen, Kaycee thought, "Jimmy Zane? What was he thinking taking this job?" Not for money. Jimmy was not the type. He had rescued her off the cliff with sheer brute strength and brains. Ellyn was preparing a triple batch of chocolate chip cookies. "How can I be so bad-mannered? I don't think I even gave Jimmy proper thanks for saving my life," she moaned to Ellyn.

Ellyn did not pause while she scraped the thick batter in the metal mixing bowl. "The circumstances alone give you an excuse for your behavior, dear. You most likely were suffering from delayed shock. The whole thing sounds awfully dangerous, Kaycee. I think you should be very concerned about the danger you're in while out on the cliff. Are you sure this is what you want to do?"

Kaycee opened the cupboard to take out the cookie sheets. She smiled. "You're right, mom, it is dangerous, but if you could've seen Jimmy. You'd know I'm in good hands. I don't think anything would stop that man."

"What do you mean? I thought he was only there today?" Karyn asked, who was sitting at the table doing her Shakespeare homework and listening.

Kaycee shook her head. "Uh uh, he's been hired full-time by the film company. His job is to watch out for the safety of the actors and actresses on the site. Since I'm the only one on the cliff filming, Jimmy has to keep me out of trouble all day long. It'll probably put him in the nut house." She paused and then glanced at her mother to see her reaction to the news.

"Well, that makes me feel much better. Jimmy is a very capable man, and he's been well trained. Didn't you say he was in the military?"

"Yep, so there's not a thing for you and dad to worry

about." She never imagined Jimmy's working for the movie company could help with the worries of her parents.

Icy wind howled around the window sashes in the kitchen crystallizing moisture on the glass.

Kaycee stood by the stove and spooned dough onto the cookie sheet.

"Doorbell," Stewart called from the front room.

Kaycee slid the pan into the oven and hurried out of the kitchen. "Who would be out on a night like this? And why can't you answer it, dad?"

"It's either a fool in love or someone whose car has broken down," Stewart guessed, turning the page of the newspaper. "Where are my cookies?" he yelled to the kitchen.

"I'm coming, dad," Karyn answered quickly.

Kaycee yanked at the heavy wooden door until it creaked open.

"Hey," Jimmy said from outside. The collar of his jacket covered most of his face.

At the sight of his bulky figure, Kaycee's heart began an erratic beat. "I don't believe after what happened this afternoon it's you at my door."

"I thought you might want to talk."

She shivered and grabbed his gloved hand, pulling on it. "Get in here, it's freezing," she demanded. She found it hard to hide her pleasure at seeing him.

Jimmy obediently stepped inside and pushed the door shut.

Stewart, sitting in front of the fire eating a cookie and holding a steaming cup, said, "Hello, Jimmy. So, you're working with Kaycee?"

"Yes sir."

Kaycee walked toward the kitchen. "You can take your stuff off out here. I have to go check the cookies."

In the kitchen, after several minutes passed and she filled the empty cookie sheet, Kaycee thought he must have stayed in the living room to talk to dad. She had no idea what to say to Jimmy. She was glad Ellyn and Karyn were still with her in the kitchen. Ellyn was now washing the supper dishes while Karyn dried them.

As soon as the swinging door opened and Jimmy appeared, they all stopped to look at him.

"Hello," he said.

"Hello, Jimmy, how nice to see you," Ellyn said.

Jimmy smiled.

Kaycee stared at him thinking he has such a nice smile. It was so genuine. His eyes crinkle up and he looks really happy. The excitement at seeing him was not the same feeling she had when they were friends so many years ago. Must be a left over adrenaline rush from him rescuing me on the cliff, she thought.

Jimmy said, "It sure smells good in here."

"Kaycee's baking again. She's such a wonderful cook," Ellyn said wiping her hands on a towel. "Come along, Karyn, they need to talk about work."

Karyn grabbed a handful of cookies and paused, giving them both a curious look, she asked quickly, "You saved Kaycee's life today?"

Jimmy actually blushed. "I guess so."

"Wow!"

Kaycee broke in, "Scram, Karyn, this isn't Shakespeare."

Karyn hurried to follow Ellyn out of the room.

Kaycee explained to Jimmy with a laugh, "Karyn's studying Shakespeare in Lit class. I just hope it isn't Romeo and Juliet, or she'll imagine us in some crypt committing suicide for each other."

Jimmy chuckled but remained in the doorway watching as she checked the cookies baking in the oven. While she took out one batch of cookies and replaced it with a full cookie sheet, the smell of baking mixed with the warmth erased the bitterness of the stormy night.

When Kaycee turned around, he had left the doorway and

was seated at the table, a cookie in each hand. She shook her head as she lifted the cookies onto the cooling rack. "Make yourself at home."

"Thanks, I've never had a problem doing that," he said.

"No, you haven't," she agreed. She turned away and set the pan on the counter.

"Is baking something women in your profession do regularly?" he asked.

Kaycee knew she looked a mess. She wore no makeup. Her hair was tied back while she baked. Her cheeks, she knew, must be bright and shiny from the oven's heat. She looked a lot different from the painted stranger Jimmy had stopped on the highway a few months ago.

Kaycee struck a pose with the spatula in one hand and the oven mitt in the other. "Yes, it keeps us humble. Especially me because I end up ruining almost everything I try to make. My mother was the one that made this cookie dough. She had to be sure the cookies would turn out since I'm baking them for Karyn's school bake sale."

Jimmy stood up and crossed the room to stand next to her. Kaycee looked at him, her face filled with curiosity.

"What are you thinking? Talk to me, Kaycee."

Kaycee squirmed away and leaned against the sink crossing her arms. "If you're asking what I think about your new job, I'll tell you. After my mother heard what happened and exactly where the filming is taking place, she was really alarmed. That is until I told her about you. After I explained that you were going to be up there everyday helping with the safety, then she was fine."

They faced each other in silence.

Kaycee shrugged her slender shoulders and said, "I guess admitting that I'll be taken care of calmed my parents anxiety. After that, how could I disagree about any of it? I just feel bad for you. How boring it'll be sitting at Palisade Head day in and out."

He shifted and looked away with a sigh of impatience. "I'm sure I'll find something to keep me busy with you around."

Kaycee reached out and grabbed his forearm covered by the soft flannel of his shirt. "I'd like to thank you again for saving my life. When I said it before at the cliff, I didn't understand that it was you who actually did the rescue."

Jimmy moved away from her. "You don't need to say a thing. Especially now that you know I'm getting paid for what I did."

Kaycee kept a tight grip on his shirt to hold him. She frowned. "Getting paid doesn't change what you did."

Jimmy laughed. "Don't get caught up in that stuff, Kaycee. I'm a cop remember. It's my job. I was just doing my job."

"So there's absolutely no other reason you're doing this. It's just for the money?"

"Of course, except I get to work on a movie set. How many times does that opportunity happen here in Duluth?"

She pushed at his shoulder. "Oh fine, I can see I'm wasting my gratitude on you, Mister Cop."

Jimmy stepped back and said, "If you want to pay me, do it in cookies. These are delicious." He returned to his place at the kitchen table.

She spun around. "My cookies, they're burning!" she jerked open the oven door. The sugar bowl crashed off the ledge above the stove, sugar flew across the stovetop. "Oh great!"

"Getting the hang of this baking thing, are you?" Jimmy asked with obvious amusement.

Kaycee ignored him as she pulled the pan out of the oven. "Thank goodness they aren't burned," she exclaimed. She walked to the table and held the pan in front of him. "There, Mr. Cop, is my debt is paid in full?"

"Not quite," Jimmy reached out to grasp the oven mitt covering her hand. His grin mischievous. "I forgot. I did want to ask you for one more thing."

Kaycee, startled at his tone, gave him a wary but hopeful look.

"Could I have a glass of milk?"

Disappointed that he was not going to be serious, that his thoughts were not plagued with hopes for their friendship in the future, she turned away. What did she expect from him? She opened the refrigerator and poured him a glass of milk, setting it in front of him with a flourish. "There, is my account settled now?"

His thick hair flopped over the front of his brow. She automatically reached over to smooth it back. Kaycee remembered doing this often when they were younger. Her hand stopped in mid-air. Their eyes locked. His were filled with amusement. She stopped and turned away with a rueful smile. "It's hard to remember we're adults now," she said as she moved to the oven. She kept her back to him, and he did not answer.

Breaking the silence, she said, "Now that you're warmed up and sweetened with almost a dozen chocolate chip cookies, I want the whole story. From the beginning, when you applied for the job to when Joe introduced us." She began to fill the sink with warm soapy water to wash the pans.

"Are you grilling me for secrets? This production is a closed set, and I'm not allowed to leak any information pertaining to the script or the people affiliated with it."

"That sounds like some kind of a recording," she teased and flicked warm bubbles off her fingers at him. "Don't you dare try to dodge the subject, Mister Cop. How did you hear about the job?"

Jimmy leaned back in the chair, stretching his long legs out in front of him.

Kaycee answered her own question before he could. "I bet I know. From my sweet sister Kathie, right? Did she tell you about the company hiring local law enforcement? I told my mom, I'm sure she told the family."

Jimmy shrugged. "If you say so."

"I hope you realize, if a movie set is anything like the modeling industry, then the whole place is like a soap opera. Everybody knows everything about everybody else. Anything you wrote on an application is common knowledge by now, especially after that stunt you pulled today."

She glanced over her shoulder at him. He looked unimpressed.

He raised one dark eyebrow and encouraged her. "Go on, tell me more."

"So, everybody also knows that we both grew up in Duluth and we know each other. The rumors about us will be going around like crazy."

The chiming of the grandfather clock that stood in the front hallway broke the silence. Kaycee looked up at the kitchen clock. "Ten, it's my bedtime," she said softly. She set the last pan of cookie dough in the oven. "I'm almost finished with these."

The legs of the chair squeaked when Jimmy stood up.

"I thought it would be easier for you if it was me working on the set instead of a complete stranger," he said quietly. He stood by the table watching her. His tall form looked lanky in the baggy clothes he wore. He sounded tired. "And you're wrong, Kaycee. I know what you're thinking about me. I would never presume that you need to be taken care of. Don't you realize how brave you were out on that cliff? You have no training for that kind of thing. I don't care how much the company tried to prep you for that experience, it's not the same thing as professional training." He moved a step closer to her. "And I know something none of them will ever know," he said softly. "You don't have a head for heights. I remember that big oak in my dad's east field. Ever since you fell out of it, you've hated heights."

Kaycee closed her eyes. She leaned into the cold porcelain of the sink. She did remember the oak. He did remember things from their past.

"You were the brave one today, Kaycee. Where you found the strength to fight off your fear, I don't know. That is, unless I'm doing you an injustice. Maybe you overcame your fear before this."

Kaycee silently shook her head no, while gripping the edge of the sink tightly.

He stood so close to her, yet she felt there was still a distance filled with misunderstanding between them. It felt like a physical separation.

"Then I'm right, aren't I? You are the one with courage."

Kaycee gave a weak smile.

"I don't expect anything from you," he told her. "I'm just glad I was there to help, and I'll be there if you need me. That's it, nothing more, nothing less."

She felt a swift brush of his hand against her cheek, and he was gone.

The sound of voices in the other room and then the slamming of the outside door revealed to her that he had really gone. Kaycee, with slow deliberate movements, switched off the stove, and began stacking the cookies in the cookie jar. "I am grateful to you, Jimmy. Once again, you're right," she whispered.

24

The first charter bus pulled in front of the Holiday Mall. The movie crew moved through the double glass doors carrying bags filled with extra warm clothes. After yesterday, the people who were not familiar with the wind off Lake Superior realized how bitterly cold it could be and wanted to be prepared.

Kaycee silently followed the others. She waited for her turn to board and once on the bus sank down into the padded seat. She held the script in front of her face. For some reason, the prep meeting had been cancelled. She was worried about which scene Lance might choose today. Her stomach churned as she re-examined the diagrams for the scene they had filmed yesterday. The other people moved past her looking for an empty seat. One of them carried a backgammon board. Kaycee noticed none of the technicians were boarding. She overheard someone say, "The boss had the technicians up on the cliff before sun-up. He's planning on taking advantage of that sky."

A few of those passing her seat stopped to give Kaycee words of encouragement.

"Tough break yesterday."

"You handled yourself great."

When the bus was filled to capacity and the passengers settled, Kaycee turned to stare out the window. Through the tinted windows, she saw the sky did look as ominous as yesterday. There was no snow as the paralyzing cold hung on. Absently, she stroked the soft fur around her cuff as the bus lurched forward.

Once they arrived at the cliff, everything was enveloped in a misty twilight. There were technicians walking around the clearing. An occasional glow from a cigarette was seen.

Kaycee stood by the bus and looked around the clearing for Joe's familiar figure. It was awhile later when she finally found him. "Joe, am I on the agenda today?"

"Nope, not today. Still too cold for any of the cliff scenes."

"So what do I do?"

Joe shrugged. He was busy reading the stack of papers clipped to his board. Then he paused to glance at her. "Take it easy. Read your lines. I don't know. Just make sure you're available for a quick makeup and wardrobe if there's a sudden change."

Kaycee said a hasty goodbye. She glanced around wondering if Jimmy had arrived on the site yet. She didn't see him, so she walked to her trailer. It was empty. Michelle was not there. Kaycee looked around at all of Michelle's belongings scattered around the kitchen and the over-cluttered living room and wondered if she should leave or wait. A chair, empty except for a fashion magazine lying open on it, looked comfortable so she sat down and pulled the script out of her pocket. Her lines blurred in her mind as she read them again. Kaycee sighed, flipping to the first page of the script.

The main character, a man in his early sixties who worked in a Wall Street brokerage, was very wealthy and respected in his field. She knew this was Richard Dawes's part. Kaycee was filled with curiosity about her pretend lover. She read on. The story was rather violent, with flashbacks to Dawes's army days when he became involved with drug trafficking. About three-fourths of the way through the script, Kaycee's character was mentioned.

Newly hired into Richard Dawes's firm as an intern, the sheltered daughter of a wealthy banker begins to work, and soon Dawes begins to pursue her. Only later is the reason revealed to the audience. Once Dawes has her not only in his office but also in his bed did the news leak out that she was not hired for her credentials. She was hired because her father was on the black list of a New York mob group. Her father refused to launder money for the mobsters and, to make an example of him, Dawes is the one who has to kill Kaycee's character. This same mob group was blackmailing Dawes for embezzling money from his clients. The tragic end of Kaycee's character takes place on Palisade Head because Richard Dawes's character is a married man, so they plan a romantic cross-country ski trip. Dawes wants the whole thing to look accidental.

Kaycee wondered what Richard Dawes was like. His name was being used to draw people to the movie. Kaycee had watched Dawes's movies with her parents. She also watched him on the set down in Minneapolis before the crew went on location. He performed each scene perfectly on cue. Each move he made was on time and executed exactly as Lance wanted.

Kaycee suspected Lance was accepting Dawes's performance however it came, whether it was perfect or not. It did not take away from the thrill she felt performing with this legend. He was experienced and well-liked by the public and the critics. She was really looking forward to meeting him.

The uneventful week continued at Palisade Head. The wind and the cold continued to stagnate the filming. The camera crew worked on the preliminary and trailer segments of the film that were tacked on to the main scenes.

At the beginning of the third week of filming, the news that Richard Dawes himself would be at the site today set the entire staff into an excited frenzy.

Suddenly, the mess tent staff was expected to have a special menu of what Richard Dawes preferred to eat. The security crew was increased so Jimmy was not the only local law enforcement at the site. The technician crew was suddenly busy in Dawes's trailer setting up the satellite and the other contraptions he expected.

The day Dawes was supposed to arrive, Jimmy and Kaycee left Michelle's camper and walked across the clearing to see if anything exciting was happening. There were people clustered around.

Jimmy said, "Somebody better clear that ice away from those metal steps or Mr. Dawes is going to have a nasty fall his first day on the set."

"Do you think he's already in there?"

Jimmy shook his head. "No way is he here yet."

"How do you know?"

"Somebody like Richard Dawes needs a big entrance. I'd say he's going to show up in a limousine, but there's no way a limo can make it up here. I bet a Humvee. That's what he'll pick."

"Why would someone as well respected as Richard Dawes need to have a big show, especially with such a small operation as this one? There's nothing going on here, let's go back," Kaycee defended.

They turned around, heading toward the trailer. Jimmy grinned. "I dunno if I'm right about Mr. Dawes. I'm only giving my opinion."

"I could see Lance doing something like having a big car and a grand entrance staged."

"I don't think I would share that bit of information with Lance," Jimmy told her as they walked away from the crowd.

"I know what Lance thinks. Richard Dawes is this movie's bread and butter. While I'm the dash of vinegar that casting threw in to make his life miserable."

Jimmy laughed. "You're the pretty new face who's going to break every man's heart watching this blood and guts movie."

Kaycee laughed as they reached the camper.

"I'm going to the communications tent. If the weather is right, the camera crew said they were going to start filming Mr. Dawes as soon as he arrives. I'll let you know so we can go watch."

Kaycee waved goodbye to him as she walked into the camper. The smell of toast permeated the small area. Michelle had brought her toaster and a small burner for a teapot. She seemed to live on tea and toast and was passing her habit onto Kaycee.

"Smells like breakfast in here."

"Almost, the water will be ready in a minute. Has Dawes arrived yet?"

"Nope, Jimmy just went to find out when he's set to film."

"You guys are going to be disappointed. Dawes has been around long enough. I'm sure he doesn't allow bystanders at any of his takes."

"He can't possibly have a closed set up here."

Michelle carried a plate of buttered toast and set it on the table next to the chair Kaycee had flopped into.

"You'd be amazed at what these A-list film stars demand and get wherever and whenever they want."

Michelle soon joined Kaycee with two steaming mugs of tea, and the girls enjoyed an hour of easy conversation.

A sharp knock sounded on the door and it was thrust open. Jimmy stuck his head inside. "He's here. Come on let's go."

Kaycee jumped out of her seat. She pulled on her fur coat, and cried to Michelle, "Aren't you coming?"

Michelle, picking up the dirty dishes, shook her head. "You tell me what happens. That'll be as exciting as being out there."

Kaycee smiled. "You're wrong about him. I'm sure he's going to be great."

Kaycee hurried out of the trailer to reach Jimmy. "I thought maybe I'd ask Mr. Dawes for an autograph for my parents. Wouldn't that be a great surprise for mom and dad?"

Jimmy stopped to give her a look of disbelief. Then shook his head. "No, I wouldn't. Think about it Kaycee. Your parents, you want his autograph for your parents, and if you call him Mr. Dawes, he's going to hate you right off. I don't think you need to bring attention to his age and your youth. You want to make a good first impression."

"What is with you and Michelle? You make it sound like

this talented man, an actor who has won Academy awards, is insecure. There cannot be an insecure bone left in his body. He has critics all over the world singing his praises. Why would he care what some small town nobody like me said to him? Besides, that's a big part of the movie, a man of his age taking advantage of someone my age."

Jimmy shrugged. "Okay. If that's what you want to do, go right ahead."

They arrived at the cliff in time to see Richard Dawes emerge from a bright yellow-orange Humvee. A woman holding a mirror in front of him backed out of the car and another woman followed, smoothing his hair around the stylish derby style hat he wore.

Lance was rushing around calling the technicians to check the microphones. A microphone was clipped inside the front of Dawes's coat and then the technicians scattered. Ralph rode the overhead boom to check the camera angle. It zoomed down closer to Dawes.

Lance yelled over the mega-phone, "On three people, Rick…one, two, three…action!"

The cameras rolled, following Rick as he walked along the cliff's edge peering over the rim with a dark look of consternation on his face. Then he turned away and hurried up the hill. The camera continued to follow him until Lance yelled, "And cut."

Richard Dawes stopped his climb and looked neither right nor left before he returned to the Humvee and got inside. The Humvee drove away.

Kaycee and Jimmy looked at each other. Jimmy said, "I told you so."

The crowd dispersed quickly. They walked away.

"Did you see how he went right next to the cliff? He never even hesitated about looking over the edge. He wasn't afraid of it at all."

"You really thought a crumbly cliff would stop *the* Richard Dawes?" Jimmy asked amazed.

"Oh, stop it. That cliff's a 350 foot drop, it would stop anybody, even Superman."

"Where are we going?" he asked suddenly. "I wanted to stay at the cliff. The stuntwoman who falls from where you were hanging out there is going to be filming next."

Kaycee stared at him and felt a shiver slice down her back.

"Not me," she said hastily. "I saw enough when I was out there. It's horrible." The memory of her helplessness and the relentless waves of brown water foaming against the rocks below her were still too fresh in her mind for her to be an uninterested bystander.

"How come they can film the stuntwoman when the wind and sky isn't right, but they don't want to work on my scene?" she asked. The worry that she might be replaced because of her inexperience and what happened during the first filming continued to bother her.

"I asked the technicians, and they said the fall is a downward shot. The sky really doesn't play a big factor in the scene. Why? Are you worried?"

"No!" she snapped. "I'm going to my trailer to warm up with something hot to drink. See you later."

Jimmy turned and bounded back in the direction of the cliff. Kaycee continued the rest of the way alone, surprised to find she felt lonely. It wasn't often anymore that Jimmy was not nearby. I've already become accustomed to him and I'm actually missing him, she thought. How ridiculous. Was he acting the same way about her? No, Jimmy acted like they were working together. It's me! I can't get him out of my mind. Not only here, but at home, where he had no business invading her thoughts.

25

Kaycee climbed the wobbly, uneven metal steps of the trailer and knocked before she let herself inside. Glumly, she plopped down in the empty makeup chair and stared out the window.

"Ice has built up under the steps again," she said listlessly to Michelle. "You better ask maintenance to clear it, or we'll get locked in here again."

"Those darn steps, they keep moving all over the place. You alone?" Michelle asked.

"Yes, and don't ask me where he is or I'll scream," she warned darkly.

"Okay, I'm not quite sure why, but I won't ask."

"Good," Kaycee muttered, more to herself.

Silence fell as Michelle puttered around the trailer putting her supplies away in the cupboards. After several minutes of Kaycee's silence while she stared into space, Michelle said, "Coffee? It's nice and hot."

"He's at the cliff watching my double fall into the lake," she blurted out, unable to contain herself any longer.

"You didn't want to see this yourself?" Michelle asked curiously. "It sounds kind of interesting."

"No, and you were right about Richard Dawes. He never even spoke to anyone. He got out of his big car, did the scene, and then climbed back in and drove away. I'm so disappointed. My parents would love to have his autograph."

Michelle sat on the arm of a chair and faced Kaycee. "Tell me why you didn't want to watch your double."

Kaycee smiled weakly. "Come on, Michelle. She's dressed to look just like me. She does look kind of like me, at least her build. It would be like watching my own death...ick."

Michelle's eyes widened behind her large framed glasses. "Ick?" she repeated. "What is that?"

Kaycee laughed. "You know, 'ick.' A mix of yucky and gross. Didn't you ever say it when you were a kid?"

Michelle blinked several times. "Ick? Yucky? If I said words like that where I came from, I'd probably have been beaten up, and I'll tell you I would've deserved it."

Kaycee smiled at the petite girl with a rough edge. Kaycee had long suspected Michelle talked tougher than she really was. Michelle came from the Bronx and whenever she had the opportunity she used it to her advantage.

Kaycee looked out the window and saw the top of the crane begin to move. She could feel the jerky movement in the pit of her stomach. Abruptly, she spun the chair away, so she faced the mirror instead.

"Don't you think you should take that coat off while you're in here?"

Kaycee looked down at the fur and stood up. "I suppose you're right. I've gotten so used to being in it."

"It is nice," Michelle stroked it as she put it on a wooden hanger. "You know it's going to shed if you don't start taking care of it," she said as she carried it to the back of the trailer. "There's a good strong breeze coming through this wall. It will stay nice and cold over here. What did you think of the one Joe's wearing?"

Kaycee burst out laughing. "I knew he was going to do something like that! The minute he saw mine I could tell he was plotting a way to get one of his own."

Michelle walked up behind her. "Why don't you let me touch up your makeup?"

"Why? I'm not filming today," Kaycee said indifferently, turning her eyes away from her mirror image.

"No, but it will give me something to do while you're taking up space in my trailer, and it might take your mind off that scene."

"What do you mean 'your trailer'? I'm the actress," Kaycee retorted.

"This is my trailer for the entire movie," Michelle argued smugly. "It's only your's for this site."

"Oh fine, get technical," Kaycee said. She leaned back and closed her eyes as the protective sheet was placed around her shoulders.

This trailer had turned into a haven for Kaycee, partly because Jimmy only came in when specifically asked by either herself or Michelle and partly because she felt comfortable with Michelle. The two of them had first met in Paris and worked together for several seasons of magazine shoots. Then they lost track of each other until they met up again in New York and worked together again for a short time.

"Besides," Michelle added, "now that Rick Dawes is here you'll want to look your best."

Kaycee caught her glance in the mirror and frowned. "No way! He's old."

"Well, then, what about Jimmy? He's single, isn't he?"

Kaycee said nothing. Then admitted, "He's working special duty so he could come up here and…help me."

"That was really nice," Michelle replied.

Kaycee looked down at her hands clenched in her lap and agreed softly. "Yes, he's a really nice guy."

"So, he's not only cute, but nice. I don't see a problem with this."

"Of course you wouldn't," Kaycee said sulkily. "I can't seem to get away from Jimmy Zane anymore. All I hear about is how great he is. How nice he is, how available he is." She stopped. Then she thought that she should add, but she could not say the words out loud not even to Michelle, "And what a fool I am to let him get away."

"Why can't people understand that Jimmy doesn't belong to me? He never has. The way that man attracts women is sickening. The crowd that follows him around is getting ridiculous. I'm so sick of wading through the stench of perfume and bodies wherever we go."

"What are you talking about?"

"Jimmy," Kaycee said. "I'm tired of helpless females who whine and cling just to get his attention. It's making me crazy. I can't concentrate and how can I play my role if I don't have any peace? If Joe thinks I'm going to continue to put up with this then he's wrong. I think it's time Jimmy finds some other job on the site."

Michelle gave Kaycee a puzzled look but kept her mouth shut.

"I'm going to tell Joe today that this isn't working," Kaycee declared, her face brightening. "Jimmy's presence is causing me more problems than it's solving. He'll just have to give him another job." Kaycee let out a contented sigh and closed her eyes. "Then everything in my life will get back to normal. He will live his life and I will live mine—separately. That is how it should be."

26

Michelle, with a smile on her lips, carefully smoothed cleanser into Kaycee's skin. How the conversation progressed from how nice Jimmy was, which Michelle agreed with, to crowds of women getting on Kaycee's nerves, she was not quite sure. Michelle was good at her job and did not ask questions. She kept her mouth shut and listened.

Michelle knew a lot more about Kaycee than Kaycee realized. The gossip that flew around the dressing rooms was cruel, but it was pretty accurate when given by the right people. Michelle had been around long enough to know whose word she could trust. Kaycee kept very close-mouthed about her private life. So Michelle was keeping her observations about Kaycee and Jimmy to herself. She liked this new job and planned on continuing to climb upward in the movie business. Kaycee Swanson just might be the shirttail she can hold onto to make it to the top.

The reporters soon would start hounding this place because of Richard Dawes. They talked to anybody and printed whatever was said. Michelle had already been approached once, but as a rule, she blew reporters off. The others working here were not so particular. Most of them were just temps hired for this site. Michelle knew none of the details about what was going on between Kaycee and Jimmy, but there was something. It was enough to cause even Michelle to become curious.

The press had not been on-site yet, but once Richard Dawes worked with Kaycee, they would come after her, too. Whether or not she wanted it, Kaycee was going to be thrust into the spotlight.

Michelle's hands kept busy doing Kaycee's facial as her thoughts drifted back to when she first met the young, inexperienced Kaycee Swanson, a rookie model in the glamorous city of Paris. The girl had been so wide-eyed and green, Michelle truly had been scared for her. Too often, she watched girls come into the business in just the same way. They usually lasted a few months, and when they left the business, it was not a pretty sight. There were a lot of ways to be exploited. Some people made a business out of doing just that. To get attached to the models she worked with would be emotional suicide. The business was so fickle she never knew who was going to make it and who was not.

After she lost track of Kaycee, she was shocked to meet up with her again in New York City. If a betting woman, Michelle would have lost. She never thought Kaycee had the staying power, but the girl turned out to be tough enough to keep modeling. In one way, Michelle was right. This was not the same Kaycee she met in Paris. This new Kaycee was cool and polished like a hard, shiny diamond. She had impeccable taste in everything from clothes to men. Michelle heard while working in New York that Kaycee had come to earn the rather unflattering nickname of Ice Princess. Unflattering, but Michelle secretly suspected the nickname saved her from receiving unwanted attention from both men and the press.

Michelle enjoyed working with Kaycee. Their personalities clicked and though Kaycee was in her late twenties, she had great skin that was slow to age. Kaycee also did not fuss with herself and that made Michelle's job easier. When she did begin applying the makeup, all she had to do was redefine the beauty of Kaycee's already distinctive features.

When Michelle finished and removed the plastic hair cap to begin brushing out Kaycee's hair, she heard Kaycee's stomach rumble.

"It must be late," Kaycee said. She stretched, feeling sleepy after sitting for so long. "I'm starving."

"Only after twelve," Michelle said, glancing at the clock. "There, you're ready. Go feed yourself." She pulled the protective cover from Kaycee's shoulders.

Kaycee stretched and yawned. "I don't know if I look any better, but I sure feel better. Thanks, Michelle."

Michelle stepped out of her work area. "Don't tell me, tell anyone you meet. Maybe the great man himself, Rick Dawes, will request my services, and I'll start making some real money."

"I could do that but then I'd lose you. I'm way too selfish to share," Kaycee teased as she slipped into the fur coat Michelle handed to her.

"I knew I shouldn't have wasted my time on you."

"Would you like anything from the Chuck Wagon?" Kaycee asked as she pulled on her gloves.

"I'll wander over there after awhile," Michelle said, turning her sanitation equipment on.

"Okay, see you later." Kaycee opened the door and let in a blast of cold before she quickly slammed it shut behind her.

She hadn't walked very far when she saw Jimmy. His long-legged swinging stride was easy to pick out. The other men working up here weren't used to walking on the icy rocky ground so they shuffled as they walked. Not Jimmy. He'd grown up with this. Winter here lasted for more than five months of the year.

It was obvious Jimmy enjoyed the outdoors and was not bothered by the cold like some. His parka was unzipped, his head and hands uncovered. He looked ready for a spring day instead of a day in late January. Kaycee walked along with her chin buried in her collar. From this distance, she felt free to stare at him as much as she liked. The blast of a horn stopped Kaycee in her tracks. She stood in the middle of what was referred to as the road, which was really only a wide path where all the snow had been worn into mud from the loading and unloading of trucks. It was a truck with an impatient driver and Kaycee was blocking him. She backed away to a safe distance. By the time the truck rumbled off, Jimmy had completely disappeared. "Where could he have gone so fast?" she thought. Lunch was being served in the mess tent, so there were more people walking around outside than usual.

Kaycee walked to the communications tent and took a quick look around at the men in there before she walked outside, ready to go into the mess tent and look for him. Then she saw him. He was on the other side of the clearing near the ring of trailers around the cliff. Kaycee wondered what he was doing over there. There was no reason for them to go over there.

Jimmy's head was down. His shoulders hunched and his hands shoved in his pockets. Nothing about him looked the same as when she saw him twenty minutes ago. He was walking in the direction of the mess tent, but abruptly switched direction.

"Where is he going?" she thought impatiently. The smell from the kitchen made her stomach ache with hunger. She hesitated, debating between the base need of food and worry about Jimmy. "How ridiculous to worry about Jimmy, he is the most self-sufficient man ever," she argued with herself. But, there was something wrong. She knew it.

Kaycee moved away from the tents and heard her name. "Kaycee."

Joe hurried over to her. He wore a dark red fur coat that came past his knees. "How are you? What are you doing these days?"

Kaycee knew that Joe only came around if he had something to say. Preoccupied, watching for Jimmy, she said, "Not much. Any idea when I'll be filming next?"

Joe flipped open his clipboard. "We're working on tomorrow. They'll inform you at the briefing." Joe gave her that searching look of his behind his glasses. "Everything else working out okay?"

"What do you mean?" she asked bluntly.

"If you have to ask, then you must be handling everything just fine," he said with a big grin on his face. He snapped the clipboard shut and buttoned his coat.

"These furs are great. I haven't felt the cold for days," he said, stepping past her.

Kaycee's thoughts immediately returned to Jimmy. This wasn't like him at all. Usually, he found her the minute the lunch bell went off. He was always hungry. Maybe he had gone to the cliff? He seemed to like it there while she was not at all crazy about the place. As she reached the crest of the ridge, she prepared herself for the blast of wind off the water. It was strong and cold. Her cold ears reminded her that she must have left her hat someplace. She gingerly stepped along the uneven rock. She stopped and looked along the slate gray stone for Jimmy's army green jacket. He was standing at the edge of the cliff, away from where the main filming action was taking place.

"Jimmy!" she yelled, but her voice became lost on the wind.

Carefully, she stepped over the slabs of granite. Small gravel made the rock slippery even without snow and ice covering it. The drop at the edge fell sharply. For her to get where Jimmy was standing she had to cross the slippery spot. "If I do slip, I'll go right over the edge." She thought closing her eyes and praying for courage. Out of breath, partly from exertion, partly from fear, Kaycee slowly crossed to the granite wall where Jimmy stood. His eyes never left the expanse of water that reached out to the horizon. The wind whipped his face, but he seemed oblivious to the cold and to her.

"Jimmy," she shrieked as she grasped onto a piece of the rock to steady her balance.

27

He looked at her, his expression bleak. Abruptly, he stepped across the rocks and reached over to lift her off her feet and pull her into his arms. He held her so tight she forgot about breathing.

"I can't do it," he told her bitterly. He buried his face into the soft sheen of her hair.

Kaycee remained still in his embrace. She put her hands on his shoulders. "What can't you do?" she repeated. Twisting to see his face, she asked, "What happened?" She stepped back, not far enough to lose the protection of his arms, but so she could face him.

Jimmy stared at her. His distress faded then disappeared. Cold anger replaced it. Anger directed at her.

"Did something happen during the filming today?" she forced herself to ask. She was frightened by what he might say, but she needed to know. "Did the stuntwoman get hurt?"

"The stuntwoman?"

"Yes, what happened during the shoot?"

"Nothing, not a thing. It was after." He groaned and dropped his arms from her shoulders. His hands clenched into fists. "This has nothing to do with the shoot, Kaycee," he cried exasperated. "This has to do with the way women act around here." He turned away.

Kaycee stared at him. He made no sense. "What? What are you talking about?"

His sudden silence unnerved her.

Then Jimmy turned on her. The intensity of his anger changed his face. He looked like a stranger…a dangerous stranger.

Her eyes, wide with confusion, searched his face. "I don't understand…please tell me what's wrong."

"You don't understand? I don't believe you. You work

here, and I've found out in the last couple of weeks the women who work here are different," he said, keeping his voice under tight control. He stepped away from her and faced the water as he spoke. "There's something you need to know about me, Kaycee. I'm old-fashioned in the way I think, especially where women are concerned."

Kaycee crossed her arms, her own anger and suspicion surfacing. "Oh, really, and what exactly does that mean?"

He glanced at her with shadowed eyes. "Women are equal in intelligence, superior in emotional situations, and physically capable of reaching whatever goals they want to reach. I've seen bravery and courage in women as much as in men. I'm not being condescending, Kaycee. Why are some modern women allowing themselves to get caught in the feminist thinking that acting sexually aggressive is what feminism is all about? It's not! Feminism is all about a woman's dignity. That's the important issue. There's nothing more precious and beautiful than what all women inherently possess inside of them. It's a gift. Something men can never hope to achieve in any way." He paused. "How can you...?"

She could tell he didn't want to say anything more, but she wasn't going to allow it.

"And this is leading where?" she questioned sharply.

"No person, man or woman, liberated or not, has the right to try and seduce an unwilling partner. Not ever!" he declared fiercely, refusing to look at her. "I don't know what goes on in New York or anywhere else in the world, but I won't put up with it. It's wrong!" His bronze skin flushed a darker shade.

Kaycee's mouth fell open from the shock she felt. This was definitely not what she expected him to say. Questions welled inside, but she couldn't voice them. She didn't want to know whom he was talking about or the particulars of what happened. What she really didn't understand was why he chose to blame her for what happened.

The sound of water rushing up the shore was the only

sound for a long time.

"I won't defend myself, Jimmy," she finally forced the words out. "Bad manners run in both sexes. I've had to deal with the same thing." Her body shook, either from cold, or what was happening.

"On the street, busts often end in propositions, but that's caused by desperation from desperate people." His eyes met hers. "This isn't the streets. I wasn't prepared for it. Damn it, Kaycee! I can't help but wonder about the choices you've made. This life…is it you? You couldn't have changed that much to accept this?" He paused. "Yes, you could," he murmured, lowering his head.

Kaycee stiffened. "I can't help what happened to you, Jimmy, but don't you dare accuse me of anything. In your job, you're putting up with a lot of the same situations I am. How many times have you been propositioned not just with sex but with money, drugs, and power? I'm sure more times than I have. By more desperate people than I know. Do you ever give in to it?"

"Temptation can be very appealing but not worth the trouble," Jimmy said distantly. "The officer who trained me for the Rangers told me that more than once." He sighed. "I've never forgotten it. I won't let myself forget it."

"I have no doubt in my mind that you have never compromised yourself, Jimmy Zane," Kaycee admitted. She paused. The sun, free of the winter clouds, touched her face with the briefest warmth. She closed her eyes. "I just want you to know I have never compromised myself because of my job. It wasn't worth it to me either. I don't know if you can believe me, but I think it was you that kept me strong. All the things you said to me. The warnings you gave were right. I like to think I was smart enough to pick up on that, but then again, I'm always quick to give myself too much credit even if it isn't deserved." Her voice trailed off when there was no change in his face.

"Everybody calls you the Ice Princess," Jimmy murmured, still not looking at her. A grim smile touched his lips. "Nobody around here knows why you're so unattainable. They think it's because you're stuck up, or just too prim and proper." He stopped at her furious gasp. His dark eyes flew to her face.

She stared at him in disbelief. She couldn't believe he would retaliate by openly mocking her. "That's just about enough."

28

Jimmy's anger left him, dissolving into nothing. He did believe what she told him. She never talked about herself and her feelings, except that first night in his Blazer. Now she was letting him in a little more. He reached out to entangle his fingers in the thick strands of hair that flew around her face. Then she stopped staring at him, her blue eyes wide and teary. His words had bruised her and he could see it. The wind blew at the tears in her eyes freezing them into miniature crystals on her thick black eyelashes.

"Did you think for a minute I wouldn't hear what the people around here call you behind your back?" he questioned. His voice deceptively soft, his hand reached behind to cup the back of her head gently holding her. "You are clever about keeping your life private, but you hope for the impossible if you think the gossip about you isn't flying around this place."

Stiff, unrelenting in his arms, she glared at him.

"I know what you want to do right now. You want to run. I can read it in your face. I haven't forgotten about the way you deal with anger. You run away. You always did. I can see the rebellious Kaycee I thought didn't exist any more. What's stopping you? You know I won't force you to stay." To emphasize his point Jimmy dropped his hands. He hooked his thumbs in the belt loops of his jeans.

Kaycee, her color high, said incoherently, "Just knowing that cliff is so close, you really think I'm going to push you aside and run? Then lose my footing and allow every nightmare of falling to come true?"

Jimmy wanted to wrap her safely in his arms again. He wanted to hold her tight and confess his true feelings. Instead he said, "Do you really think I would allow that to happen? Tell me now, do you want to leave or listen to what I have to say?"

She looked at the ground and said bitterly, "I suppose you'll force me to listen at some time. If not now, then later."

Jimmy raised his eyebrows at her. "Does that mean you'll stay?"

Kaycee turned her head away and snapped, "Yes, I'll stay."

"Good. I'm not criticizing you. I'm not trying to tell you how to live your life, and I'm certainly not one to judge others. I can recognize the envy in the voices of those who gossip about you. I can recognize good judgment, and everything I've heard about you shows that you have it. That's why I'm so angry that your life is connected to people like this, to an industry like this with its unethical reputation."

"But I'm not one of them, Jimmy, can't you see that? I follow my own set of rules."

He shrugged, unconvinced, but once again, he moved close to her and settled his arms around her shoulders.

"Not everybody working here is a bad apple. Don't let the bad control how you feel about the rest."

Jimmy, with a heavy sigh, dropped his arms. "Ain't that the truth. Like I said before, when I'm doing police work, I expect the unexpected. I should have known better than to let my guard down."

"I'm sorry, Jimmy. But there are many sincere, dedicated people on this crew, people worth knowing."

"Why are you apologizing?" he asked. "It wasn't you who offered me anything illicit. And why do you insist on beating yourself up about the past? Let it go, Kaycee. We all did stupid things. Everybody does stupid things, I think it's called immaturity."

"If you feel that way, then why did you just give me the riot act?" she questioned.

"At work I can be objective," he admitted reluctantly, "you aren't involved." Afraid he'd revealed too much, he stepped away. "You're cold." He took her gloved hand out of her muff and rubbed it briskly. "We should head back."

Kaycee nodded in agreement. Her head ached, and she did not like being on the cliff.

As they started over the rock, she kept her head turned away from the drop off as, sure-footed, he led her across the ridge onto level ground. They walked hand-in-hand until Jimmy left her at the door of the bus. She stopped and held onto his hand for a moment longer. He smiled and pressed his lips against the fuzzy material of her scarf. Kaycee climbed onto the bus and waved out the window before she sat down.

Jimmy watched the bus drive away. He had tried everything to forget this girl, Kaycee Swanson. When she first left Duluth, he wanted to wipe her out of his mind completely. By the time he gave up ever doing it, he had traveled all the way across the country and settled in Texas. He finally decided he did not want a life that far away from his roots. Worse, Kaycee's big blue eyes continued to haunt him. He knew she wasn't living in Duluth and decided it was foolish for him to stay away when he wanted to go back. He felt the electricity she brought into his life. It hung in the air whenever Kaycee was near. She wore him out, frazzled his nerves, and drove him to distraction. He inhaled the cold air. Its sharpness touched all the way down into his lungs. Anything else just wasn't living!

29

Kaycee adjusted her sunglasses against the harsh glare of the sun dazzling off the white snow. Several inches of new snow had fallen over the last two days, and this morning the sky had cleared. After the cold and snow, the warm spell had the film crew scrambling to take advantage of every available minute of sunshine. The scene they were filming right now was the day before Kaycee is to be pushed off the cliff edge. The day of brief romantic bliss between her character and Richard Dawes cross-country skiing. Lance insisted on bright sunshine the day before and menacing blackness the day of the murder. The filming was all back on schedule after the paralyzing cold. The entire Duluth shoot was almost finished. Today was her first full-length scene with the leading man.

"I'll be glad when this segment is done," Dawes confided in her. His breathing was heavy as they walked through the wet snow in the valley of the cross-country ski trail. "I hate snow and cold, and I've never felt cold like they have in this forsaken country."

Kaycee laughed softly. She found it impossible to complain about the weather on a day like this one. She felt too warm in her thermal ski outfit. It was the same outfit she wore hanging off the cliff.

"I don't know," she replied, smiling shyly at him. Unwittingly, she leaned too close to him and the loose black curls of hair brushed against his cheek. He moved his head into her hair and inhaled the fresh scent. His smile was toothy and white and looked almost too perfect.

"I'm enjoying the fresh air and exercise. We're getting paid to cross-country ski. America is wonderful."

He gave a shake of his head. "Of course you're enjoying it. I'm the one stuck carrying your blasted equipment," he quipped keeping the same smile on his face for the benefit of the camera. Kaycee shrugged. She lowered her eyelashes coyly from his bold look.

"I'm sorry I can't help you with it," she said concentrating on watching his lips move. She pulled on her lower lip nervously with her teeth.

The director watched Kaycee's innocent, sensual play with Rick and whispered, "This is fantastic. I can't believe she's doing so well her first time out with him." He looked through the camera. "The sparks are really flying between these two. It's magic. Who would've thought with a rookie?"

His assistant nodded. "Right, Lance, you're right."

In the snowy valley, isolated from the movie world of cameras, Kaycee and Rick remained in the same spot while Rick struggled to keep control of the ski equipment. He turned and took a moment to study the slope in front of them.

"I can't believe we still have to climb that," he grumbled.

"It's in the script," she said, staring at Rick with what she hoped was an adoring expression. His face had deeply tanned grooves on either side of his sexy mouth. It almost looked too grim. His hair was mostly black with some gray at the temple. She could not pinpoint his age. What did it matter when every movie he made turned out to be a blockbuster?

When the filming began this morning, Kaycee felt more than a little overwhelmed, but in her mind, business was business. So when Lance yelled, "Roll 'em!" she fell into character and didn't look back.

They started to walk again, remaining shoulder to shoulder, and Kaycee listened to him complain, amused.

"I know. I should have demanded they change the script. There's no reason you shouldn't be carrying at least half," he groaned with a heavy sigh. "Are we almost to the top? I'm tired."

Kaycee looked around. "It's just a few yards further I think."

Rick suddenly stopped. He leaned forward to look closely into her face. Kaycee felt herself instinctively avoid contact with him but then caught herself and leaned into him thinking, "What's he doing? This isn't going to be a spontaneous kiss? I can't kiss a stranger convincingly when I'm not prepared for it.

"What's going on down there?" Lance hissed into the two-way radio.

He saw Ralph look in his direction and shake his head. "I don't know, but let's keep rolling. Whatever Rick's doing it plays into the scene."

Lance, with a dissatisfied sigh lowered his radio. "Fine for them, but I'm having a nervous breakdown."

Silence continued in the valley except for the call of sparrows in the nearby trees. Rick slipped off his glove and reached toward Kaycee to brush away a strand of hair clinging to her cheek. Tenderly, he caressed her skin with his fingertips. His voice raspy, he said, "I realize this isn't in the script, but I have to rest a minute."

Kaycee watched him, astounded that he could ad-lib so easily.

A crease appeared in his forehead when he continued to stare at her. "I don't remember seeing you in any films before, but your face is familiar. Why?"

Kaycee stared into his eyes and kept a smile of sweet contentment on her lips. She admitted softly, "This is my first acting job."

Rick looked surprised but masked it in the next instant. "Really? I'm impressed. I never would have known."

Kaycee felt giddy at his compliment, but there was no time to dwell on it.

Rick adjusted the load of ski equipment on his shoulder, and they began to walk once more.

"Thank you," she said hastily as she followed close behind him. She hadn't expected him to pay much attention to her let alone compliment her. Richard Dawes was known to be a tyrant with rookies. He had treated her not with patience exactly but with tolerant indifference. She hoped that continued.

The hard crust of the snow was quickly beginning to melt. Rick began to break through into the deep wet drift underneath before Kaycee did. As soon as it happened, they heard Lance yell, "Cut."

Rick immediately dropped the ski equipment in a heap on the hill. Kaycee stared at him in amazement. There were still several feet left to climb before they reached the top. Rick stepped over the pile, flexing his shoulder, and began to stomp up the hill.

Kaycee, not knowing what else to do, followed him. The last few feet they sunk with every step. As they reached the top of the ski trail, the cameras had moved back.

"Nice touch on the hill, Rick," Lance complimented him.

Rick looked at him and then grumbling, he walked away.

Kaycee's heart pounded hard against her chest. She wiped at her face covered with sweat.

"Nice job," Joe said, walking over to where Kaycee stood alone.

She smiled. "Thanks! Am I glad that's over. I had so many butterflies in my stomach, I'm surprised I didn't lose it in the valley.

"Any later in the day and you never would have made it through that valley," Joe said as he gestured to the deep footprints. "At the base of the valley I'm sure the snow is a lot deeper. You two would've sunk completely away. At least Rick would've for sure. I'm not so sure about you. You're light, you might have made it."

"Rick wasn't too happy about it."

"I could tell."

"I hope nothing went wrong so it has to be reshot."

Joe shook his head. "They'll review the film right away.

Everything looked great from the angle I was at. I'm pretty sure you'll only have one last scene to do with the famous Mr. Dawes, Kaycee."

"Yes, when he shoves me off the ledge. How pleasant. I am so looking forward to it." She made a face.

"One consolation for you," Joe interjected with a grin, "the guy who does it is an Oscar winner."

Kaycee laughed out loud. "A very small consolation," she agreed, "but I guess it will have to do."

One of Joe's assistants interrupted them. "Are we breaking for lunch now?"

Joe glanced at his watch and nodded yes.

"Take a break, Kaycee." He looked at the blue sky. "Compared to last week, this is almost tanning weather. We can't film the other scene until it's cloudy. That won't be today. If the last take turned out you're done for today."

Kaycee hurried past the jumble of cords and camera equipment the crew was hastily packing together. They needed to move it away from the melting snow. She paused to lift her face into the rays of the sun and unzipped her jacket, stuffing her hat and mittens in the pocket. She wanted to find a spot where she could enjoy the sun and think about the filming sequence she'd just had with her leading man—that had such a nice ring to it.

When she reached the trailer so she could change, Jimmy was standing outside, lounging against the steps and eating an apple.

"What's so interesting?" she asked.

Jimmy didn't look up right away. Slowly, he bit another chunk from the apple and chewed it. "His mistress?" he questioned. "You're playing the part of an old man's mistress?"

"Oh, hush," she said laughing. "It's a role, remember?"

He grinned, flipping the manuscript shut. "I haven't read the entire script yet," he gave her a wicked look, "are there any bedroom scenes?"

Kaycee shook her head vigorously, "No!"

"You know, maybe I should be there to protect you in case Mr. Dawes gets carried away?"

"Mr. Dawes is a professional," she said primly. "Professionals don't get carried away by anything."

Jimmy's eyes swept over her.

"I wouldn't be too sure about that," he murmured. "He's never been faced by Miss Kaycee Swanson."

Kaycee pushed against him with both hands. It was like pushing on a tree trunk. "Will you stop teasing me?"

"Even the mighty Rick Dawes might be tempted by you."

Kaycee melted into giggles. "Stop! I'm starving and you sit here making jokes about my character. Let's go eat. First, let me change, I'll only be a minute."

When she returned outside, fifteen minutes had passed. Jimmy glanced pointedly at his watch.

"Hmm, one minute? I believe that was more than one minute."

Kaycee ignored him, flipping her hair back. He put his hand up and felt the silky stuff move across his fingers. Kaycee did not even notice.

"Are you ready for food?" she quipped. "Because I am."

"So you told me before," he said as he slipped the manuscript in his pocket. "It's usually me saying those words. The shoot must have gone as planned if you're so hungry. How was Mr. Dawes?"

"He gave me a compliment," Kaycee exclaimed over her shoulder as they walked toward the Wagon.

Suddenly, a stranger holding a camera stepped directly in front of her and snapped a picture. Kaycee screamed, slipped, and fell back. Jimmy caught her arm.

Another man behind the photographer moved quickly forward and held a microphone up to her face while other cameras began going off all around her.

"You're the love interest of Richard Dawes in this movie?"

Kaycee looked desperately at the men and the cameras and then at Jimmy.

"A rumor is going around that you and Rick Dawes are also involved off the set. Is this true?"

"What's your name?"

"Where are you from?"

Kaycee backed away. Before she said anything, Jimmy pulled her behind him and spun around in the other direction, pushing her ahead of him. They dodged between the big tents, and the people hurrying into the mess tent for lunch.

Jimmy tried to block Kaycee from view until the reporters were left behind.

When they finally stopped, Kaycee looked around and saw they were back at the cliff where she had found Jimmy, and they were alone.

"Where did they come from?" she asked with a shaky laugh. "I'm used to cameras, but that was ridiculous."

"I never saw them," Jimmy said. He was angry. "One minute they weren't there, the next they were. You haven't had a scene with Rick before, so they didn't pay any attention to you. That scene with Rick on the cross-country trail gave away who you are, Miss Swanson."

"Great," said Kaycee. "Can't we bar them from access to the cliff or something? If they mess up the shooting, Mr. Dawes is going to be furious."

"Tough," said Jimmy. He glanced around to be sure they were alone. "How about if I run back to the Wagon and grab us some food. We can eat it here, kind of like a winter picnic."

Kaycee gave him a warm smile. "That sounds like a fantastic idea. It's so warm with the rocks around us I'm sure we'll be comfortable."

30

Jimmy left the ledge with her blessing until Kaycee realized she was a virtual prisoner here. She could never walk across that ledge by herself. She leaned against the sun-warmed rock. Cliffs of white snow and brown tree trunks surrounded the lake as far as she could see. Dark green spruce and evergreen dotted the shoreline, leaving white trunks of birch trees stark like bleached bones in between them. Kaycee looked at the sky and watched the gulls wheel around the blue sky. An ache started in her chest because she knew soon she was going to have to say good-bye to all of this again. Each time she had to leave her home and return to the Cities, it was harder for her.

She thought gloomily, "That's what old age does to a person. Gone is the pioneering spirit, replaced by the longing for the comforts of home."

She leaned forward to look at the water. There was an overhang of rocks, so she couldn't see directly below. Slowly, she inched forward just to catch a glimpse of the height and see if it scared her still. The water lapped against the pebbled shore not as angry in the sunshine, but the drop…her heart started pounding. Sweat broke out over her entire body. Her head whirled into a rush of blackness. Kaycee fell back against the solid rock behind her and closed her eyes. The fear was still there and worse than before.

All that was left of this movie was her final scene. There was no question in her mind that she was going to do it. Rick Dawes hated being here, and he would not have much patience with anyone who slowed down his plans to finish the filming and then leave. Add that to her being an amateur actress doing a scene that scared her silly…it wasn't good.

She heard the scrape of leather against rock and saw Jimmy come around the corner. He carried a paper sack and a thermos tucked under his arm.

"Hey," he said with a conspiratorial wink. "I ditched 'em, ditched 'em all," he declared with a Texas drawl. "Them there reporters didn't stand a chance against me. I learned from the best Texas has to offer how to outsmart rustlers, well, in our case, reporters, and I done it good."

She reached for the paper bag. "Bring that food over here before I faint," she instructed, then she brightened. "Of course I'm light headed, I haven't eaten all day. My blood sugar must have dropped."

"What are you talking about?" he asked, setting the bag on the dry flat rock that would serve nicely as a table.

"Nothing, I just felt a little faint before."

"Probably all that exercise on the hill," he said, opening the paper bag and taking out two foil-wrapped packages.

"What is that?" she asked.

The heat rising from it made the air steam with a delicious smell.

"It's a little concoction from my camping days," he said secretively, "but it must be served just so."

"Whatever it is, it smells wonderful."

Jimmy opened the hot foil and set it down in front of her. "Voila!" he exclaimed. "A campfire supper—chicken, potatoes, and vegetables all cooked to perfection in tinfoil. The easiest pans to wash," he said proudly. "Sam, the cook in the mess tent liked it when I started ordering them. So he added it to the menu. I had to reserve two of these this morning. If you ordered something else I would've eaten two of them myself, one for lunch and one for dinner. I'm not much on eating supper alone. I don't like my own cooking, and dad's out of town. Sam, on the other hand, is a super cook."

"But it's your recipe," Kaycee said and took a bite of the chicken. Spicy, but not too spicy, the meat fell off the bone.

"Yes, but I didn't have to fix it. That makes all the difference," he smiled.

Neither of them spoke for a while, their eyes on the sparkling water of the lake as they ate. Kaycee wiped her hands on the napkin and sighed.

"That tasted so good. Now I understand why you've been looking so healthy lately."

Jimmy swallowed his last mouthful. "Is that another word for fat?"

Kaycee turned to look at him. Somewhere he'd discarded his jacket and now wore only a flannel shirt tucked into his blue jeans. There wasn't an ounce of extra flesh on his tall, rangy frame.

"Healthy is not another word for fat," she said firmly. "But you'd better watch it. When you settle down someday with a wife and three square meals a day, then it might catch up to you."

He didn't seem to hear her. After a moment he said, "That's not in the near future, anyway."

Kaycee couldn't help feeling relieved. He had just answered the question she had never dared to ask him. They were together almost every minute up here, but he hadn't called at the house since that night she baked cookies. Where he went and with whom after work, she had no idea. She only knew that ten years was long enough for Jimmy to fall in love and make commitments. He might have married and divorced. This thought made her suddenly feel sad. She kept her tone cheerful, "Don't be silly, Jimmy, you'll find the right woman, and it will all fall into place."

He looked straight at her. His stare unwavering. "You're right," he said briskly, rubbing his hands on the sides of his jeans. "I just have to remember to be patient."

He stood to clean what was left of their meal off the rock. Kaycee was full and felt incredibly sleepy with the glare of the sun forcing her eyes to close.

"Getting tired? It must be the fresh air."

Kaycee yawned and closed her eyes when she felt Jimmy grab her arm. "Come on, sleepy head, up you go. The buses are loading early."

Kaycee sat up. "Why?"

"I don't know."

Later, they rejoined the film crew milling around outside the communications tent.

Jimmy asked, "What's going on?"

"We're waiting to hear tomorrow's schedule."

"Oh, does everybody need to listen?"

The technician shook his head. "Naw, just the technical crew."

Jimmy started walking away and Kaycee followed. When they were away from the crowd she turned to him and said, "Thanks."

"For what?" he asked, surprised.

"For everything. For lunch, for rescuing me from the press, for taking this job to help. I really appreciate it."

"We've been friends a long time, Kaycee. This is what friends do for each other."

"Announcement," shrieked the intercom. "Everybody quiet on the set."

Kaycee and Jimmy stopped walking and heard the ripple of laughter as it went through the crowd.

"The press is here taking some pictures and asking for interviews. They have permission, so cooperate."

Kaycee glanced at Jimmy and they both grinned.

"Only if they don't plow you over with their enthusiasm," he whispered.

"Quiet everybody! We have a weather report for tomorrow, and the clouds are moving back in. If they look right and we can film, we might wrap this thing up tomorrow."

Kaycee gave a soft sigh of relief.

"Wish you could get it over with?" Jimmy asked.

She shook her head. "It won't matter either way. I don't think I'll ever be ready."

The speaker squawked, "The crane crew needs to meet at

the cliff edge right after this. Harness check for those involved with the cliff scene report to the cliff. The rest of you enjoy the sunshine."

"I guess you won't be taking the early bus back."

Kaycee shook her head. "Not now that I have a harness check. It sounds like a horse race. How do they know about the clouds?"

They walked up the ridge, and Jimmy pointed to the horizon over the lake. "See that?"

A thick mass of dark gray clouds stacked to look like fluffy skyscrapers was lined up across the lake.

"Where did that come from?"

"That's a storm headed this way from the northeast. The lake might divert it, or it may hit us. Anyway, it's that cloud cover they need to finish your scene."

When they walked down the ridge, the crane engine was not running. Kaycee walked over to the technician holding the harness. "You aren't in costume, Miss Swanson. You have to be wearing the outfit you'll use in the scene."

Kaycee gave a moan. "I didn't realize. I'm sorry. Now I'll have to walk all the way back."

He smiled good-naturedly.

"It'll only take me a half hour. I'll be back by then."

He nodded. "We'll be waiting."

"I'm going to roast, Jimmy," Kaycee said as they hurried away. "Do you realize the lining in those outfits? And I'm sure I'll have to put on everything, that awful spandex and the thermal underwear included."

"Yeah, even you must be feeling the sun's warmth. I just remembered you left that animal in the trailer," he teased her. "Just remember only last week you almost froze. Tomorrow might be another day like that. Which do you prefer?"

"No question for me. Give me too warm over freezing any day. I just hope if it's like this I don't sweat too much. That wouldn't look right on film either."

As they neared her trailer, the same press group they'd seen before was standing there.

"Oh great, the press."

Jimmy said, "Ah, ah, ah, Miss Swanson, you are now a star and have orders to be nice. I suppose it's good publicity for the movie."

"Of course it is, but I don't have time. Maybe you could pose for the cameras instead of me?"

Jimmy scowled. "Not hardly, now smile pretty."

The reporters pressed forward with their microphones. Jimmy intercepted them. "Miss Swanson is late for an important scene," he said. "After she's finished, she will be glad to answer questions about the film and her career."

He stepped into the group holding onto Kaycee's arm as he did and kept her moving forward until she reached the steps of the trailer.

Kaycee only had to smile and wave.

"Nice touch, where did you learn that?" she hissed to him under her breath.

"I must have seen it in a movie," he admitted, keeping his body between her and the reporters until she could shut the door of the trailer on them all. Kaycee peaked out the window and watched as Jimmy faced the people and the cameras started going off.

When she reappeared outside, all was clear.

"I sent them over to Rick Dawes's trailer," he told her. "That guy needs a lot of stroking to be productive."

"I'm just glad they're gone," she sighed. "Now I can think about answers to the questions they'll be asking me. I'm not allowed to give away any specifics that happen in the movie. It's in my contract."

"Thorough, aren't those lawyers?" Jimmy remarked. "What happens if you slip?"

Kaycee grimaced. "I'm not sure, so I'll just have to be careful."

The harness fitting took more time than it should have. By the time they finished, Kaycee thought it fit her exactly the same as it had last time.

The set was being closed down as she stood outside her trailer in the gathering dusk. There was no light pollution up here so the sky over the water shone with bright stars. The big dipper stretched out above the northern sky. The temperature on the cliff top remained unusually mild. Kaycee knew that now that the sun was gone, the cold would return fast.

The reporters had left the site. Their demanding questions and the unblinking eyes of their cameras wore her out. She tried to remember what her answers sounded like but not much came to mind. "What do I care if I sound like a naïve rookie or somebody who is just plain ignorant," she said to herself. "I'll find out tomorrow in the newspaper with everybody else."

Jimmy had stayed away during the interview. He warned her that the reporters asked him questions about his job on the set. Neither of them knew what to say. Kaycee wanted to talk to Joe before making any kind of statement and Jimmy agreed.

Kaycee knew it was safer if Jimmy was not around when she was interviewed or pictures were taken. Cameras cannot lie. Early in her career, she learned that lesson. Emotions and feelings hidden under the surface when caught in the lens of a camera became plain to see. In a photograph, the hidden became obvious.

Right now, Kaycee was having a hard time fighting her feelings for Jimmy. Too much soul searching would cause her to face what was becoming increasingly obvious to her. But it was too risky. If she made the mistake of voicing how she felt, then there was no way to ever take them back. She desperately did not want make a complete fool of herself.

Kaycee heard a sound behind her and turned to see Jimmy's tall figure emerge from the shadows of the tent. She knew he would come. For some reason, with the warm wind, the black lake, and the remembered beauty of the day, Jimmy would be there, too. "This is truly one of the most beautiful places I've ever known," she said when he stood behind her.

"I know," he agreed. His voice sounded as hushed in the velvety darkness as hers had been.

"We leave, searching to find something better. It isn't until we come back that we realize it was right here in front of us all the time." She gave a soft sigh.

The most natural thing to happen was for Jimmy to wrap his arms around her, settling her slim body into the warmth of his own. She thought, "Should I tell you how I feel? Should I tell you I'd almost forgotten what love feels like, but it all comes back when I'm with you?"

The hush was broken by the sound of laughter. The parking lot was empty. In about half an hour, the bus would be picking up the last group of people from the site. The sound came from the mess tent where the rest of the crew was waiting for their ride.

She and Jimmy were alone in the dark, peaceful silence under a sky studded with stars.

Feeling oddly defenseless, the darkness hiding his features from her and hers from him, she asked, "Why don't I see the Northern Lights anymore?" Her eyes scanned the horizon. "When I was a child, I remember always seeing it, winter or summer. I remember seeing it more when we were camping up north." Kaycee relaxed against him and felt his breathing. The warmth of his arms with the strength of him pressed against her back. She half closed her eyes wishing this moment to go on and on.

Jimmy remained holding her but silent.

"The brightness of the light used to pulsate through the sky in waves," she continued, a throb in her voice that hadn't been there before. "Sometimes I could even see different colors. Where has it gone?"

Jimmy moved slightly and said, "Inuit legend says the aurora borealis is the laughter of unborn children. Maybe there isn't much cause to laugh anymore."

"That's so incredibly sad. And I hope it's not true," she said, turning in the circle of his arms to press her face into the warm flannel of his shirt. What she should do is move away, put some space in between them. It was too painful to be this close. To fully realize she had waited so very long to find someone like Jimmy and he could never be hers in the way she wanted him.

"I wish I knew something profound to say."

Kaycee sighed and lifted her face. Their lips brushed against each other in the darkness. The warmth of skin as they touched in the cool night air shattered any preconceived ideas she might have that Jimmy was too close to being her brother for there to be any physical attraction between them. His lips moved slowly. She had no trouble responding. All of the feelings she'd fought to hide from him burst to the surface, the tide of emotion that swept through her left her drowning and dizzy, clinging to him. The earth must have moved out from under her feet and left her helpless. The feeling of the roughness of his skin against her; this is where she belonged, with him and nowhere else.

A deep shattering shudder ran through Jimmy's powerful body as he raised his head and pulled her closer still. She felt his heart thundering in his chest. She marveled at the control they possessed over each other. After all these years, there was a connection between them.

Neither one spoke. There was no need for words as they continued to cling tightly to each other in the darkness.

31

Through the dark streets of the East End of Duluth, Kaycee drove home from the Holiday Parking Ramp. She hummed to the music on the radio. What was she feeling so darn happy about? Nothing had changed. Nothing except that now she knew without any doubt it was Jimmy Zane's fault she could not settle down. How long had she been comparing the men she met in her life to his image? Kaycee parked her car on Sixth Street and ran up the front walk. She still felt the rush of excitement, the rush of feeling more beautiful than anyone else in the world, because she was in love with a wonderful guy. Her worries about the future would just have to wait while she enjoyed this moment.

Walking through the front door she heard, "Kaycee, you home?" from Karyn upstairs.

"Just got here," Kaycee yelled back.

"Phone's for you."

Kaycee kicked off her boots and picked up the receiver as she slipped off the fur.

"Hey, Kaycee," Jimmy said.

Kaycee felt her cheeks flame as if he was suddenly in the room looking at her.

"I know this is pretty sudden, but would you like to go out tonight?"

Kaycee's heart started pounding. Unable to answer, she lowered herself into the chair next to the phone.

"I was going to ask you today, but with the reporters and all, I completely forgot."

Kaycee dragged her fingers through the tangles in her hair. How could he talk to her so calmly? His voice alone made her feel like a lovesick teenager.

"Forgot what?" she managed in a steady voice.

"There's a party for Sally and John Thomesen tonight,"

he explained. "It's their tenth anniversary party. I thought you might want to go. They wanted you to come."

Kaycee's palms were wet. She saw Jimmy every day but then his good looks, his height, and his strength were just a part of him she took for granted. Now all she could remember was his mouth on hers, the strength of his arms as he held her, and the width of his shoulders as she touched him.

"Kaycee?"

"I'm here," she croaked.

"You're probably worn out. Today was pretty rough after having to deal with the snow and Rick Dawes."

If she wanted, here was an excuse to stay home, where it was safe. "I'm not tired. Tell me the plan," she blurted out. She wanted to keep him on the line. She wanted to hear his voice.

"The party is being held at a local bar, you'll remember it. When we were in high school it was a hangout for college kids. As a matter of fact, it still is. Maybe it's not something you'd be interested in. I know you're busy."

"No, no," she protested hastily. "It sounds like fun. Ten years, they must have been married right after high school."

"Yeah, they have a bunch of kids already," he told her. "I talk to John once in a while. He works at the county courthouse."

"Really?"

"Do you remember John or Sally?" Jimmy asked suddenly.

Silence fell.

"Man, do I feel foolish. You don't know them do you? I must've hung around with John when I was playing football."

"I haven't seen any of these people in ten years," she defended herself. "I might not remember the names right off the top of my head, but I'm sure I'll know their faces when I see them."

"Oh, so you're willing to go?"

"Of course, what time?"

"Around eight, and don't worry, I won't forget your curfew."

"Thank you, I'll be ready," Kaycee said. She hung up the phone and lowered her head, onto her arm.

"Who were you just talking to?" a voice asked. "Was it a new boyfriend?"

Kaycee whirled on the chair to see Kathie in the shadows of the living room. She was dressed in flannel pajamas and holding a book in her hand.

"I'm quite certain that's a romantic novel and not a school book. And you shouldn't be reading without the light on," Kaycee reprimanded her and tried to change the subject.

Kathie grinned at her sister. She stood and walked toward her. "Don't you try to change the subject. Did you meet some actor or the director on the set? Is it Rick Dawes? Are you going out with him tonight?"

Kaycee frowned. "Rick Dawes is twice my age. You've got to be kidding."

"That isn't a yes or no," Kathie said, still grinning.

"No, gross. It'd be like dating one of dad's friends."

"Then who is it? Come on, Kaycee, fess up. I won't stop bugging until you do."

"I have just realized what your future occupation should be," Kaycee gasped. "You would make an ace reporter."

Kathie paused and looked pleased at the comment.

Before Kathie could question her further, Kaycee jumped off the chair and vaulted up the stairs. She left the fur coat unattended on the chair.

Kathie walked over to the chair and stood looking at the coat. Kaycee kept track of the fur coat every second it was in the house. Kathie was dying to try it on. She glanced up the stairs before she reached for the sumptuous, white fur. Kathie's hand and another hand reached for the coat at the same time.

Startled, Kathie looked up and saw Karyn. Karyn shook her head and held a finger to her lips.

"I get to try it on first," Kathie mouthed fiercely.

Karyn tiptoed down the rest of the stairs, and the two girls tiptoed out of the front hall into the privacy of the back sun porch where a large antique mirror hung behind the couch. In this room, they had no fear of interruption while they played dress-up with Kaycee's fur coat.

Upstairs in her bedroom, Kaycee was scrambling to get showered and dressed before Jimmy arrived. She was ready in time and waiting by the front door with butterflies in her stomach.

When she heard him on the front porch, Kaycee opened the front door. "I'm ready," she said, zipping her jacket. She gave him a hasty smile as she walked past him toward the car. She was so nervous. Now everything between them was different. It was complicated.

When they pulled into the parking lot of the Reef, Kaycee gave a sigh of relief. After the stilted uncomfortable conversation in the Blazer on the way here anything, even a packed college bar, was preferable to this.

"I can't believe this place is still so popular," she said.

"It's the location," Jimmy replied. "I work here sometimes when I'm off duty. The people are pretty much the same that have always been coming here."

"And what kind of people would that be?" she asked, not caring for his sharp tone.

Jimmy glanced. He said quickly, "You mean you don't know? I thought…well this was one of Tod's old hangouts. I thought you might have been here with him."

Kaycee was silent. Then she said, "No, I was never in a bar underage. I was too scared to even try." Kaycee appreciated that Jimmy did not offer any comment and flung open the car door to get out.

Once inside the building, Jimmy took her hand and led

her through the crowd of people. They walked past a huge model ship displayed in a glass cabinet. There were ship wheels hanging from the walls and fishnets strung from the ceiling. Music blared from the jukebox, but in the back area was a stage set up for a band.

"Live music doesn't start until nine," Jimmy told her with a smile. "Then the excitement really starts."

"Starts?" Kaycee mouthed with a wide-eyed look at the crowded bar. Each room they walked through was full of people. Every table they had passed was being used, and there were people standing and waiting for a place to sit down. Jimmy took her down a hallway that led to the private banquet rooms. When they walked through the only open door, Jimmy was immediately greeted with loud friendly calls from both men and women. Kaycee glanced around at the unfamiliar faces of the people and then at the room. A plain yellow tablecloth decorated a buffet table along one wall. The whole area was decorated with crepe paper and balloons, giving it the look of a child's birthday party.

As they walked toward the bar, Kaycee was stared at—politely, by most of the women, but the men gaped. Kaycee whispered to Jimmy, "What's the matter with these guys. Do I know them? Why are they staring at me?"

"Because you look exactly the same as you did in high school except that you're more glamorous, that's why."

"I am not."

"You have the same hair style, you're dressed about the same as you always were back then. I guess whether you realize it or not, this is who you really are Kaycee, not the model or the actress. You haven't changed your appearance a bit. Come on over here. It looks like Sally and John are taking pictures by the cake."

Kaycee followed him. She tried to recognize the people she went to high school with. Some of the faces tugged at her memory, others she knew she'd never seen before. When she saw the couple posing in front of a ridiculously large white sheet cake, she recognized Sally Reasling right away. Kaycee had gym class and Spanish and countless other classes with her during school. Sally had never been considered one of the popular crowd, but she was always involved in school activities. Kaycee thought she remembered that Sally had run for senior class president, or one of the officers their senior year, but couldn't remember if Sally had been elected or not.

"Kaycee Swanson!" Sally called out excitedly. She rushed over and threw her arms around Kaycee's shoulders giving her a tight squeeze.

"You are so beautiful," Sally took a good look at her and said. "But then you always were."

Sally was plump and pretty with apple red cheeks and wavy brown hair that fell to her shoulders. Her blue eyes shone with a light Kaycee did not recognize. Her bubbly personality had not dimmed a bit. It was when she told Kaycee about John and her three boys that she literally glowed with happiness.

"Jimmy, go and talk to the guys," Sally said.

Jimmy stood next to Kaycee and looked like he wanted to stay. He glanced at Kaycee.

Sally said, "She'll be fine with me, Jimmy. John's over there at the bar, go and talk to him."

Sally turned to the photographer and said, "Kaycee this is Tim. Do you remember him? He always had a camera in front of his face. He took pictures for the Greyhound Newspaper in high school."

Kaycee smiled. "And you're still taking pictures?"

"After high school I decided this is what I like to do. I became a professional photographer."

"And a very successful one," Sally added. "He worked with Jace Montgomery when he went on that expedition to the Antarctic. Some of his photos ended up in National Geographic."

Kaycee nodded like she knew who Jace Montgomery was.

Then Sally led Kaycee around the room and introduced her to everyone there. She also took the time, with the subtly of an experienced hostess, to explain if Kaycee should know them or not before the introduction. Soon, a crowd of women came over and jumped into the conversation. Some of the women stood with Sally and Kaycee, others sat at a table next to them. Sally said to the group, "Okay, everyone listen. Kaycee, please give us the whole scoop on this movie thing you're doing!"

"I'm really such a small part in the movie I haven't seen a lot of the filming, only the part that's being filmed on Palisade Head."

"Well, you know more than we do," a woman named Connie piped up. Kaycee remembered Connie worked with John at the courthouse. "So, spill it all. Who is the leading man?"

Kaycee talked about the scenes that Joe had told her were acceptable for the public. She could not mention the ending of the movie and what happens to her character. When she finished, the questions began.

Kaycee laughed at what they thought the movie site was like. She shook her head, "It's freezing on that cliff." She looked up and saw Jimmy. Then she had a brainstorm, she began to tell the women about Jimmy's first rescue. She only left out who the actress he rescued was.

The group of women turned as one to look at Jimmy.

"That is so romantic. Jimmy has to be involved with this actress now," one of the woman said.

"I don't see how she could ever let him go after he saved her life."

Sally grabbed Kaycee's arm. "Let's go and get something to eat before the food is all gone."

When they walked to the buffet table, Kaycee picked up a plate. "Sally, I'd like to know what your beauty secret is."

Sally stopped and looked at her. "What do you mean secret? My entire life is a completely open book. I think having kids and a husband answers every mystery in life, so there's no need to have any secrets."

"That's not the secret I'm talking about. You have to look in the mirror," Kaycee said. "You just shine, and you haven't aged since I saw you last."

Sally laughed. "Now that's impossible, and I don't know if I agree with you. I think you're even prettier than high school, so I'm hoping that as we age there's something added to all of us that makes our looks more pleasing, if not to ourselves, then to the people who love us."

Kaycee picked up the spoon in a large bowl of fruit that smelled delicious. She began spooning it on her plate.

"That could be true for you because you've already found someone who loves you. But what about me? I'm still single."

Sally giggled and then lowered her voice to say, "You make me feel guilty. My husband of ten years tells me that all the time, and you know I have never bothered to believe him."

"Next time he says it, if I were you, I'd believe him."

"Thank you, Kaycee. Hopefully, John will compliment me again sometime, and I'll try to remember to say thank you. Look at this monstrosity of a cake. We are going to have tons of it left."

"The boys will love it."

"That's what scares me. Three boys high on frosting," Sally shuddered. "That isn't a pretty picture. Take another piece, you're so thin."

Kaycee laughed.

They returned to the table. Kaycee pushed the plate of food aside and ate the frosting off the chocolate cake, roses and all.

"I can't believe you're actually eating that," a thin woman with long blond hair said. She was sitting directly across from Kaycee.

Kaycee licked the frosting off the fork and smiled. "It's my favorite part."

"Aren't you terrified of gaining weight?" another woman asked.

Kaycee shook her head.

"Do you and Jimmy still spend a lot of time with each other?" the blond who first spoke asked.

All of a sudden Kaycee knew this woman. Nancy Winslow, she was a year older than Kaycee and one of Tod Mathisen's favorite dates. She was Tod's on again, off again girlfriend all through high school. Kaycee found out after Tod had dumped her that he was dating both of them at the same time. "Not really, but right now we're working together," Kaycee said in a clipped tone.

"I'm amazed at how closely you resemble your sister."

Kaycee frowned. "Which of my sisters do you know?"

"I can't remember her name, there are so many girls in your family," Nancy said with a bite in her voice, and then she paused and looked around the room. "I'll just ask Jimmy. Where is he?"

Kaycee felt a rush of dread when Nancy mentioned Jimmy's name. Why, she had no idea. She barely knew Nancy. All the same, when Kaycee looked toward the bar she hoped Jimmy was not walking toward them.

32

A television screen was at one side of the room and the loud noises coming from it sounded like a hockey game was playing.

Jimmy leaned against the bar with a group of men watching the screen.

"Jimmy," a feminine voice called loudly from across the room. "Jimmy Zane, come here."

Jimmy turned around and the first person he saw was Kaycee. It was not her voice he heard, but she had the strangest look on her face. He left his beer on the bar and walked across the room. Jimmy's eyes swept over the group Kaycee was sitting with. He recognized most of the women at the table. One of them was Nancy Winslow. What was she doing here?

He stood behind Kaycee's chair. "Hi, ladies," he nodded to them.

"Tell me something, Jimmy," Nancy began, her voice high-pitched. She leaned forward and acted like she was going to lower her voice but did not actually do it.

Jimmy wondered if she was drunk. "What could I possibly tell you, Nancy, that you don't already know?" Jimmy asked in a teasing voice, but there was tone of steel in the words.

Nancy fluttered her eyelashes. "Oh, Jimmy, you're such a tease. I can't remember when exactly this happened or where, but you introduced me to one of your girlfriends a while back. I could have sworn it was one of Kaycee Swanson's sisters. Which one was it, Jimmy?"

Nancy turned to the woman sitting next to her and added in a hushed tone that was clearly audible to everyone, "Why do you think Kaycee's sister didn't tell her she dated Jimmy?"

An uncomfortable silence fell over the group as they

watched Jimmy and Kaycee.

Jimmy's anger began to build. He had no idea what Kaycee was feeling, but he knew she was used to hiding her feelings. "Nancy, I hope you have a designated driver tonight," he said, sounding like a cop. "Where's your husband, Phil, anyway?"

Nancy was clearly taken by surprise. "I can catch a ride with somebody," she cried defensively. "I won't be driving. Phil couldn't make it. He's…he's…" She fell silent.

"I wouldn't get behind the wheel tonight." Jimmy warned. He slid Kaycee's chair back away from the table and took her hand in his.

"I'm hungry, will you help me fix a plate?" he asked, leading her to the buffet table. Jimmy hissed into her ear. "Don't you dare let Nancy think she got the best of you. You'll hate yourself if you give her the satisfaction of ruining Sally's party."

Kaycee glanced up at him.

"Don't you realize that's exactly why she planned that little ambush?"

Kaycee relaxed her expression to a smile. "Wasn't she always like that in school? I think she just likes misery."

Jimmy moved down the buffet putting food on his plate until he looked at it and was satisfied. He was not hungry, but he knew they had to stay. If Kaycee had her way she would have walked out without another thought. Jimmy knew that is exactly what people like Nancy Winslow wanted to happen. It put them at the center of attention. Kaycee did not care, but he did. Nancy did not deserve to get the better of Kaycee.

They walked over to the bar where he could force some of the food past his dry throat.

The men soon surrounded the two and began to ask questions about the filming on Palisade Head.

While Jimmy was occupied with his food, Kaycee found it much easier to talk to the guys. She told them stories about the technicians and the prop men and the machinery they were using. Men did not want to know who the handsome leading man was or who was making the most money. They wanted to know who was going to die and how.

Jimmy finally pushed his plate away and joined the conversation. "I think you've told enough secrets about the production. Remember guys, all of that was top secret and Kaycee will get in trouble with the press manager if any of it leaks out."

Kaycee smiled, her eyes flicked over Jimmy. "But wait a minute, I haven't had a chance to tell the best story of the entire shoot. The one about you, Jimmy." Jimmy watched as Kaycee changed right before his eyes. She became the model again. The model he had stopped on the freeway coming into Duluth. The poised, calculating woman who thought she was going to con a local cop out of a speeding ticket. Jimmy knew now she was angry, really angry. Nancy had done what she wanted by mentioning Jimmy and one of Kaycee's younger sisters. She set the fuse inside of Kaycee, and Jimmy knew when it was going to explode. Not in here, but when they were alone.

Jimmy heard someone asking him, "Who was the actress, Jimmy? Was she anybody famous?"

"Did you get some kind of reward? She's probably loaded. You should ask for a reward."

Jimmy watched as Kaycee abruptly walked away from the group. She returned to the table and picked up her jacket.

He shook his head. "I'm on the payroll. Why would I ask for a reward when I was doing my job?" he replied with annoyance. He pushed past the men and walked toward Kaycee. She had stopped to talk to Sally.

Kaycee fell silent when he arrived.

Jimmy said with a smile, "Thanks, Sal, for great food. Tell John goodbye. He's busy watching the game." Sally jumped at Jimmy's cue.

"No wait, I'll get John. He wants to say good-bye," she cried and ran across the room.

The two stood together, but not a word was spoken.

Sally returned with John in tow.

"Jim, you're off already," John said with a slap on Jimmy's back. "Don't be a stranger. The kids miss seeing you at the house."

Jimmy smiled. "Tell them I talked to my lieutenant and made a request to visit their school, so they'll be able to start the siren on my squad."

Both Sally and John laughed. "We won't hear the end of it. That's great."

"Jimmy loves kids. Did you know that?" Sally asked Kaycee unexpectedly.

Kaycee shook her head.

"Please, if you ever have the chance, come to dinner at our house with Jimmy. Then we can visit."

Kaycee gave her a hug.

"Thank you so much," she said softly. "I'll never forget how kind you were tonight." Kaycee turned and walked out the door.

Jimmy was right behind her. He ignored her attempts to knock his hand off her arm.

When they walked outside of the bar, Kaycee jerked out of his grasp. She hurried across the parking lot to the Blazer and waited impatiently for him to unlock her door.

Jimmy climbed in the driver's side and put the keys in the ignition, but he waited in silence. Kaycee put on her seat belt and refused to look at him.

"Go ahead, get it out," he said suddenly.

Kaycee jumped.

"I know you've got something to say, so do it." He leaned back in his seat.

She said in a small, cold voice, "I don't know what you're talking about."

"Of course you do. Nancy Winslow wanted to start a fight and she did it. Now you're back to being angry and not talking to me."

"I'm tired Jimmy, that's all."

"What is it you're so angry about? That Nancy told you I dated one of your sisters, or that Nancy knew and you didn't?"

Kaycee snorted she was so angry. "You know nothing about me, Jimmy Zane, so don't play smug like you can read my mind." She took a deep breath. "I'm late and tomorrow is going to be hard enough without my catching pneumonia in your truck tonight."

"It's nice out, you won't catch pneumonia," he said mildly. He heard her groan of frustration and shook his head. Then he reached over and started the Blazer. "Whatever you're thinking, Kaycee, it's probably wrong, but if you haven't the guts to ask me for the truth, then why should I bother explaining anything."

Kaycee glanced at him out of the corner of her eye when he pulled up in front of her parents' house. "Thanks," she mumbled.

Jimmy said quickly, "See you tomorrow."

She jumped out of his Blazer and escaped to the house without a backward glance.

33

The house was completely dark and silent. Kaycee moved quietly around the upstairs getting ready for bed. How could her blissful day with Jimmy have ended like this? How could he have dated one of her sisters? It was unthinkable. She couldn't imagine him with anyone else, let alone one of her sisters.

Kaycee never once bothered to think about why she was so upset in the first place. Who cared who Jimmy dated before?

Bleary eyed from lack of sleep, Kaycee stared out the window from her usual seat on the bus. At the early morning meeting, they were told breakfast would be ready for them when they arrived. When the bus stopped, the passengers cleared off quickly. Kaycee had no plans to eat anything until she was done filming today. She remained in her seat feeling crabby and miserable.

As soon as she got off the bus, her day would begin in full force, and she was not ready for it. There was the filming on the cliff, and she had to face Jimmy.

"What's the hold-up?" Jimmy asked loudly from the front of the bus. "You too busy daydreaming to know the bus stopped?" He moved down the narrow aisle toward her. His shoulders hunched forward so he wouldn't hit his head on the low ceiling. Kaycee jumped out of her seat looking desperately for a way out, but she was neatly boxed in. Jimmy stopped to rest his arms against the backs of the seats a few feet in front of her. Kaycee took a deep breath, mustered all the anger she could, and with a defiant tilt to her head and the grace of a dancer, she walked directly at him. She hoped, but doubted, he would move and let her pass. When she reached him, he did not touch her but continued to block the aisle.

"Is this the plan you've come up with?" he asked coolly.

"You're going to ignore me and then run off? You're acting just like the old Kaycee, the thirteen-year-old. Why can't we talk about it, face it, and then we can get the whole mess out in the open and settled? Holding a grudge only makes you the bitter one."

Kaycee glared at him. "I have every right to hold a grudge against you, you traitor. You turned my own flesh and blood against me. Not even my family told me that you dated one of my sister." She stopped. There was no softening in her lovely face.

"Think about it, Kaycee," he pleaded. "We were friends, yes, but that was all. Why would anyone in your family think it strange for me to ask Cyndy out on a date? You and I never dated. You've reminded me of that over a dozen times since we've been working together."

"So you admit it was Cyndy."

"Yes, it was Cyndy. I asked her out exactly twice and that was it." He stepped closer to her and lowered his voice. "Kaycee, it wasn't until last night that we allowed any of our other feelings to change our relationship."

Kaycee shrugged her shoulders slightly and looked away. Her insides trembled, but her voice remained cold. "And look what's happened to our friendship the very next morning. It's better to just put what happened behind us and forget it."

Jimmy said softly, "May I ask why? I thought we were moving forward. Friendship is a great start, but we're finding out there's so much more between us. Don't you want to find out where this first taste of intimacy will lead?"

Kaycee moved to step around him, and he moved out of her way. "I have to go."

Jimmy called to her, "Watch out. There's been a major change in the weather."

Kaycee ignored him and stepped out into the parking lot carrying most of her winter gear in her hands. The wind slapped her in the face first and then whipped its icy fingers through her unzipped jacket. With uncovered fingers, she dragged the material together and struggled along the frozen rutted ground. Why did she pick today to misplace the fur and leave it at home?

Getting ready at home this morning was a complete fiasco. She was already late for the meeting and could not find the fur anywhere. She had to leave without it. Now as she battled against the wind, she was already chilled to the bone.

Michelle held the door open for her as she walked into the trailer. "You poor thing. You don't handle this wind very well at all." Michelle studied her stark, pale features.

Kaycee shivered. "I know, and I'm supposed to be filming today."

"Sit down," Michelle told her firmly, "this is going to take awhile."

Michelle slapped a mudpack on Kaycee's face and told her not to move.

There was a knock on the trailer door.

Kaycee stopped herself from turning to look, wondering if it could be Jimmy.

"Come in, it's open," Michelle called, hurrying over to the door.

A man bundled in a hooded parka and flannel scarf came inside. "I'm looking for Miss Swanson."

"Come on in out of the cold," Michelle said quickly. "That's Miss Swanson under there. You can talk to her but she can't answer. I'll give you the answers."

Kaycee kept her eyes closed and nodded.

"Joe sent me to tell you the scene with Mr. Dawes will be shot first. Mr. Dawes wants to return to the studio as soon as possible if the scene can be filmed at all today."

Michelle asked, "Has there been any word from the weather service?"

"The wind is supposed to drop. I don't know about the temperature. Joe said the scene with Mr. Dawes and Miss

Swanson will be shot if the wind drops, even if it stays cold."

"Well, Miss Swanson has had an unavoidable delay and needs at least an hour to get ready. I hope the wind doesn't stop before that," she told him.

With a shrug, he let himself out.

Michelle placed a warm washcloth over Kaycee's face to loosen the dry mud.

When Kaycee could talk she asked, "An unavoidable delay?"

"Yes, the condition of your face is an unavoidable delay."

"So you're implying that the way my face looks today, it would be better suited for the scene when a week later I wash up on shore?"

"Something like that, but it's not going to happen. Not with my reputation on the line," Michelle declared. "You'll have to act the hysteria, not look it."

"Somehow, I don't think hysteria will be a hard part for me to act," Kaycee muttered. "I'm rediscovering how disappointing the men I choose can be. It doesn't surprise me in the least that I'm to be murdered by one of them."

"You must have seen the paper this morning?" Michelle said.

Kaycee remained perfectly still. "Now what? No, I haven't."

Michelle was silent until Kaycee heard the rustle of a paper in front of her. She opened her eyes. "Mystery Woman on Set of Movie at Palisade Head is a Duluthian," the headline read. The headline didn't upset her until she saw the photograph of Richard Dawes and Kaycee walking through the snow in the valley. Richard Dawes looked magnificent carrying the ski equipment across his back like some kind of Swiss skiing instructor. Kaycee looked awful. Her sunglasses were pushed off her face and she was squinting. "Oh no," she moaned. "That looks absolutely horrible. How could they have printed such a picture?"

She closed her eyes wondering what else could go wrong today.

"Richard Dawes has a personal manager who has to preview photographs of him before they are printed. I guess you don't get the same treatment."

"The newspaper, and today Rick Dawes gets to push me over the edge. This day is unbelievable."

"Stop wrinkling your forehead," Michelle said.

"I know some people will be thrilled to see a picture like this in the paper," she told Michelle without malice when she handed it back to her. Kaycee did not care anymore.

An hour later the loudspeaker announced, "The wind has dropped. Let's move people." Crewmembers and technicians rushed out of the tents and the trailers. Everybody wanted to see the final scene with Mr. Dawes. Kaycee felt the excitement when she stepped out of the trailer. Not only was this Dawes's last scene, but there were only a few segments left and the filming at this location would be over.

Kaycee was going to have trouble leaving here. The crew did not share her sentiments. They would be thrilled to get away from the difficulties of the snow, the wind, and the cold, all caused by the crazy unpredictable big Lake Superior.

Kaycee walked slowly down toward the cliff. The yellow Humvee was parked next to it with the engine running. Kaycee smiled and thought, "Richard Dawes wasn't kidding when he said he wanted to leave immediately after filming."

The film crew was busy reshooting the scene where Dawes runs away from the murder scene. Kaycee walked up with the other bystanders just in time to watch the final sequence.

Dawes leaned over the edge of the cliff so far he tilted like he was going over himself.

Kaycee felt goose bumps rise along her scalp. His face took on the twisted, crazed look of a deviant as he scrambled away from the ledge and ran toward the ridge. Half way to the top, he slipped and slid on his stomach, stopping close to the edge of the drop-off. Kaycee did not remember if it was part of the script or not, but it sure looked real. She covered her mouth and gasped.

Dawes regained his balance and crouched down, keeping his body low to the ground as he ran up the ridge. At times he was on all fours and then he disappeared. Only when the scene ended with the word, "Cut!" did anyone in the group move.

Kaycee realized she'd been holding her breath.

Everyone broke out in applause for Richard Dawes's performance.

When he reappeared over the ridge, he gave a quick wave of his hand in their direction before he disappeared into his Humvee.

Kaycee shook her head with wonder at this man. She looked up and smiled, waving back at Joe when she saw him. Joe looked warm in his fur, and Kaycee saw that now Lance was wearing a fine-looking dark red fur coat of his own. She regretted not having hers with her. She could have worn it over the thermal cross-country outfit.

The technicians were not wasting a moment. As soon as the gear was being set for the next scene, they motioned for Kaycee. She was being strapped into her safety harness when Joe walked over to brief her about the scene.

"We are going to do the scene before you go over the edge," he told her.

Kaycee nodded.

Joe paused while the technician tested her lines. "She set?" he asked.

The technician nodded.

"Come over here," Joe led the way to the edge.

Kaycee followed him. A swimming feeling from the height caught at her, adding to the butterflies in her stomach, but she ignored it.

"This is where he will push you off," Joe said, raising his voice over the crane's motor. A few feet below there's a wide safety ledge with a canvas pillow to cushion your fall. You need to end up within the markers," Joe pointed at the markers camouflaged by the ground, "before he can start to get you close to the edge. We don't know how difficult this will be, so we're going to keep shooting as much as we can. If we make it all the way to the push, roll and fall, then we'll keep shooting as long as you two make it work."

Kaycee nodded as she leaned over the lip of the cliff to study the air bag on the ledge below. Suddenly, she felt her feet slip. Before she could panic, a strong grip grabbed a hold of the back of her jacket and held onto her. Kaycee's heart raced. She didn't need to see who it was. She knew it was Jimmy and felt better just because he was near. She listened intently to Joe's instructions. Once Joe cued them, the crew returned and began to take their places. The technicians stayed with Kaycee and had the crane lift her to her tiptoes and then lower her to be certain everything worked.

"Ready on the set!" Joe yelled. "Call Mr. Dawes."

A hot blanket was wrapped around Kaycee until the filming started.

Rick Dawes climbed out of the Humvee. He stood patiently while his makeup and wardrobe were checked, and then he walked across to where Kaycee waited. They were going to walk along the edge of the cliff for twenty feet.

"Ready on the set," Lance said through the loudspeaker. "One, two, three…roll."

Richard Dawes took her gloved hand in his. They walked a few steps then stopped to look at the lake. Rick put his arms around Kaycee, cuddling her into his body. They were approaching the marks on the rock where the push was to take place.

"Shall we go down and look at the shoreline?" Rick asked her.

With a look of fear, she looked directly at him, Kaycee shook her head. Burying her face into the curve of Rick's shoulder. At the drop-off, Kaycee did not need much acting ability for this part.

"Come on, honey. This is the true wilderness where our forefathers landed. I had family members from the Hudson Bay Company that trapped furs out in this country side-by-side with the Ojibwa Indians."

Kaycee hung back. "I'm afraid. The ground doesn't seem stable enough," she insisted.

"Well, if you're going to be a coward, I'll go and take a look by myself," he said in an aggrieved tone. He had an obvious look of anger on his face.

"No, wait," Kaycee called to him. She gave a frightened laugh. "You're right, I'm just being silly, but hold onto my hand. If I slip, don't you dare let go of me."

Rick grasped both of her hands tightly in his and declared with earnest flamboyance, "I would never let any harm come to you, my love." He lied to her with a charming smile. "It would break my heart."

Kaycee smiled happily up at him. "I just know everything is going to work out for us," she cried. "Your wife will surely sign the divorce papers soon and then we can be married. I'll be so happy." She turned away from Rick to look at the lake. The wind ruffled her hair and brightened her cheeks.

He said softly, "No, we'll be so happy, darling."

When they reached the markers, Rick stopped. He became mesmerized by the sheer drop-off. The wind whipped at his hair while he stared down the cliff. It turned his face and ears bright red. Kaycee followed him and timidly leaned toward the edge. Rick moved his head to watch her. A glazed look came over his face.

Kaycee cowered back. "This is really dangerous," she said nervously. "Why aren't there any safety fences blocking this?"

"It would ruin the view," Rick said harshly. "You wouldn't

expect them to fence in the Grand Canyon, would you? Of course not." His voice softened. "That would be ridiculous."

Kaycee shook her head. "Let's go back now," she said hastily. "I want to go back. It's cold, and I don't like it here." She stepped back and her foot slipped on some gravel.

Rick grabbed onto her and held her under the arm until she regained her balance. "Be careful," he said.

Kaycee stared at him. She did not remember that line. She searched her mind for the line before Rick pushes her.

"Cut!"

"What's the problem?" Lance yelled. He walked quickly to where they stood. Kaycee had already moved away from Rick and the cliff edge.

"She forgot her line," Rick said with a sneer. He was surrounded by people who wrapped him in a warm blanket and handed him a cup of something hot.

Kaycee was told sharply, "Stand still," while a technician checked the straps under her jacket. She flinched at how cold his hands were. Then a heated blanket was wrapped around her and a cup of hot coffee pushed into her hands. "May I please see a script," she said to a technician.

"Here," a familiar voice said.

Kaycee looked up into Jimmy's face and almost burst into tears. His head was covered with an army green hat. His cheeks a darker shade of bronze from the wind and he looked so dear and comforting. He held his script and flipped it to the page she asked for.

"Thanks," she said, quietly moving closer to him. She held the steaming coffee under her chin to warm her mouth. Her eyes quickly read through the lines.

He said, "The suspense is building."

"But we'll never finish, it's freezing out here."

"The wind's dropping, that will bring the temperature up a little. They aren't using the helicopter to film this, the wind is shifting too much."

"Then how?"

Jimmy pointed to the metal cage on the crane. "They're going to try that. Let's hope it works so this scene can be done."

Joe hurried over to where they were standing. "After this take, we're going to break for lunch," he told them, stamping his feet. "If it gets any colder, I don't think we'll be able to continue."

Kaycee clutched the blanket closer around her. "What is Mr. Dawes going to say about it?"

Joe glanced over his shoulder at the man in question. "He's cold, too," was the only comment Joe would make. "Are you ready to continue?"

She nodded.

Jimmy took the coffee and the blanket. "Are you done with the script?" he asked.

Kaycee shook her head, scanning the words on the page. She knew the lines, but not the one he had said earlier, and the physical directions were mixed up. Mr. Dawes must be ad-libbing some parts. It was one thing when he did it to catch his breath walking up the hill, but it was another when he was doing it on the edge of a cliff.

She turned to Jimmy, wishing he wouldn't leave her. Both of them had laughed when he said he needed to protect her from the leading man, but now she wanted him to be right there in case something did happen. She handed back the script but held onto his arm. "Don't go too far away," she said, "please." Her gloved fingers slipped slowly from his arm.

Jimmy nodded. "I'll be right here. If you need me, just say my name so I can hear you."

Kaycee nodded, took a deep breath, and faced Richard Dawes once again. She hid her apprehension behind the stupid, bubble of happiness her character was living in. Rick's expression when he looked at her was one of barely veiled insolence.

"You missed your cue," he said in a low voice.

Kaycee anxiously searched his face. "You aren't following the script," she accused him softly. "What do you expect me to do?"

He smirked at her. "I was just testing you," he said.

Kaycee shivered. "Don't you agree it's too cold to be doing that?"

He looked at the sky. "What else is there in this place?"

"Why don't we finish the scene so we can really warm up?" Kaycee suggested, clinging to his arm. They were closer to the edge than they had been before but she refused to look down.

"You don't like heights, I take it?" Rick said, narrowing his eyes at her. "It isn't so bad, and you're wearing a harness to protect you."

Kaycee frowned at the sound of menace in his voice. She turned to the script girl who looked almost blue from the cold. "Could you please cue me?" she asked, raising her voice. "I can't recall where we left off."

The girl gave her the cue.

Lance yelled, "Roll 'em."

Kaycee's lines clicked into place, and she repeated them without flaw.

The scene went on until Lance yelled, "Cut!"

Kaycee instantly released Rick's arm and rushed to where the technicians waited to remove the harness. When they finished, Jimmy brought a warm blanket and wrapped it around her. By the time they reached the trailer she was visibly shaking. Jimmy opened the door for Kaycee but remained outside. "I'll bring some lunch," he said. "Michelle, you hungry?"

"No, I'm not like the model here. If I eat three meals a day, I turn into a Macy's parade balloon."

Jimmy laughed then slammed the door.

"I see you will need a little touch-up on your makeup,"

Michelle observed dryly. "First, you should thaw out."

"It feels colder than the first day we filmed," Kaycee said with chattering teeth.

"Oh, do you mean the day you almost froze to death?" Michelle asked sarcastically. "Then why are they still filming?"

Kaycee shrugged.

Michelle piled a down comforter on top of her. "Where's the fur? You could be wearing that between takes."

Kaycee pulled the comforter tight around her while Michelle helped her take off the boots.

"I couldn't find it this morning. I have no idea where my mother put the darn thing. I just hope she didn't try to wash it for me. We're probably still filming because Rick Dawes wants to go home...today."

"He hates the cold. Why would he insist on being out in this?" Michelle wrapped her feet in another blanket.

"That's hot," Kaycee said in surprise.

"It's a heating pad. I couldn't survive here without it," Michelle confessed with a smile. "When your feet get toasty we'll put it under the down comforter."

"Thanks, Michelle, I already feel a lot better," Kaycee told her sincerely. "The suit they gave me does a good job, but that darn wind. Jimmy says it's supposed to die off some more later on. Then maybe Mr. Dawes will get his wish, and he can finish filming today."

"After you eat, I'll work on your face. Right now, close your eyes for a little while," Michelle advised her. "I'll be as quiet as I can."

Kaycee snuggled into the thick comforter and did rest her eyes. They burned from lack of sleep, unshed tears, and the cold wind. "Only for a minute," she told herself, expecting the disturbing events of the last two days to once more keep her from sleeping.

The smell of hot coffee woke her. Kaycee thought she

was home in bed.

"Hey, sleepy head, hurry up and eat, then I have to do a rush job on your makeup."

Kaycee sat up. Jimmy was sleeping stretched out in the other chair. He had his hat pulled over his face as he leaned back in the chair, almost tipping it over. He never seemed affected by the cold. He didn't even have a blanket on him. Kaycee looked down at herself. No wonder he didn't have a blanket, she had every blanket. She stood up and flipped the comforter over Jimmy before she walked into the kitchen. The food was on the kitchen table set around the bottles and tubes of Michelle's cosmetics.

"It sure smells good," she said. "How long was I out?"

Michelle shrugged. "About a half hour, I'm glad you could rest."

Kaycee couldn't believe she had fallen asleep. She sat down hoping Jimmy would wake up soon so she could talk to him about Richard Dawes and how strange he was acting.

Michelle sat across from her and picked up one of the sandwiches. "I've read where the cold affects all people differently. I've heard where it can make people quite insane." She took a small bite of the sandwich. "I think I watched a movie about that but the people were snowbound someplace."

Kaycee said quickly, "So it doesn't apply to this situation at all."

"Did Rick make any comment on the newspaper this morning?" Michelle asked her.

Kaycee shook her head. "There wasn't time for it. They were pushing us through the scene pretty fast."

The loudspeaker announced, "People, you have fifteen minutes to get ready and be out at the cliff."

Kaycee took a swallow of the lukewarm coffee and stood. "We better get busy."

Once the loudspeaker had sounded, Jimmy awoke. Kaycee had her back to him but watched his movements in the mirror while Michelle applied fresh makeup to her face.

"I know you don't like the foundation to be this thick, but the wind blows it off too fast otherwise. You'll have to suffer through it this time," she said sternly.

Kaycee sighed. "Joe complained that I looked like a washrag again."

"I'll kill him if he did," Jimmy said from his chair. He grinned when both of them turned around to stare at him. "I'm only kidding."

"Well, stop. We have a deadline," Michelle admonished him.

"I'm going to the com-tent to check the weather. I'll meet you at the site," Jimmy told Kaycee as he pulled on his outdoor gear.

Kaycee gave Michelle a look in the mirror.

"What did I do?" Michelle asked defensively.

"You know if you weren't happily married to a mailman in the Bronx, I'd think you had a crush on Jimmy."

Michelle placed her hands on her hips and said, "Nobody who chooses to live in this refrigerator could tempt me. I don't care if he's Adonis."

A second blast sounded from the loudspeaker and Kaycee jumped from the chair and hurried to put on her ski outfit.

"Don't forget your stuff," Michelle cried, grabbing her hat, scarf, and mittens off the chair. She helped Kaycee tie her boots.

"Good luck!" Michelle called before she ducked back inside and slammed the door.

Kaycee hurried away from the trailer and then started to run until Jimmy grabbed her arm. "Wait a minute, you could turn an ankle on these frozen ruts. With the thaw, the trucks really tore the ground up."

Kaycee slowed her pace but still hurried. She did not want to keep Richard Dawes waiting to finish his last scene. Once they reached the ridge, she stopped.

"It's warmer," she said in disbelief. "Is it me or does it feel warmer than it did?"

Jimmy nodded. "The wind died and it went up ten degrees, so the weatherman was right."

"I'm so glad, I can't wait to get this over," she said anxiously. She started down the hill toward the people waiting for them.

"I wanted to ask you about that, but we didn't have the chance. What's up?"

Kaycee glanced around before answering him. "I don't know exactly, but Rick Dawes is acting kind of weird."

"I've been telling you that since the man got here," Jimmy reminded her.

"I know you have, but this is different," she said uneasily. "Or it might just be my imagination. I just feel like some of the time he isn't acting, and that he really would like to kill someone...me."

Jimmy didn't laugh at her.

"I'll stick as close as I can to where you're filming. Don't be afraid, Kaycee, you have the safety harness on and Dawes doesn't."

The scene on the cliff quickly turned from the romantic interlude to tragedy. Rick Dawes's character never gave away what he was going to do to Kaycee's character. He treated her with the same loving concern he'd used right up to the point when he pushed her.

They were kissing. "How odd it feels to be kissing a stranger," she thought. Kaycee kept her mind blank when Rick leaned into her pressing her backward. She forced herself to relax in his grasp and to keep her eyes closed. It was hard to do.

The grip he had on her suddenly changed. The points of his fingers dug into the flesh of her upper arms.

Kaycee's eyelids flew upwards. She was staring into Rick's face. His eyes were open and looked black, sinister.

Abruptly, he moved. His expression was a furious grimace that sent chills through her body. He looked capable of murder right now. She twisted her body and fought him. She couldn't stop herself. Self-preservation kicked in. It was too soon.

"Cut!" blasted through the bullhorn. "Kaycee, you reacted too soon. You didn't wait for indecision at all. Remember you don't suspect a thing, yet."

"Okay, I'm sorry," she said, breathing heavily. She wiped her mouth off with her scarf.

"Good fear expression," Lance added. "Use it in the right place next time."

"Thanks, I will." She moved reluctantly back into position. When she looked at Rick, he had a less than complimentary look on his face.

"It's so blasted cold," he snapped, "would you at least let me say my lines before my lips freeze."

Kaycee nodded. "Sorry, you're too good of an actor. I forgot it wasn't real," she murmured in explanation.

Rick snorted and grasped her shoulders. "If there are anymore stupid mistakes to keep me here longer than I have to be, it might not be an act," he said in a threatening tone.

Kaycee gasped, her mouth dropped open for a moment. "You can't be serious."

"I'm not," he quipped.

Then Lance gave the order and Rick began to speak the lines she recognized from the script. His fingers tightened. He shook her once, then again harder. With a strength she didn't expect from him, he dragged her stumbling, resisting body to the very edge of the cliff. He held her arms tight behind her back as he dangled her over into the space beyond but he held on. The words he said were just a jumble that Kaycee could not hear. Her heart thundered so loud all she saw was the water below and the depth of space in between. Darkness clouded the edges of her vision. She could see the ledge, the huge airbag, and the swirling water beyond. The ground under her boots crumbled away. With a shriek, she threw herself backward, fighting the hands that held her. Her abrupt movement caught Rick off guard. He stumbled back giving her seconds to regain her footing. Frantically, she broke one arm free and clawed at him. Her gloved hands slid uselessly against his slippery coat, unable to find a grip. Kaycee threw her body sideways. She caught hold of his torso and clinging, kept her arms around his waist, anything to stop her from going over the edge.

"Let go," Rick leaned close to her ear and hissed. "Let go. Let go right now, or we're both going over." His voice, harsh with anger, penetrated Kaycee's fear. Kaycee remembered where she was. She relaxed her grip long enough for him to fling her away from his body. She hit the edge of the ground hard. Then she rolled, the rocks were sharp. Desperately Kaycee scraped at the ground. Her hands moved constantly, searching for something to stop her fall even as she continued to slide over the edge. Her eyes, filled with terror, stared up at him beseechingly until she started to scream. Her screams increased as her hands, the only part of her body left for the camera to see, continued to claw at the ground.

Rick stood watching her go over the edge until the tormented scream escaping her lips, one of undeniable primal fear, ended. Not until the sound of that scream abruptly stopped did he turn to go.

34

The sound of her shrieks echoed eerily off the walls of rock surrounding her as Kaycee plummeted through the air. Abruptly she was silenced when the harness caught around her torso, slowing her fall. Her body slammed into the air bag waiting on the rock ledge, and the force of the hit knocked her senseless. The canvas bag was hard even as the air deflated with the weight of her body. Blackness engulfed her until she felt the bag move underneath her. The next instant, she was not alone. Cold hands cupped her face, and suddenly, she was being kissed. Kaycee pushed at the hard body and the warm flannel. She pushed, moving her face away, gasping for breath. She opened her eyes and wheezed, "Jimmy?"

"You're all right?" he asked, grasping her arms to stand her up on the pillow. "You're not hurt? You hit that bag so hard I was sure you'd broken something."

"If I could breathe properly, I'd feel a lot better," she snapped. She held onto her ribs as she shifted her weight. She ached all over but felt no sharp pain. Kaycee tried to steady herself on the half collapsed bag but couldn't.

"Everything okay down there?" Joe yelled from above.

Kaycee could have sworn she heard laughter. A hot flush filled her cheeks.

Jimmy tried to help her but she pushed him away. "Back off," she said fighting to catch her breath.

He stood with his hands on his hips watching her struggles.

"Help me," she demanded when it became obvious she couldn't make any headway on her own. "I can't move with this sack and the harness holding me down."

Jimmy placed one boot on the folds of the air bag. Then he reached out to grasp her arm and haul her ungracefully over the edge. The bag shifted uncontrollably, throwing them both off balance and Kaycee onto her knees.

"Are you hurt?"

"If I wasn't before, I am now. I'm not a sack of potatoes," she cried, struggling to stand. Once on her feet she looked up the side of the cliff. From down here it wasn't as far down as she thought.

A row of faces peered down from above, watching them. "Get me out of here, Joe," she yelled up the cliff.

"We're working on it."

Kaycee leaned against the wall and took several deep breaths. Her ribs did not hurt anymore and neither did her back.

Jimmy leaned negligently against the side of the rock near the edge with his arms crossed over his chest watching her.

"What is taking them so long?" she muttered, shivering violently. With quick movements she rubbed her arms and stomped in place to keep circulation going.

Jimmy, strangely, wasn't offering her any comfort.

"Come over here with me. There's some protection from the wind."

Kaycee ignored his offer. "This is crazy. What's the hold up?" she yelled.

The sound of the crane roaring into life above them brought her head up. She caught her breath.

"That whole last scene, you weren't acting at all, were you?" Jimmy asked. "That scream you let out, it was the real thing?" He shook his head moving toward her.

Kaycee felt close to tears, but she did not want him to see. She moved away from him. The edge of the airbag tangled around her boots and sent her sprawling forward. Right under her nose was the open expanse of black water. The wind whipped into her face bringing tears to her cheeks. Violently, she scrambled backward stumbling across the folds of canvas when Jimmy caught her in his arms. He lifted her away from the canvas and held her sheltered by the protection of his body.

"Jimmy," she croaked. Tears streamed down her cheeks eroding the heavy makeup. Black mascara blurred her vision.

"I-I think I'm going to be sick," she exclaimed in horror. She tried to break away as her stomach heaved.

"It's okay, love," his voice soothed her. As he helped her out of view near the rock, he held her shoulders until the spasms stopped. Her mouth trembled as he wiped her lips gently with something soft and warm.

"Oh, no, Jimmy," she protested weakly, "not your shirt. How disgusting." Jimmy continued wiping the black from her cheeks and under her eyes. He held her close to him until the trembling in her limbs eased.

"Kaycee," the bullhorn cried from above. "We're ready to bring you up."

Jimmy held her chin and inspected her face. "You look fine, now get into position." He led her to the open and pulled hard to check on the line.

She smiled weakly at him. "I still look awful."

"Michelle can fix it," he reassured her.

"Sorry about your shirt. I'll wash it for you."

He shook his head. "Don't worry about it."

Kaycee held onto him. Her eyes wide, shining with unshed tears, she continued to stare at him, wanting his strength to make her strong.

"Ready!" they yelled from up above.

"I'll hold your legs until you can reach the rock so you won't scrape against it," he told her as the line tightened.

She moved her body, tensing so she would be ready when the crane lifted her.

She slowly rose in the air and yelled to him, "Where's your jacket, Jimmy? You're going to freeze down here." The harness tightened so she couldn't speak. Why did he insist on taking such chances with himself? Kaycee looked up and saw she was at the lip of the edge. Hands reached out and grasped the line. They pulled her in and undid the harness.

35

Forgetting about her own fear, she pulled the harness off. "Hurry, he's down there without a jacket!" she shouted anxiously to the technicians. "Does anybody have a blanket? He's going to need warm blankets. Joe? Where's Joe?"

She watched as the harness was lowered down the side again. The crane jerked then stopped, swinging in the wind. There was a grinding noise she'd never heard before. Kaycee held her breath, when, ever so slowly the motor stopped making the noise and the harness continued to move. The wind blew cold, and Kaycee shivered, completely occupied with Jimmy on the ledge exposed without a jacket. Why was it taking so long?

Joe walked over and Kaycee turned to him. "Thank goodness, you're here."

"He'll be fine, Kaycee. We'll have him here in a minute." Joe patted her shoulder. "He didn't put on any safety equipment either." Joe shook his head. "Just wait until I have a talk with him. He's taking this job way too seriously by jeopardizing his own life. You better get back to the trailer. You're blue with cold already and don't you dare get sick when we're almost done here."

Kaycee started walking back up to the ridge. She overheard one of the technicians saying, "I've never seen anything like it. He heard the lady scream, and he ripped his jacket off and went over the side."

"He looked like a monkey climbing down that rock."

"Crazy, completely crazy," another added.

Kaycee hurried away. She couldn't listen any more. The sick feeling had returned to her stomach. Against the gray of the rocks, she saw army green. Jimmy's jacket. It lay near the lip of the cliff where he must have tossed it before going over the edge. Without pausing to think, she hurried to pick up the parka. Kaycee knew why he had done it. It was because of her. She didn't deserve him. She'd battled all the ghosts from the past and defeated them, but now she couldn't get past Cyndy.

* * * * *

Kaycee walked over and picked the jacket off the ground. Smoothing the bulk over her arm, she went back to where the men stood watching over the edge. The crane's engine again made the grinding noise. The line jerked and slipped several feet. Whatever was happening below sent the crew scrambling. The wind caught the telescoping pole held by two men who were trying to hook the swaying cable. Jimmy was on the other end of that cable. Kaycee hid her face in his jacket, the helplessness of hanging in mid-air and unable to do anything to help yourself felt so real. She inhaled sharply. She could smell Jimmy's aftershave in the material of his jacket. She hugged it tight.

The crane roared and then ground to a stop. She looked up to see the men gathered in a tight group near the edge of the cliff grabbing the line. Then Kaycee saw them pull Jimmy up and over the ridge. The group surrounded him, blocking Kaycee's view. She hurried over and handed one of the technician's Jimmy's jacket. Jimmy was wrapped in a blanket, breathing heavily from the climb. The side of his cheek was bleeding. He must have hit the cliff.

"Get him to the medic's tent, on the double," Joe snapped at the technicians.

Kaycee had never heard Joe raise his voice before.

"He's all right, isn't he?" she asked the technician fearfully.

"I'm sure he's fine. It's just a precaution. You know how careful Joe is."

Kaycee stood watching the group. Joe saw her and walked over. "I thought I told you to get going."

Kaycee anxiously watched Jimmy walk away and asked, "He's going to be okay?"

Joe laughed. "I'm surprised you, of all people, even have to ask. By the way, I'm going in to view that last scene to make sure it's a go. I already talked to Ralph and he says it looked perfect. Ralph's judgment is usually right on target."

Kaycee slowly walked a few steps then stopped. "If something's wrong with it when are we going to reshoot? The same time that we do the other scene?"

Joe shook his head. "I really don't know. I think there's something seriously wrong with the crane." The operator is going to have a look at it, but if he can't figure out what's wrong, a mechanic will have to be called. You get on the first bus tonight. It's a great excuse for an early evening for you. I think you need it."

"Do me a favor, Joe? Will you tell Jimmy that I took the first bus home so he won't worry about me? On the ledge…I was pretty shook up," Kaycee glanced at him and then away.

Joe nodded. "Sure, not a problem, Kaycee."

"Thanks." She turned and wearily walked up the hill.

A second messenger delivered the news that Jimmy had a few scrapes and bruises but otherwise he was just fine.

The first messenger arrived completely unexpected. He delivered a message that shocked both Kaycee and Michelle. Joe received word from the studio there was no need for Kaycee to reshoot the scene with Dawes.

"What a relief." Michelle said it first so Kaycee did not have to.

The main office, when faced with waiting for repairs on the crane, decided not to reshoot the shot off the cliff. They planned to use the footage they already shot five weeks earlier.

As she left the trailer, Kaycee paused to take one last look at the filming site. A desolate slab of basalt at the top of the frozen world, yet this place held many special memories. Hastily, she wiped her eyes. It was horrible to say good-bye to Michelle. This time they exchanged addresses, and Kaycee planned on writing a mushy letter filled with sentiment she could never have said out loud.

Kaycee walked away carrying a duffel bag filled with personal belongings left at the trailer during the weeks of filming.

The second part of the message was the official notice that she was released from the Palisade Head camp and was to report at the Minneapolis office on Monday. Two days from today.

In two days, her former life was to resume like none of this had ever happened. How am I going to do it? she wondered.

The bus rumbled up the road, and in the twilight, Kaycee walked across the parking lot to board for the last time.

36

Piano music, a gentle peaceful sound in the background of many voices speaking at once, grated against Kaycee's nerves. She pressed her temple to briefly ease the pain in her head, but it did not really help.

"You're still troubled by the headaches?" Drake Edwards asked her. As her manager, he was always worried about her health. With concern, he handed her the glass of sparkling water she asked for.

Kaycee gave an indifferent shrug.

"I'm sorry, Kaycee. I know you aren't having a good time, and this is supposed to be a celebration."

"I know that, Drake, and I do want to be here. This is important to me, too. I'd be crazy to wish myself anywhere else but here."

They looked at each other and laughed.

"Really, Drake, this is my big screen debut, isn't it? I wouldn't miss it for the world. Stop fussing."

Drake frowned. Her smile could not erase his worry. He knew her too well. Not only as her manager but also as a family friend. Drake had gone to college with Stewart. He knew the entire family, and they knew him as Uncle Drake.

Kaycee glanced away. He did not look pleased. "What's wrong?" she asked with a sigh.

"I don't mean to nag you," he hesitated.

Kaycee smiled at him. "I think you do," she said delicately but with a touch of iron.

"Well, now that you mention it, I do. I'm worried about you, Kaycee," he said quickly.

Kaycee gave a distracted smile. "There's nothing wrong with me, Drake. I'm just feeling restless, that's all. It's probably spring fever."

Drake was unconvinced. The almost translucent quality

of her skin reminded him of an extremely expensive china doll his mother had owned. Her rich black hair cut in the simple shoulder length bob framed her face like an Egyptian queen. She was willow thin, thinner than before, and, when dressed in a long heavy gown of white that shimmered when she moved, it caused him to recall her nickname, the Ice Princess. Tonight she looked the part. Slightly aloof from the boisterous company, alone, yet content to be so.

Drake smiled. He liked Kaycee. He liked her professional attitude. It was the only reason he agreed to represent the eighteen-year-old almost ten years ago. True, Stewart and his family were his friends but it was not enough to induce him to represent their daughter unless he discovered she had potential. He recognized her ability for modeling and now, after reviewing her performance in the movie, he realized she could go far in the movie business, too. She was good, surprisingly good. When she began taking acting lessons and took an interest in acting, he had started doing his homework by looking into commercials. The movie contract came up so fast it shocked even him. He liked what he saw. Her character was convincing. The audience was going to love her. He had great hopes for her future, but right now he was worried about her. Ever since she returned from Duluth, there was something bothering her. Hopefully it was something she would work out soon. He already had other phone contacts about upcoming parts in movies. Drake did not want to present any of the new offers to Kaycee until she had seen herself on the big screen. She needed to see the result of all the hard work and appreciate it. "Then, we can really get the show on the road," he said, rubbing his hands together in anticipation.

"What was that?" Kaycee asked.

Drake shook his head. "Nothing, just thinking out loud. Why does a beautiful unattached girl like yourself insist on standing by the wall at this gala event with an old codger like myself?" He turned to stare at her. "Why aren't you mingling? Don't you want to see any of the people you worked with on the set of the movie?"

"Like whom? Rick Dawes?" she said with a laugh. She had caught a glimpse of him when she first came in and pointed him out to Drake. "He was the only actor I worked with. There wasn't anybody else at the shoot in Duluth except technicians and behind the scenes people like that. I feel like a fraud being here. Nobody even knows who I am."

"Richard Dawes recognized you. I saw it in his face."

Kaycee shuddered. "He is one I'm not looking forward to seeing again. Do you think the producers and directors come to these things? Unless maybe Joe and Lance might be here. I'd like to see Joe."

Drake watched in amazement at her sudden change. "I'm sure they will be here tonight. Who is Joe?"

Kaycee smiled. "Do you know I never remembered what his full name was? I couldn't ask for him if I wanted." She frowned thinking back. "Joe could be a nickname for some strange foreign name."

Drake watched her as she spoke of this Joe. Maybe this was the reason for her restlessness. She'd fallen for some guy. He chuckled. If she'd fallen in love, she'd have enough brains to find out his name.

Kaycee, her interest in the group of people that filled the ballroom renewed, left Drake and began to walk casually through the many elegant rooms. The high ceilings were bright white and the walls were either deep green or mauve or smoky blue. The plush champagne carpet cushioned the floor so her high heels made no sound. Kaycee glanced at faces as she passed, smiling at the people she recognized but never speaking more than a few words to them. By the time she circled the area, she realized neither Joe nor any of the other people she worked with at the site were here.

Right before the screening began, Drake rushed through the rooms looking for Kaycee. He finally saw her standing near the windows staring down at the freeway. Drake slowed his pace. He was huffing and puffing from moving so fast with his bulk. He watched Kaycee look up as a man approached her. She gave a disinterested smile and turned away. He continued to talk but with a polite smile she walked away. The man stopped in mid-sentence, an amazed expression on his face. Drake hoped she had not treated any of the filmmakers who were interested in her the same way. He hurried over to intercept her before she disappeared into the group walking toward the theater.

"This entire evening feels like a dream world. Look at this place, it's like a palace in Spain," Kaycee said to Drake. "I never could have imagined that in one year I'd be previewing my first movie. This instant success part of the movie business is really difficult. Much harder than the actual filming was."

Drake smiled. "Success is never what we expect."

"All those phone calls."

"The first thing after a press release come the phone calls."

"Yes, but talk shows, news shows?"

"What did you think of the game show offer?"

Kaycee laughed. "I may be a rookie but not that much of a rookie."

"How is Camille working out?"

"Thank you, Drake. She's fantastic. She takes care of all the calls, lines up the schedule, and then tells me how to dress and where and when I'm to show up. I won't be able to keep her though. Now that there aren't the interviews and publicity shots, I have nothing for her to do."

Drake looked at her. "After the premiere, the rush will start again. I wouldn't get rid of her altogether, Kaycee. Tell her the problem and ask if you can call her back when you need her."

Kaycee nodded, then asked, "How much of the social is left?" She was anxious to see this movie. If just for a time, she could go back into the world of making it, back on the cliff with Joe and Michelle, and mostly she would be with Jimmy.

When they turned the corner, Kaycee saw Rick Dawes walking across the room toward her. Her heart began to pound. He couldn't possibly be looking for her. Not now, when he looked noticeably tipsy. He walked normally but wore a silly grin on his face. Richard Dawes's reputation was not one of friendliness.

"Kaycee, my dear," he called to her cheerfully, waving his half empty glass in the air. When he reached her side, he reached out to run his fingers down the naked flesh of her arm.

Kaycee flinched. The fact he remembered her name was a shock, but it did not stop her from moving away from him.

"You certainly didn't look this delectable in that frigid hellhole we were in up north," he said, amused at his own words. "We never did find the chance to get acquainted. It's blasted difficult on location. Everything's screwed up. There's never any privacy, and people always breathing down your neck wherever you go. Don't you agree, my dear?"

Kaycee turned to Drake, glad that he stood next to her. "Richard Dawes, my manager, Drake Edwards."

Drake held out his hand but Rick merely nodded and did not take it. He tried to slip his arm around Kaycee's waist but she was too fast. Before Rick could blink, Kaycee put Drake between the two of them.

Rick frowned but side-stepped around Drake's bulk and said to Kaycee, "After the show, we should sneak off some-where and have a drink or dinner and talk. This isn't New York, but there are some decent restaurants. I wanted to in-vite you before, of course, but as I said, there wasn't the op-portunity." He pressed close to her again. "I find you a fasci-nating creature," he murmured in a silken voice. He looked her up and down. His expression showed he was certain his advances would be accepted. The hunger in his eyes made her stomach tighten. The many men she had to put up with looking at her in the same way while she was a model, Kaycee refused to tolerate it any longer, not from anyone. In high heels, she looked down at the top of his head where the hair was thinning. Richard Dawes was definitely an attractive man, but he was already showing the signs of excess that were wearing him down. Puffiness around his face, jowls forming in his cheeks, all of these showed that he liked rich food, high living, and alcohol. The scene at the cliff came to mind with a startling clarity. Something in his expression when he looked at her right now sent goose bumps across her skin. "He isn't a nice man, no matter how good of an actor he is," she thought. Masking a shudder, she stepped back, again putting space between them.

"I thank you for the honor of your invitation," she began with a distant smile, "but I am already engaged for the remainder of the evening." She briefly held her hand out and took his. "It was such a great experience working with you. Good-bye." She dropped Rick's hand, turned, and placed hers under Drake's elbow and said, "Shall we find our seats in the theater?"

Drake looked at Richard Dawes and saw his narrowed eyes. Kaycee looked neither right nor left as they walked away from the actor.

37

The plush velvet seats of the theater reclined. Several waiters walked up and down the aisle taking drink orders. At the front was the stage and hidden behind the maroon curtains edged with gold tassels was the screen.

"Excited?" Drake asked, settling his bulk gracefully into the narrow seat.

"Of course," Kaycee said quickly. "I can't wait to see all the pieces of the movie put together. Now I'll finally be able to see it in order. My part in the movie was so small."

"An important part," Drake added with emphasis. "The length of the part doesn't matter, it's the quality," he said. Then he nodded at the truth of his words.

Kaycee laughed. It was a genuine laugh, one of amusement. The musical sound caused Richard Dawes to turn in his seat and shoot a disdainful look in their direction. Drake smiled and nodded at him then turned to Kaycee. "What's he really like when he's working? Did you have fun with it?"

Kaycee shot him a stare of disbelief. "After what just happened, how can you even ask that?"

"Then why does Richard Dawes recognize you by your laughter. Something at the film site must have made you laugh."

Kaycee fell silent then shook her head. "I don't know. I barely saw Mr. Dawes. He was either in his Humvee or getting in his Humvee except while we were filming."

It took time for the guests to find their seats and settle themselves. "First is the producer's speech," Drake explained to Kaycee to pass the time while they waited. "The stockholders and executives responsible for the funding of the movie are included along with cast members in tonight's festivities."

"That explains all the pomp and circumstance," Kaycee said with a smile.

The lights began to dim, and the producer walked out to stand in the spotlight.

"Are your parents coming to the opening?" Drake whispered to her.

"I'm sure they are," she said, though she wasn't sure at all. She remembered warning her parents that the premiere would be coming up, but she never bothered to confirm any plans with them. The last couple of weeks, she had deliberately put off calling home because she knew as soon as she heard her parents' voices, she was going to break down and cry. How could she tell them she was homesick? What kind of fool at the age of twenty-eight became so homesick they cried?

"The studio has quite a program of events lined up for two days to promote the opening," Drake was saying to her. "I'll send you a copy of the itinerary to give to your parents. Everybody's invited to all the events."

He fell silent as the producer left the stage and the curtains slowly opened as the film was already rolling. The soundtrack blasted the room.

Kaycee leaned forward. The music sent chills up her spine.

"A macabre story of the underworld," the narrator said.

This was not the kind of movie Kaycee usually rushed out to see, so she watched not knowing what to expect.

The story was good. Her admiration of Rick Dawes became reestablished as she watched him professionally. His acting caught at you and dragged you into his personal fight for power, his all-consuming greed. The only light side of the film was the brief romance with her character. There were many scenes of him on the phone talking to her that she wasn't a part of, but sympathy for the girl was nurtured carefully along until the film of the winter get-away with Kaycee's appearance and the shock of her calculated, cold-blooded murder. It was definitely cold-blooded murder on his part. Kaycee recognized herself but did not feel like the girl moving across the big screen.

"That hat looks hideous," she whispered to Drake.

He smiled and nodded.

The cliff scene began. The horror of the episode still haunted her even though she had already viewed the clip. The camera focused on the crazed light in Rick's eyes as he held her in his arms next to the cliff edge to comfort her. Then it flashed briefly to Kaycee's face. The unsuspecting innocence she recognized in her expression shocked her. She hadn't felt a bit of trust for Rick Dawes during the actual filming, but at this moment on the screen, she seemed oblivious to everything except the joy of just being in his arms.

The struggle between them began, and the camera focused on Rick mostly and the depth of the cliff's drop-off. That is until it swung in on her figure clinging to the edge of the cliff, staring up at him with huge haunted eyes that almost looked silver in the camera's eye. Sympathy for her love of this monster filled even Kaycee for an instant. She had always secretly despised her character because she had not seen the huge flaws in this man's character. Now after seeing the whole scenario of the movie laid out in one sitting, she could dredge up a small bit of pity for the stupid little twit.

The actual film slowed during the fall to create the sensation that the audience was falling with her. Snow, rock, and dead leaves floated around her. When she caught herself on the overhang of rock and desperately began to climb to safety, Kaycee heard the people watching the movie around her sigh in relief. She was being buffeted by the relentless wind when she lost her hold and plummeted down the cliff face at the jagged menacing rock and into foaming mass of brown water at the bottom.

Kaycee clung to the armrests of her seat. The falling sensation in her head and the pit of her stomach actually made her slightly sick. Briefly, she shut her eyes and took a shaky breath. Drake reached across to pat her arm in comfort. When she opened them, Rick was already away from the cliff, on the road running to the resort. The remainder of the movie moved fast. Rick did not waste any time getting out of the area. He returned to the city and went on with business as usual. When the body of the girl was found, the father went crazy. It took him awhile to find out who was responsible and then he wasted no time in plotting against Rick Dawes's character. Kaycee wondered why a wealthy powerful man did not have his paid henchmen keep track of what his daughter was doing in order to protect her.

The final scene was of a huge explosion, and the audience was left wondering if Rick was caught in it or not.

"So, it's a cliffhanger." Kaycee shivered as the eerie movie music started up again with the credits. "My character won't be returning."

Drake shifted his weight. "Don't be too sure about that, stranger things have happened in the movies. Don't forget to watch the credits."

As the credits began, several people stood up immediately to leave the theater. The loudspeaker overrode the music while the announcement was made that supper would be served in thirty minutes. Kaycee remained in her seat, scanning the words as they slowly rolled up the screen. She read each line of the credits feeling a thrill when she recognized someone's name. Finally the heading: Location—Palisade Head, Minnesota.

Kaycee leaned forward to concentrate. Jimmy Zane's name appeared as Helicopter Pilot, Stuntman Safety, First Aid Crew, and, tacked on the last line, Personal Escort for Miss Swanson.

"Personal escort?" she said out loud. "Personal escort?" she repeated. "They didn't use those words in the credits. Drake, they listed Jimmy as the personal escort of Miss Swanson. Listen to it. It sounds as horrible to hear as it does to read." She turned to face Drake. Angry, her face flushed with embarrassment, she said, "Drake, they called him my personal escort. My parents are going to read that."

Drake stared at her, coming fully to attention. "They what?" he asked.

"The credits, didn't you read the credits?" she demanded, standing in a fluid movement. Her hands worried at the beaded handbag she held.

Drake sat forward and struggled to his feet. "I don't know what you're talking about."

"Then you didn't read it?"

He shook his head. "I'm really sorry, Kaycee, I didn't. But whatever it is, I'll take care of it. Don't upset yourself tonight. Tomorrow I'll talk to them. I'll find out how we can get them to change it."

"They can change it?" she asked with relief. "They can still change it? They have to change it. The wording is totally unacceptable. My mother will die if she reads that."

"I'll call and make an appointment with the editing staff or whoever tomorrow," he assured her.

"Thank you, Drake. I can tolerate anything except 'personal escort.'" She shuddered. In the modeling industry, those words carried an ominous cloud with them, filled with unspoken meaning that respectable models did not even think about.

"Whatever you want, Kaycee," Drake murmured, wiping his brow with a handkerchief.

38

The dark silence in the apartment was the only greeting Kaycee found when she arrived home hours after her curfew. She flicked on the lamp next to the couch and reached for the telephone. The time had come when she must make the phone call home. The pounding in her head still persisted. The hour was later than she usually called. She realized the time for excuses had ended. After the filming at Palisade Head ended, the communication between her and the family had been sporadic. It was entirely her fault. She put off the call because she missed them terribly. Kaycee dialed and then waited. Nervously, she tapped her fingernails on the glass tabletop as she slid onto the couch feeling drained. Suddenly there was her father's voice. He did not sound sleepy at all. "Dad!" Kaycee greeted him. "It's me, Kaycee."

Tears sparkled in her eyes when she heard his excitement. She listened to him tell her mother who it was. "No, everything's fine. I just want you and mom and everybody to start packing. The opening for the movie is at the end of the month," Kaycee laughed. "The whole family is invited—Maris, Will, Cyndy, Tony, everybody. Drake says it's going to be a fantastic party with two days of events to kick everything off. I guess most of it's promotional, but who cares? The company pays for everything—the hotels, the banquets. You guys only have to get down here. Drake said he's putting a packet together for you explaining everything." She paused to brush her tears away while he told Ellyn.

"Yes, it's formal. Pull out all of the dress clothes you have in the back of your closet, you'll need them."

Kaycee slipped her shoes off and stretched. "No, not a problem. I think the girls should stay here. You can all stay here if you like." She laughed. The tension eased away now that she actually faced talking to them. Then Ellyn took the phone. At the sound of her voice, the tears again slid down Kaycee's cheeks. Closing her eyes, she listened to all the news about the family.

"The house sounds just as hectic as usual. No, I'm not sending it. Drake's secretary will send it. Call me when it gets there so I'll know what's going on, too. I miss you so...love you, good night."

Kaycee set down the receiver and leaned her head back against the smooth leather of the cushion. "That wasn't so bad," she thought. Now she must plan and get everything ready for their impending visit.

* * * * *

Until the movie was officially released in theaters, Kaycee had a brief respite from the obligations connected with it.

Since she was no longer modeling under a contract, she decided to try freelance modeling for Minneapolis-based businesses. She wanted enough photo sessions to keep her busy but nothing that would tie her down too much. The premiere was fast approaching and with it her family's arrival.

To be back doing the familiar routine of modeling after the uncertainty and fear she had faced up at Palisade Head was reassuring. The weeks flew past and spring took hold of the Twin Cities. Replacing the ugly gravel-covered boulevards was pale spring grass. The skinny almond trees that lined the downtown streets bloomed bright pink, decorating the stark sidewalks lined with office buildings made of reflective glass.

Kaycee passed all of this in a distracted dash. She held a slip of paper in one hand as she peered at buildings looking for an address. She turned off the main street and started into neighborhoods with brick buildings. Today, she was looking for a small bridal store off the metro area of downtown Minneapolis. The appointment for fittings was this afternoon and the actual photo shoot was for the end of next week. After this appointment, Kaycee had the rest of the week off. She planned to begin preparations for her family's visit and the opening of the movie.

When she found the small storefront, she walked inside and found herself in what looked like a large sewing room. There were no display counters, nor any wedding dress adorning clothing dummies. There was nothing but long tables draped with different types of materials. Kaycee stood inside the door and looked around for a few moments. "This can't be the right place," she decided and turned to leave.

A woman suddenly appeared from the back room. Kaycee placed her age at a few years over forty, and she was probably five feet tall. She was dressed in what looked like a serviceable ankle length dress. Several pencils protruded from her tightly curled mass of black hair. She wore a measuring tape wrapped around her neck and a wristband pincushion filled with pins. "Hello, hello," the woman called when she caught sight of Kaycee. "Please do not go so quickly. May I help you?"

Kaycee realized she must be in the right place. The woman's speech held a heavy Latin-American accent. She said with a smile, "Yes, I do believe you can help me. I'm looking for Espana Bridal Shop."

The woman's face brightened in an excited grin. "You have found it. I am Lucia Rodriquez-Sanchez. You are the model for the photography shoot?"

Kaycee held out her hand and Lucia grasped it with both of hers, holding it tight without shaking it. Her hands were rough from hard work. She had a strong grip for such a small person.

"I am Kaycee Swanson."

"Of course, of course, I recognize you from your photographs. Welcome to our shop." Lucia waved her hand at the cluttered, completely unorganized, undecorated warehouse-looking room. "We have not been open long, and the business started coming in so quickly we have not the time to organize. But we will. Come, come I will show you the gowns we can choose from."

The store might look like a warehouse, but Kaycee's viewing of the gowns certainly was not disappointing. They were magnificent. The first gown she tried on brought tears to her eyes it was so beautiful. A simple wedding gown with seed pearls outlining the collar and a flowing skirt of heavy satin, the train was ruffled and spread in a rose shape along the square of deep blue carpet Lucia had her stand on. It was the kind of dress she pictured herself in on her own wedding day.

"Let's add the veil for effect," Lucia said. She bubbled with excitement in her charming accent. "I am just so pleased with how well this gown suits you. I can't believe it was the first you picked out. How fate guides our paths!" She left the room and then hurried back carrying a heavy lace veil with a small faux diamond tiara to hold it in place. Lucia placed a stool next to Kaycee so she could position both pieces on her head. She smiled. "Will you turn this way?"

Kaycee turned and Lucia smiled again. "Perfect." Lucia was thrilled this experienced model had agreed to accept the small photo shoot for her family business. Lucia had been in Minneapolis long enough to recognize Kaycee's face and appreciate that nothing shady or unsavory had been voiced about her in business practices or her private life. This is what the sisters thought was important for the representation of their product. A wedding is an important part of a person's life and must be presented in a respectful way.

Kaycee ran her hands down the material of the gown. "This is exquisite."

"Gracias. Come here, dear," Lucia said. She reached over to adjust the back of the gown. "Oh, I see the trouble. You are too thin. Your chest, it is too small. That is why the material does not hang right, but we can fix it. If you gained a little weight it would all go to your chest, I'm sure of it," Lucia said with a knowing nod.

"I'm not so sure gaining weight would help, but I do have cups at home that help. I can bring them over," Kaycee said, smiling at Lucia's bluntness.

Lucia frowned. Her face puckered as she studied Kaycee's figure. "I am not sure if cups will help with this dress. Perhaps we should look at something else for you."

"But the gowns will be adjusted before the shoot, right?"

"Why no! There will be no time for fittings like this dress will need. Only temporary adjustments can we manage before Friday. The photographer is scheduled for Friday morning." Lucia looked at her and then anxiously clasped her hands on either side of her face. "You did not know this?" she exclaimed, her voice rising. "That Maria, she does nothing that she is supposed to. Why do I trust her?" Lucia swung around and rushed into the next room.

Kaycee studied the dress in the mirror. She knew enough about adjustments to know the seams, if tacked properly could look good enough for a photo shoot. Of course, adjustments were taken care of by the designers and their flock of people. The models merely show up at photo shoots and have the clothes peeled onto their bodies right before walking into the studio or out onto a runway. Kaycee was beginning to worry about how prepared Lucia was for an actual photo shoot.

In a few moments, Kaycee heard loud voices speaking in Spanish. A younger, slimmer version of Lucia hurried out of the back room with Lucia directly behind her. Lucia stopped the angry woman and said quickly, "Kaycee, this is my sister Maria. Tell her what the mix-up is in English, Maria."

"I said Friday to the photographer of this week and Friday to the model of next week. This cannot be. We have to have you both on the same Friday."

Kaycee frowned. "There's no chance the photographer

will reschedule. But I doubt any of the dresses will fit me without being adjusted."

The two women fell silent and looked at each other. Lucia said anxiously, "Does this mean you will model for the photographer this Friday?"

Kaycee briefly thought of all she had to do on Friday and nodded yes just the same. "Yes, I will. I just don't know about the clothes fitting me."

Lucia and Maria both smiled and then laughed. "You are so good, Kaycee, gracias." Lucia clapped her hands as she moved toward Kaycee. "You do not have to worry about it. The fit is our worry. If we could just take some measurements and do a few adjustments right now then you can leave. Do you have time?"

The remainder of the afternoon was spent going over the limited inventory of the shop. There had not been the time for Lucia and Maria to build their supply of wedding dresses. While Kaycee examined the gowns, she noticed the stitching in the embroidery was impeccable. Never had she seen any needlework done this well before. It looked handmade. "The work on this bodice is amazing," she commented as she studied the stitching in the mirror while Lucia paused in arranging the yards of material in the train. "Ah, yes, my sister Maria did that," she replied. "She, too, was trained by Papa in Mexico."

"This is all hand-stitching? Everything is hand-stitched? You definitely aren't charging enough for the product," Kaycee said.

"Will you turn this way? Something still does not look right."

Kaycee turned and saw in the full-length mirror her bare back with the deep scoop of the dress. The bones in her back clearly stood out. "You're right, Lucia. I am too thin. A long veil will be necessary if we chose this one," Kaycee said, chewing her lip as she studied her reflection. The bones in her cheeks did look sharper. When had she last eaten a complete meal? She could not remember.

Suddenly, she worried that she might not be able to show the dresses to their best advantage. She looked down at the front of the gown and her hipbones looked too prominent against the satin overlay. She searched her mind wondering if they had stuck out like this in the other gowns.

"Lucia, is this how you picture the dresses when the prospective bride is wearing them? Not worn by a scarecrow like me."

"Ah! You are lovely, Kaycee. You just need a little more meat on your bones. You stay for supper with my family tonight, and I will put some weight on you. Not too much like me, but just enough, si?" she said, motioning to her own round hips and bust.

"Oh, Lucia, I couldn't. It would be an inconvenience for you," Kaycee protested weakly, though it sounded tempting. The appetizing smells coming from the upper living quarters above the shop were wonderful.

"Ah, my sister and her children come over whenever they like without any word. They eat a lot more than I am sure you eat. There will be plenty of food for everyone." She smiled then patted Kaycee's bare arm. "Besides, my children think you are a celebrity and will ask for your autograph. It will be fun. Let us finish here so we can go upstairs."

Kaycee and Lucia had decided on four wedding dresses of different styles. They were engrossed in discussing the alterations for them without making the alterations permanent when Lucia's sister Maria returned with her three young boys in tow who looked from age three to nine. The boys, all black-haired, paid no attention to the dress shop and raced upstairs. Their footsteps echoed off the wooden floors.

Maria joined in the discussion and knew exactly what alterations had to be done. Between Maria and Lucia, with Kaycee being the dress dummy who remained silent and unmoving, they finished quickly.

Kaycee listened to the two women argue constantly, sometimes in Spanish and, when they remembered Kaycee was present, in English, so she could understand what they were arguing about. Kaycee laughed when Lucia sheepishly said to her after the fittings were done, "I am sorry," and shooting a condemning look at her sister. "This is the only way we work together."

"Please don't apologize," Kaycee protested as Maria helped to slip the satin from her shoulders. "It makes me feel very much at home. I have four sisters of my own," she explained.

Both women smiled and nodded approvingly.

"Being here with you brings back many memories that make me rather homesick," Kaycee admitted to the strangers.

In the small confines of the dressing room, cluttered with fabric and every sewing notion imaginable, along with a small desk inches thick in paper work waiting to be taken care of, she felt at home. Kaycee had been accepted by the two women who fluttered around her yet didn't treat her for what she was—a stranger. They cared because this is their life, and she had become a part of it, even if it was temporary.

"We will have everything ready and pressed for Friday, don't you worry," Lucia said when she saw Kaycee's anxious glance at the gowns.

Kaycee was out of her element when it came to preparing the gowns, so she decided not to worry and trust the seamstresses to do their part. The two women, though a bit unorganized, knew their business. It was the unorganized part that caused Kaycee concern. For some reason, she felt responsible for the success of this photo shoot.

The three women walked up the narrow stairs located at the back of the shop to Lucia's apartment. Kaycee found it closely resembled the office she had seen downstairs. Lucia casually walked through the room, tossing pieces of clothing over her arm after she removed them from the floor, chairs, and the kitchen table. The children had deserted the front room to play somewhere else, their voices clearly audible throughout the apartment.

Maria walked into the kitchen, opened the refrigerator and began removing containers of food and putting them on the countertop. Lucia opened the oven to check what was inside and, muttering to herself, slammed it shut. She lifted lids off steaming pots and stirred each carefully, sniffing the steam as she did.

Kaycee saw the kitchen table held the children's abandoned schoolwork and began stacking schoolbooks and papers to carry them out to the other room. An ancient sagging chair was covered with bedraggled, well-hugged dolls wrapped in scraps of cloth. Pillows littered the couch. Trucks filled with wooden blocks lined the floor. Kaycee carefully stepped over it all to set the books on the table. Her parents' house had looked like this at one time. Cluttered, messy, and well-loved. Her apartment never would. Was the sterile life she was living right now to be her destiny?

The children trooped into the kitchen and took their places around the kitchen table. Solemnly, they watched Kaycee. She smiled at the group, and they returned her smile joyfully and began to speak with eager young voices, high-pitched at full volume. Maria stood by the stove with a stack of plates ready to begin dishing the food onto them. "Children, our guest is Señorita Kaycee Swanson," Lucia said formally.

The smaller children said, "Oooooh," in one voice.

Kaycee grinned at them. "And you are?" she spoke to the first boy who stared at her with his mouth open.

"Petro, close your mouth and answer the lady," Maria snapped.

"Petro, how nice to meet you," Kaycee quickly replied.

The rest of the children were able to voice their own names in a quick manner.

"All right, Maria shall say grace," Lucia said. She was sitting in a small niche by the window feeding a toddler in a high chair. The children bowed their heads and said the prayer before meals Kaycee knew so she joined in.

The food was dished onto plates by the adults and consumed by the children. After they finished and cleared their plates, the three women could then take their turn to sit and eat. A bottle of wine was opened, and they sat down.

"Wonderful," Kaycee said pushing her plate away.

Lucia critically studied her plate. "You are sure that is all you will eat?"

"I wish I could eat more. I've never tasted authentic Spanish rice and enchiladas before."

Lucia complained, "No wonder you stay so skinny, you eat like a bird."

Later that night when Kaycee returned to her apartment, she smiled as she slid the foil packages into her empty refrigerator. When she told Lucia how good her food tasted, she packed most of the leftovers for Kaycee to take home.

After seeing the abundance of food in Lucia's refrigerator, Kaycee's food supply was sadly lacking by comparison. Her family was arriving in three days, and she needed to have food for meals on hand, but with Kathie and Karyn staying at the apartment she especially needed snack food.

Tomorrow, she would start getting ready by making a detailed grocery list. As for tonight, after working on the dresses with the two sisters, she was completely worn out.

For the next two days, Kaycee cleaned her apartment. She made the extra beds in the spare bedroom. She filled the pantry cupboards with chips and crackers and whatever else caught her eye in the grocery store and stocked the refrigerator with pop and beer. Friday afternoon about five o'clock the family planned to meet at her apartment, and then they would go to check into the hotel.

As he promised, Drake had secured a limousine for Saturday night to take the group to the theater and the formal supper after. The family could leave their vehicles in her apartment building's garage. They would be able to ride together.

Friday morning arrived, and Kaycee woke feeling the thrill of excitement. It was all coming together after months of work and constant waiting. Best of all, her family would be here to hold her hand when the public saw her performance in the movie.

Kaycee grabbed her purse and hurried out of her apartment with time for only one last look before her family saw it. With a critical eye, the contemporary look of the large living room was something out of a home magazine. Everything with a proper place and a proper place to put it, she thought, pausing for a moment to really take in the feeling of the place.

"Oh no!" she exclaimed softly to herself. "This will never do!" The room was shiny and new and unlived in. Her mother would be heartsick. The fact that every piece of furnishing depicted luxury without regard to expense would mean nothing to Ellyn. It most obviously was not a real home. Even the presence of the family photographs, placed lovingly in their frames lining the mantel over the white brick fireplace and resting on every available tabletop, did not seem to add any presence to the room. Quickly, she glanced at her watch and set down her bag. A feeble attempt to rearrange the room did not help. With a sigh she gave up. She had to leave now to make it to the hairdresser. Kaycee's responsibility for the photo session was the hairstyle. Lucia had given Kaycee no specific style for the photo shoot. She had said to her, "Kaycee, you worry too much. Just wear your hair in the style you wish for your own wedding."

Lucia's confidence scared her. This decision-making was new territory for Kaycee. All the years she'd been in the modeling business, professionals had made all the decisions, carefully choosing all the accessories to be used. Now, out of the blue, it was being left totally up to her.

This photograph session was a big step for the small bridal shop of Lucia and Maria. The results from this single photo shoot could cause a major increase in their finances. Kaycee had no idea what the details of their financial status consisted of, but she knew what compiling a pamphlet cost, and it did not come cheap. She could volunteer to redo the modeling if something else went wrong. But any other mistakes would cost money to fix. Kaycee had been able to rearrange her schedule, but other professionals would not be so generous.

"First things first," she said under her breath, as she walked into the hairdresser shop. The shoot has priority. Everything else she had to worry about would have to wait.

39

The weather outside was perfect with a sky so blue it blinded her as she walked the few blocks from the hairdresser to Lucia's. Kaycee had chosen this particular beauty parlor so the downtown traffic could not complicate her day more.

The first surprise was when she walked in the front door and Lucia told her they had a garden in the back of the shop that they were going to use for some of the photographs. Kaycee wondered what kind of garden there could be in the middle of downtown Minneapolis.

Lucia and Maria fluttered nervously around Kaycee while inspecting her hairstyle and anxiously showing her their finished work on the dresses. With Lucia and Maria leaning over her shoulder, watching her every move, Kaycee was getting more nervous than she already was and needed some breathing space. "Okay, ladies. I think I should begin to get dressed. The gowns look wonderful. But before I do, why don't we look over the garden to see how it will work into the layout?"

Her idea luckily met with instant agreement from the two women. They hurried ahead of her toward the back. Maria opened a set of French doors that Kaycee had not noticed before. When she walked outside to see Lucia's garden, which was in fact a Spanish hanging garden and not the spring version of a Minnesota garden Kaycee expected to find, the first thing she saw was lush green ferns framing a stone fountain with a statue of Our Lady set in the middle of it.

"She is the one who makes our garden grow so beautifully," Lucia said proudly.

Kaycee voiced her pleasure as they looked around the small but beautiful area. Above was a glass dome that heated the room. Poinsettia, hibiscus, and azalea plants already were blooming with pink, peach, and white flowers. Several trees and other ornamental bushes were beginning to open their spring blossoms.

Maria brushed leaves off the stone bench with her hand before sitting. "We have the bench and over there is a lattice arch. Tell us what you think. Will it work for the camera?"

Kaycee exclaimed, "Of course it will work! It will be perfect. Let's get ready. I can't wait to hear what the photographer says when he sees this."

The afternoon hours flew by for Kaycee. Maria and Lucia's relatives all showed up at the shop to help with the dresses and to watch the photographer shoot the pictures. The scenery was changed twice from outside to inside. And the willing hands of the family members made the changes go quickly. Once the photographer packed up his equipment and left, the family began to leave a few people at a time until it was the three women left at the shop.

"Can you come to my cousin's for supper tonight?" Maria asked as Kaycee walked out of the dressing room in her street clothes. "It will be a celebration. Everything was wonderful."

Kaycee handed over the wedding gown. "No, I…"

Lucia walked in from the garden and called exuberantly, "Oh, Kaycee, everything went so well. You were fabulous, the garden was fabulous, the photographer was fabulous." She smiled wider. "Didn't you notice how handsome he was, Kaycee?" she asked. "He was flirting with you, wasn't he?"

Kaycee looked at her with disbelief. "You have to be kidding. If he was flirting with anyone, it was you. How can I compete with that luscious accent all of you have?"

Maria and Lucia laughed.

The dressing room had been cleaned out to give Kaycee room to change during the afternoon, but now it had returned to its previous state of clutter.

"We will miss you," Lucia said to Kaycee.

She picked up her purse. "It will only be for a few weeks. I'll be back when the proofs are ready. Tonight I have…"

Lucia gasped. "Tonight is your movie." She turned to shout something to Maria in Spanish.

"It's late. We must say good-bye. You must go quickly."

"It's all right, Lucia," Kaycee interrupted. "The premiere isn't until tomorrow night. My family is arriving tonight."

Lucia did not seem to hear. She waved her hands at Kaycee to get her to the front door.

"I know my family would love to meet you. Maybe not this time but some other."

"Of course, when you or one of your sisters gets married you will come here to buy your dress," Lucia said.

"Wait, Kaycee," Maria yelled from inside the shop."

They both turned to wait for Maria who ran to the entrance carrying a plastic garment bag.

"Take this," she said, thrusting it into Kaycee's hands.

"What?"

"This will bring you luck for your movie and your future," Maria explained. "Please, please accept it."

Lucia saw what the bag held and nodded her head.

"No, not one of your dresses. It's too much," Kaycee argued. "You have already paid me."

Maria said. "It has nothing to do with payment. We do this because we care about you. Now go, it is late."

The two women disappeared back into the shop and slammed the door. The bell jingled cheerfully. Kaycee had just had the door slammed in her face and she felt wonderful. Smiling, she held the garment bag safely off the street and stepped toward the curb to wave down a cab.

Carrying the heavy gown slowed her down, but it was such a kind gesture, as well as an extremely generous one. Kaycee peeked under the plastic and saw it was the rose lace wedding gown she admired the most, and it had a hefty price tag. It was way too generous of them but something that came straight from their heart.

40

"If only I had a dog to mess up the place," Kaycee muttered. She tossed the throw pillows at the pristine couch, then stepped back to look at it with a shake of her head. She rearranged the photos trying not to keep them straight but ended up putting them back into order. "Dogs slobber and cause all kinds of chaos. Of course, having a dog isn't an option. The hours I keep would give any animal a nervous condition. Music!" she exclaimed out loud. "That would definitely add something. Well, at least noise."

The telephone rang as she switched on the compact disc player.

"Hello?" she said distractedly as she discarded a rock and roll CD for a country western one instead.

"Kaycee," her father yelled cheerfully into the phone. His voice jumped out from the receiver at her. "We're all here standing in your garage."

"Dad," she cried scrambling to her feet. "That's great! Do you remember how to get up here?"

"Sure, sure. It's a snap," he replied chuckling.

"Well then, hurry," Kaycee said and hung up the phone. She took a breath to steady her excitement. Then she ran to check the rest of the apartment. The kitchen looked fine. The music played loud enough to ease the silence. But how did she look?

After the day she'd had, it was a question that made her uneasy. She brushed her hair back from her face. She looked tired, but it was not a physical tired. The photography shoot was done and in a more than satisfactory manner. Now, she and her apartment must pass inspection by the people she cared about most in the world. After that, the rest of the weekend would be a cinch. Only the hard-nosed public of the big screen would be critiquing her. If she passed her mother's inspection, she felt confident she could handle the public.

The buzzer sounded, and Kaycee ran to the door. She threw it open and the excited voices in the hallway stopped. A crowd of her people, the Swanson family, stood at the door in complete silence.

In one breath everyone said, "Kaycee!" All began to push in at once. They grabbed her hands, hugged her. A jumble of hair, arms, and hugs was all Kaycee could glimpse until she saw the shining silver of her father's head above the rest. The others moved quickly inside, laughing and talking as she waited and then slipped into the arms that held her tight for a moment.

"Kaycee," Stewart said, a smile tugging at his mouth. "You are even more beautiful than the last time I saw you."

Her heart swelled with gratitude. "And you look tons better than the last time I saw you. You're face is tan, have you been golfing already this season?"

"Why, yes. The snow's been off the courses for a month now. It's cold, but there aren't any lines at the tees."

She squeezed his arm as they walked inside where the rest of the group congregated.

Karyn and Kathie pushed past their father and each grabbed one of Kaycee's arms. "Kaycee, where are we going to sleep?" they demanded in unison.

Kaycee stared down at Karyn. "Who the heck are you?"

Karyn blushed. "Cut it out, Kaycee."

Kaycee couldn't believe Karyn had slimmed out of the last bit of youthful plumpness. Her face had lengthened, giving depth to her cheekbones, and her eyes were touched with a light coat of eye shadow. She looked like a woman. "I'm sorry, sweetie. You took me by surprise, that's all."

"It always has to happen," Ellyn said softly from behind them. "No matter how much I try to prepare myself for it, when they go through the last stage, it breaks my heart."

Kaycee turned to embrace her mother, who seemed, for

the time being, not to have changed.

"How do you get used to it?" Kaycee murmured. "I'm not their mother and it drives me nuts."

"You have to. This is the entire reason for having children, to send responsible adults out into the world to help make it a better place."

Kathie cleared her throat impatiently behind Kaycee. "Yes, and in two months I shall be one of those responsible adults," she said pertly.

"God help us," Ellyn whispered.

Kaycee giggled.

"You haven't forgotten my eighteenth birthday, Kaycee?" Kathie asked. "I'm expecting a super great present from you."

"Never would I forget your birthday," Kaycee said. She released her mother and turned to face her sister. The thick ponytail was gone, replaced by a shoulder-length bob that made Kathie look more mature. "New hairstyle?" Kaycee walked around her sister to get a full view of her shiny blond hair.

"Kathie swears she's going to be discovered at your premiere," Karyn broke in, ducking to hide behind Ellyn at Kathie's look.

"That's right. I want to look as sophisticated as I can," Kathie said, patting her hair to keep it in place.

Kaycee hugged her. "I'm sorry to tell you, but photographers don't like sophisticated. They want innocent. Then they can change you into whatever suits them."

Kathie paused. "Then tomorrow, I'll go back to innocent, but tonight, I am going to stay sophisticated. Now where are we sleeping, and if you say on the couch, I'm going to scream."

"There are two bedrooms open. First come, first serve."

Both girls instantly let out a shriek and raced through the living room into the back hallway to the bedrooms.

Ellyn laughed as the shrieking continued for many long minutes before silence fell.

"What in the heck was that all about?" Stewart called from the kitchen. "Wine, Ellyn? Our daughter must have bought out the liquor store."

"Don't you know, dad? I'm practicing in case I end up in Hollywood," Kaycee said with a grin.

"I'd believe you, except you don't own a wine glass, and none of the bottles have been opened. I'm betting you don't have a corkscrew either."

Ellyn walked toward the kitchen and said, "Kaycee just let loose the girls in her bedrooms. She has no idea the pandemonium that could follow. And, of course Kaycee owns a corkscrew, and I'm quite certain she has a beautiful set of wineglasses too. You just don't know where to look."

Ellyn left and Kaycee walked over to shut the apartment door.

"Don't let her bluff you, dad," Kaycee called out, "the only reason I have any of those things is because mom bought them for me."

Kaycee turned and reached for the doorknob and saw Jimmy Zane standing in the hallway watching her. Time stopped. She stared at him. For a moment, she wasn't sure if he was real or just a figment of her imagination. The khaki dress pants and button down shirt gave it away. She never pictured him in anything but his flannel and blue jeans.

"Hey," he said with that quirky grin of his. He seemed uncertain of his reception.

Her heart ached and began to pound. "Hi," she replied, croaking over her suddenly dry throat. She wanted to move straight into his arms and feel the warmth of him like they had up on the cliff.

"Kaycee!" her sister Cyndy yelled, appearing suddenly around the corner with Tony. Jimmy seemed to expect them.

"Cyndy, Tony," she said numbly as she was caught in her sister's tight hug.

"Look who we found all alone at the hotel," Cyndy said,

grabbing Jimmy's big hand. "So we brought him with."

Stewart walked into view behind Kaycee. "Cyndy, Tony, it's about time," he said. "Jimmy, too. Come in, what are you standing in the hall for? Join the party." Kaycee stepped aside and allowed them to file inside before shutting the door. She watched as Cyndy released Jimmy's hand and hugged her father.

Kaycee avoided them and slipped quietly to hide in the kitchen. She needed a moment to recover after seeing Jimmy so unexpectedly. All of the symptoms of this hopeless infatuation she thought time and distance would help her control leaped to the surface the minute he showed up at the door. Just seeing him made her happy and miserable at the same time.

Ellyn was busy poking around in the refrigerator. "There's plenty of food to have dinner here tonight," Ellyn said, looking up. In her arms she held two heads of lettuce and a tomato. "Let's make pasta and stay in," she said cheerfully. "It's so much cozier here. We'll be eating out in public the rest of the time. What do you say?" She set the vegetables on the cutting board and began opening the plastic on the lettuce.

"Sure, I guess." Her mother made it sound like it was Kaycee's dream come true to have everyone stay here for dinner. How little she really knew her daughter. The muffins and cookies and bread baking episodes while she lived at home should have given her mother a clue of how wrong she was.

Soon, pots were boiling merrily on the stove. Her mother was mixing a cake batter in the mixer.

"This will do just fine for dessert," Ellyn told her.

"Great, mom, great," Kaycee said, stirring the steaming hot water overflowing with pasta noodles.

Her mother had come up with a pasta bake, salad, and cake for the meal. Kaycee was just shocked that she had all the necessary ingredients to create any kind of a meal.

"I didn't know Jimmy planned on coming this week," Kaycee finally found the courage to say. Ellyn spooned the batter into the baking pan.

"None of us had talked to him either. We met up at the hotel. You know your father. Once he saw him, he asked if he had plans for dinner tonight and invited him along. The more the merrier with this group." Ellyn paused to scrape the bowl and give her oldest daughter a curious look. "You don't mind, do you?"

Kaycee refused to look at her. She crouched down, looking for a colander to drain the pasta. "There will be plenty of food for one more. What happened with Maris?" she changed the subject.

"She's joining us tomorrow for the premiere," Ellyn said quickly. "Kaycee, I've wanted to ask you something but not over the telephone. We haven't heard from you very often, but we thought you needed some space after being cooped up in the house with us for so long." She paused. "Is there another reason you haven't been keeping in touch?"

"I've been busy, mom. You've seen some of the appearances I've made on the talk show circuit?"

"Of course I have," Ellyn said indignantly. "I brought along the videotape of every single one for us to watch when there's quiet."

"Spare me," Kaycee muttered rubbing her temple.

"What, honey?" Ellyn said, washing the mixer beater under the faucet.

"I don't think anybody wants to watch me talk about the movie that much," Kaycee said with a frown. Lucky with this group there was never a quiet moment of any kind.

"I'm going to start setting the table," Kaycee said. She carried out the cloth napkins and placemats.

"You get those two girls to help you," Ellyn called. "They don't need to sit in front of the television the entire time."

"But, mom," Kathie yelled from the couch. "Kaycee has

satellite, 152 channels," she wailed.

"We aren't watching this, young lady," Stewart said, staring at the screen with a perplexed frown. The heavy metal beat from the stereo system filled the room. "Change it or pass over that remote."

Kathie pouted but quickly changed the station.

Kaycee walked out of the kitchen into the apartment full of people. All of the noise receded into the background when she spotted Jimmy sitting on the couch by Tony. The two were deep in conversation.

"Tony misses Jimmy," Cyndy said, walking over to stand next to her sister. "Those two were inseparable in the days before marriage," she laughed and set her wineglass down.

"Who served you wine?" Kaycee asked, suddenly remembering her duties as a hostess.

Cyndy looked at her, grabbing the placemats from her hands. "'Who served you wine?' My, don't we talk properly?" She looked her sister up and down curiously. "Dad did. Who cares? If he hadn't gotten me a glass of wine, I'd have gotten it myself. We're family, Kace, don't be so formal."

"I guess my hostess skills are somewhat lacking," she said stiffly. "I don't get much practice. I'll get the plates."

Kaycee, holding the stack of plates, walked back into the dining room.

Cyndy stood looking at the guys. She turned when Kaycee came in and watched her sister juggle the plates to the table.

"You can ask for help, you know," she said, setting her wineglass down again.

"Yes, I know, but I didn't have enough strength," Kaycee retorted.

"I think you should leave the plates in the kitchen, then everybody can just fill them in there. It saves time."

Kaycee placed her hands on her hips and stared in exasperation at her sister. "Why didn't you tell me that before?" she gasped. "This is heavy."

Cyndy shrugged. "Because you're being so hoity-toity to me, I thought you should work a little harder, beat some of that out of you."

Kaycee laughed. "Hoity-toity…please. I haven't heard that word since we were kids. I am leaving the plates here on the end of the table."

"Did you know you haven't changed a thing in this place since the last time I was here?" Cyndy told her. "When was that? Oh, let's see, when you moved in."

"What needs to be changed?" Kaycee asked indifferently.

Cyndy giggled. "Well, nothing really, but I rearrange my apartment all the time."

"Oh," Kaycee said dryly. "For what reason?"

Cyndy turned to her, one dark eyebrow raised in question. "Because I buy new furniture or new decorations. I get tired of looking at things in the same place or just to change. I guess I really don't need a reason to do it. I just do it."

"I must not get sick of the way my apartment looks. Probably because I'm not here very much."

"No, more like you're not interested in it," Cyndy interjected bluntly.

Kaycee shook her head slightly to clear it. "You always do speak your mind, Cyndy. I guess I forgot how blunt you can be."

"Blunt? I'm only being honest. If you cared about this place you would take care of it. Plain and simple, isn't it?" Cyndy began folding the napkins and placed them on the table. "And that means more than hiring a cleaning service. We need silverware."

Kaycee, unable to think of any kind of a response to her sister's sarcasm, spun on her heel and collected all the silverware in the drawer.

"You know, I think you're right, Cyndy," she said returning to the room. She was glad to find she had not left. It had been too long since the two of them had talked like this. And there were some things Kaycee wanted to know. "I guess I've never thought much about it. Once it was furnished, the only thing I felt was relief the decorating was over."

"What decorating?" Cyndy said laughing. "The only decorations I see are photos of the family. I hardly think that is considered decorating."

"So, I'm not the homey type, so what?" Kaycee said with a reluctant smile at her sister's well-aimed jabs.

Cyndy paused to look across the room at the two handsome men on the couch. Kaycee couldn't help following her gaze. The two men were so different from each other, their personalities and physical appearance. Tony was slight of build, blond, and intellectual looking, almost aristocratic in his features, soft but attractive. She glanced at Jimmy. There was nothing soft about him. He was all bronze and muscle from his love of the outdoors. His large well-shaped hands cradled a bottle of beer. He was solid, but he proved to her how gentle he could be.

"What's up with Jimmy?" Cyndy interrupted her thoughts, watching Kaycee's face curiously. "You haven't spoken to him since we got here." She tapped her chin with the lip of her glass before sipping her wine. "I really think you're trying to pretend he isn't here at all. Why?"

Kaycee stiffened. She didn't want to talk about Jimmy yet. "That's ridiculous."

"I thought you two had finally grown up and quit playing games with each other," Cyndy said after moving to the other side of the table where she carefully began to place the forks and knives.

Kaycee watched her sister. Cyndy had changed a lot since she married Tony. She used to act like Kathie, or at least Kaycee remembered her acting like Kathie. It was years ago. Right now, she looked like one of the happiest of the Swanson sisters.

"Well, haven't you gotten tired of the fighting yet,

Kaycee?" Cyndy asked with a sigh. "I can't tell you how much better it feels to be in love and to be loved. All of that energy shouldn't be wasted on arguments when it can be used in a much more productive manner."

Kaycee's mouth fell open. "I'd prefer you not share the details of your love life," she gasped out. "And I have no idea what you're getting at anyway. Jimmy and I are nothing to each other besides friends, acquaintances really. We aren't in high school anymore. I don't know why this family can't understand that. We might have been close, but that was a long time ago, and neither of us wants to return to that."

Kaycee's stubborn set to her face made Cyndy smile. "Did you know Jimmy and I dated a couple of times when he moved back?"

Kaycee began straightening the napkins and silverware at each place, desperate to be occupied and not look at her sister. She could feel the heat rising in her face.

"All he did was talk about you. 'How is Kaycee doing?'" Cyndy mimicked gruffly. "'Are there any steady guys in her life? Is she coming home? Is she coming home any time soon?'" Cyndy shook her head. "He's sweet, but he drove me crazy. All my life, I've been compared to you. The last thing I wanted to do was go out on a date and talk about you and your fabulous new career. I was always following in your footsteps."

"That's insane," Kaycee cried. This was the first time she had ever heard any talk of this.

"No, not really," Cyndy argued matter-of-factly. "Oh, it wasn't your fault. We look so much alike, and me coming along the next year. Some people thought we were twins and I'd been held back in school so there wouldn't be any confusion. Isn't that crazy?"

Kaycee felt deflated. "It sounds awful," she replied, rubbing her forehead distractedly. "How you must have resented me and rightly so," she added quickly. "But I had no idea.

I'm so sorry. That's what happens when you grow up in a small town."

Cyndy quickly disagreed with a shake of her head. "Don't get on that subject," she warned. "Tony and I would give anything to move back to Duluth."

"You would?" Kaycee asked stunned. "I thought you were so happy out East you never wanted to return. Like with the funeral."

Cyndy snorted. "Getting tickets, planning airline flights around two work schedules? It's completely nuts. We missed our flight, that's why we couldn't get home for grandma's funeral. I'm still so furious about it." She frowned. "Don't you get it, Kaycee? We don't have anyone out East. No family whatsoever. I have to rely on strangers for everything, and I don't trust people easily. It's so hard not having the parents and you guys around."

Kaycee remained quiet thinking. She remembered it was hard when she lived in New York, but that had been temporary. She could go and do whatever she wanted. There was nothing but her job to tie her down.

"I already told Tony we won't have kids until we can move back," Cyndy told her, keeping her voice hushed. "Don't tell mom this, she'd lecture me for weeks. What would I do with a new baby and just Tony? Oh, don't get me wrong Tony's great about everything, but what does he know about babies? I'd be scared to death with a helpless infant to care for all by ourselves. We're starting to look for work in Duluth—" She paused glancing behind to be sure they were still alone. "At least Tony is looking for a job." She crossed her fingers. "Don't say anything yet, we want to surprise everybody."

Kaycee leaned against the table completely astonished by Cyndy and her announcement. "That would be great!" she gasped out finally. "I hope it works out for you."

"Anyway, Kaycee, what about Jimmy?" She returned to the subject Kaycee wished to avoid, a speculative look in her brown eyes, the only difference between the two sisters' coloring. "He will always be one of my favorite people. Do you want to know why?"

"Do I have a choice?"

"No," Cyndy said with a grin. "First, because he always stood up to you no matter how big a fit you threw." She laughed at Kaycee's frown. "You were such a spoiled brat. Unlike everybody else, he wouldn't let you tie him around your finger. Second, because he introduced me to Tony. It wasn't long after our dating, if that's what it was, that Jimmy introduced me to Tony. By then I figured I'd grown up enough to know exactly what I wanted to do with my life until I met him. Tony changed everything. When we fell in love with each other, I found out nothing else mattered except that we should be together. Lucky for me, he wanted to get married. Mom and dad would never have spoken to me again if we'd run off together but I didn't care. The rest? Well, you know the rest," she said with a laugh. "Man, is my throat dry…must be talking too much." She strolled into the kitchen to refill her wineglass. "The table is completed, mother. When is dinner?" Kaycee heard her ask.

She stared across the living room to where Tony laughed at something Jimmy was saying. Tony didn't look like God's greatest creation, but he should, at least after how Cyndy talked about him. Then she looked at Jimmy. She hadn't seen him since that day on Palisade Head. He looked good. He always looked good. Her heart ached. Now she must admit to herself that it was all just an excuse. The argument she had needed to break away from him and return home to her solitary life. Now, it was probably too late to repair what she had done. What a fool I am, she thought. Once again she let the man of her dreams slip through her fingers.

Cyndy was right. She was tired of fighting. She was tired of being ignored. She was tired of being mad. Did he hate her? He'd forgiven her in the past; maybe he could forgive her one more time? She spun on her heel and walked into the kitchen. Dinner would break up the little reunion between Tony and Jimmy, and she might find the chance to talk to him.

"Come and get it," Kaycee called when her mother and Cyndy set out the baked ziti on the countertop.

"It's about time, I am starving," Stewart said, marching into the kitchen ahead of the rest.

Kaycee poured milk into tall glasses and then stepped aside to let her father lead the way to fill his plate.

"Kaycee," Kathie called from the bedroom.

Karyn was already waiting in the kitchen behind her father so Kathie was in the backrooms of the apartment by herself.

"Come and eat, Kathie," Kaycee yelled back and turned to see Jimmy look at her, give a sheepish grin, and then walk by.

Kathie yelled something else, but Kaycee did not hear her.

With an exasperated sigh, she heard Kathie's muffled voice again.

"What does she want?" she glanced at Karyn, who refused to lift her head, a strange expression on her face. Now curious at what trouble her sister was up to, Kaycee walked toward the bedroom. Kathie made an astonishing entrance into the living room.

Already seated at the table that faced where Kathie walked out were her parents, Cyndy, and Tony. Kathie called in a voice high with excitement, "What do you think?" She paraded into the living room dressed in the wedding gown Lucia and Maria had given Kaycee that afternoon.

"Oh, Kathie, you shouldn't have," Kaycee heard Karyn's anguished voice behind her.

A crash was heard from the table bringing Kaycee's attention away from Kathie. Ellyn dropped the plate of garlic bread on top of her wineglass, shattering the crystal. "Oh, good heavens," Ellyn cried.

Someone behind Kaycee made a sharp hissing intake of breath. She turned to see Jimmy staring at Kathie with his lips clenched tightly together. He turned away and disappeared into the kitchen.

Kathie, thrilled with the reaction, pranced gaily through the room. With the grace of a professional, she draped the train over her arm and did the wedding march to the dining room table.

"Isn't this a fabulous dress?" she asked. "I do not believe what you paid for this thing," she said to Kaycee as she held up the price tag.

Kaycee stepped forward with a look of forbearance on her face. "I didn't pay for it," she said, crossing her arms across her chest.

Kathie frowned. "You didn't? Why? Aren't you going to keep it?"

"Oh, thank goodness. Were you going to show us first before you decided?" Ellyn exclaimed.

Kaycee glanced at her mother, wondering about her tone of voice.

"What do you mean you didn't pay for it?" Kathie persisted.

"It must be for a show, Kathie," Cyndy broke in. "You're so rude wearing something that doesn't belong to you and doesn't belong to Kaycee. Go and take it off."

"Oh no, Cyndy," Kaycee said, "it does belong to me, but I didn't buy it."

Silence fell over the people in the room like a curtain. Even Stewart looked uncomfortable and could not raise his eyes from the table.

"You own a wedding dress and didn't tell anyone?" Ellyn said, staring at her daughter like she didn't know her.

Kaycee glanced at everyone's face and suddenly realized

what they must be thinking. "No, you don't understand. I'm not secretly planning on getting married or anything. Friends gave the dress to me. You couldn't possibly believe that I'm planning a wedding without telling any of you about it?" she asked, unnerved by what she saw in the faces around her.

Her mother looked quite upset. "What kind of friend gives someone a wedding dress? Please explain Kaycee." She ineffectually attempted to clean up the glass from the table.

"Friends and business associates, people who design wedding dresses. I just finished a photo session for a private business, and this was a gift they wanted me to have," she said logically. "You couldn't possibly think I would buy a wedding dress without talking to both of you first?" She looked at her mother then her father, astonished. Her eyes swept the room. "It seems you all thought the same thing," she answered her own question since nobody else spoke up.

Ellyn's eyes dropped to her plate filled with pasta, sauce, and broken bits of glass. "I guess I didn't know. It's possible. We really have no idea what goes on down here. I tried talking to you about it before in the kitchen but you're always so close-mouthed when it comes to your life here. We've barely heard a word from you since you left Duluth. Your father suspected that you might be romantically involved with someone and just not ready to talk about it with us yet. We've tried to be patient, Kaycee, but you have to admit Kathie's appearance was—"

"Was like a bomb going off," Stewart supplied the description.

"I guess I need to apologize to both of you," Kaycee began. She spoke to her parents. "I'm sorry. I didn't mean to shut you out of what's been happening. My life has been so public lately, I thought you knew what was going on and didn't need to hear all the details from me. I can see now that wasn't the case. And just for the record, I would never consider accepting a man's proposal who hadn't first spoken to my father about marrying me, let alone choose a wedding dress without first speaking to my mother."

Kaycee heard Cyndy laugh and break the heavy silence that followed Kaycee's outburst.

"See, mom, she isn't so much like me."

Ellyn shot Cyndy a sharp look.

"What does that mean?" Kaycee asked, silently thanking Cyndy for interrupting.

"Your sister planned her entire wedding before she asked me anything," Ellyn explained quickly.

"It was my wedding, and I didn't want to bother you with the boring details until Tony and I settled on what we wanted to do," Cyndy defended herself, turning to Tony for confirmation.

"She had already put the money down on her wedding dress when she showed it to me," Ellyn said, her tone showed she was still miffed about the whole thing. Then she smiled. "Luckily, Cyndy has excellent taste. It was a little pricey, but then wedding dresses are a big cost item."

"I paid for it myself," Cyndy told Kaycee.

"She certainly wouldn't allow me to pay for it," Tony added dryly.

Cyndy turned to him with a smile. "You already were paying for the honeymoon, darling. That, with your student loans, was almost too much." They reached for each other's hands.

"Oh really, stop…the honeymoon's over," Kathie quipped from behind them.

Kaycee looked up at her, still adorned in the gown, and frowned.

"Young lady, you owe your sister an apology," Ellyn said sternly, giving Kathie a look they all recognized as the last look before punishment was dealt. "You will do so now and return with Karyn to the bedroom to put it exactly where you found it."

Kathie, with a tragic look on her face, spun around, tripping over the length of the material. "Sorry, Kaycee," she called over her shoulder. "Hurry, Karyn, I'm starving. Kaycee, what ever happened to the white fur coat you wore in Duluth?"

"No chance for that, Kathie, it belonged to the studio and that's where it is."

"Too bad," Kathie said as she disappeared.

Kaycee was finally able to fill her own plate and walked into the dining room to find a place to sit. Cyndy and Tony squashed together making room for Kaycee on one end and Jimmy on the opposite end.

The giggling started soon after Kathie and Karyn joined the family at the table.

Cyndy was the worst. She thought the whole incident hilarious. "We should have known better, mom. Kaycee's going to be worse than me when it comes to marriage," she laughed. "It took Tony ages to convince me to marry him."

"What?" Tony cried in surprise. "You trapped me, remember?"

Ellyn and Stewart looked at each other.

"I've never understood why—" Jimmy broke in, speaking directly to the group for the first time since he arrived.

Everyone stopped what they were doing to listen.

"—a family that has such a great role model for marriage as your parents insist on treating the marriage vow like a hangman's noose. Cyndy was scared to death to accept Tony's proposal. He practically had to—" Jimmy paused. He looked unsure of how to continue.

"Drag me down the aisle by my hair like an old caveman would do?" Cyndy finished for Jimmy.

Laughter greeted her honest reply.

"As I remember it, yes, that would be correct," Jimmy agreed, followed by more laughter from the others.

Stewart broke in. "I would like to thank Jimmy for that generous compliment," he said after getting everyone's attention. "With two daughters married, it's nice to hear that we are good role models." He raised his glass to Tony and then Jimmy. "And I would also like to say I appreciate not being the only male at this family gathering, and I appreciate Jimmy agreeing to put up with us again so Tony and I have at least a fighting chance when it comes time to decide who has to do the dishes."

The women at the table jeered loudly at the men when they began to protest.

"Who are you trying to kid?" Karyn said when it was quiet once more. "It will be Kathie and I slaving over the dishes when all of you have gone back to the hotel."

Karyn's words brought another shocked silence. She sounded just like Kathie. Ellyn shook her head. "It happens to all of them, that streak of teenageritis." She sighed. "I was only hoping that Kathie would have moved out of the sassy stage before Karyn went into it."

"I can't believe Karyn is a chip off the old block," Cyndy said laughing. "Just like the rest of us."

41

On Saturday evening, Kaycee had made it from the limousine into the lobby of the fancy theater without feeling too nervous, but once the overhead lights flicked twice in succession, the cue to take their seats, she rushed into the ladies' room for a few needed moments of silence.

The ladies' room of the exclusive theater held couches and chairs with toiletries a woman might need along the counters. Kaycee hurried past and into the back to lean against the cold tile wall. She closed her eyes tightly. "This is it," she whispered. Her heart pounded hard against her chest.

The preliminary event inside the theater had probably already started, and after that was the movie premiere. Right now, it wasn't clear why she felt so nervous. Critics and reporters and their columns were not something new to her. She faced live audiences whenever she walked down a runway in a modeling show. What was different about this? She heard the outer door to the ladies' room open. Kaycee hastily moved to the sink and turned on the faucet. She began washing her hands, and, if need be, she could splash cold water on her flushed face.

"I can't believe he's here."

Kaycee heard a woman on the other side of the wall talking.

"How long has it been since you've seen him?" the same woman asked.

"Three years. He left three years ago," a different voice replied. The voice had a heavy southern accent. "I don't know if I can ever forgive him for leaving Texas, but my, isn't he just as handsome. He's even better looking than I remember if that's possible."

"He always was dreamy."

Kaycee swallowed hard, staring at her reflection in horror. It couldn't be Jimmy they were talking about, but how coincidental a conversation? Shamelessly, she listened, hoping to hear more.

"I still don't think I can completely forgive him for leaving me," the woman repeated with less conviction. "He never left word where he was going. He just disappeared."

"At least you know where he disappeared to. Are you going to talk to him tonight?"

"Why, darling, of course I am." A musical laugh filled the room. "I just want him to think I'm not going to, it makes it so much more interesting to keep a man off balance."

"Does he know you're here?"

"If he doesn't, it won't be for long. I plan on making my presence known to everyone within a mile of him."

Kaycee wanted to know what the women looked like. She had to know who this woman was. Kaycee walked out of the back room into the vanity area smoothing her gown. Kartiel, the Parisian designer she worked for so many years back, had designed the dress for her. Kartiel dyed the satin just the color he thought suited Kaycee best and intricately beaded it with sequined accents around the waist. The yoke of the gown was simple but dramatic. The high style of the bodice swept around the neck and then double crisscross satin straps left most of her back bare. There was no room in this creation to hide any flaws. She moved into the area covered with mirrors.

The two women barely looked at her when she walked into view.

Kaycee recognized one of them immediately and her heart sank. When she worked for the Paris designer, the company had several location jobs in Austin, Texas, modeling for George Mattson's company. George spoiled his only daughter to distraction. Virginia Mattson especially liked the designer Kartiel, so she also flew in her father's private jet to Paris whenever one of his new lines was being introduced. A tall, blond-haired beauty with extremely striking features, Virginia was the epitome of Texas aristocracy. Kaycee modeled for her on more than one occasion, but the two had never been introduced.

The woman with Virginia was a redhead and attractive as well, but a stranger to Kaycee.

"Is that a Kartiel design?" the redhead suddenly spoke to Kaycee.

Kaycee hesitated then nodded. She recognized the voice, so it was the blonde heiress that Jimmy had dated.

"Really?" Virginia broke in excitedly. "It must be from his new designs. I've never seen anything like it before." She looked at Kaycee's dress with interest.

"No, actually, it's rather old. He designed this one five years ago."

Virginia's vivid blue eyes studied Kaycee's face for a moment. "You modeled for him. I remember you now. But I still don't recall seeing this design." She flicked a bright pink lipstick over her lips while watching Kaycee in the mirror. "You haven't been with him for years. Moved on from the business, have you?"

Kaycee nodded as she moved toward the door but had no intention of enlightening them any further.

"I'll have to remind him how attractive the style of your gown is, but then, it isn't one that would work for everyone," the blond said knowledgeably.

"Definitely not," the more petite-framed redhead agreed. "I, for one, would drown in all that material."

"Enjoy the show," Kaycee said as she opened the door and departed.

Once in the hallway she gave a sigh. She couldn't compete with someone like the heiress, but she wasn't giving up on Jimmy either. With her purpose clear in her mind, she was determined to face him and be honest with him. She had to tell him how she felt and face the consequences. But for

Kaycee to reveal her feelings to Jimmy was easier said than done. Kaycee hurried down the corridor to where her family waited to meet her. Jimmy would be there, and she planned on sticking to him like glue until they left tonight.

Drake intercepted her. "Come on, Kaycee, the cast is going on stage before the show starts to be introduced. We have to hurry," he said taking her arm and leading her in the opposite direction she wanted to take.

Kaycee opened her mouth to protest, but Drake rushed her down a narrow hallway that led backstage. "Drake, slow down or I won't be presentable to go on the stage," Kaycee demanded.

He looked at her. "You must not look in your mirror enough," he told her unsympathetically and kept moving at the same pace.

An attendant was holding the stage door open. He was dressed in the uniform of the theater staff. Drake hurried her past him without a word.

They walked into a large room next to the stage where the cast members were gathered finishing their drinks and talking quietly. They all stopped to look at Kaycee and Drake before disregarding them. A few who knew Kaycee smiled or waved. With the publicity interviews, some of the individuals in the group had been on the same talk shows with her. She learned quite a bit about the other actors by listening to their interviews. Usually, the host started with Kaycee being introduced to the other cast members. The talk show hosts seemed to find it quite amusing she had worked only with Richard Dawes. The cast realized after watching the entire movie that the model was no threat to the creditability of their performances in the movie.

"Come on, everybody," a man in a tuxedo said in a stage whisper. "Let's go out on the stage in a single row. People like to see all of you, not just your heads. Mr. Dawes, if you would lead the way."

Kaycee fell into the back of the line and followed two women younger than she. They were dressed in clothes that looked more like the rock star circuit than a Richard Dawes movie. She could see Richard Dawes splendid in his black and white tuxedo. The stage was dark when the spotlights hit her. Kaycee fell into her modeling role, walking sedately across the stage. Her gown flashed like a cut diamond in the glare of the lights. The applause was loud and deafening. The cast members stopped, turned, and waved at the audience until the producer and director spoke a few words of introduction and gratitude for their attendance, and they all filed off the opposite side of the stage.

42

O nce out of the glare of the lights, Kaycee searched the crowd for her parents. They were supposed to be in the reserved section at the front. Slowly, she walked down the stairs.

"Kaycee."

She turned her head and said with a throb of relief in her voice, "Jimmy, do you know where the family is?" she asked, instinctively reaching for him. She was so glad to see him. Jimmy took her hand as they moved into the crush of bodies. The crowd was all moving forward toward the stage to see the celebrities they recognized.

"My father and I are only about ten rows back from here," he said close to her ear. "We lost your family in the rush. Come with me."

The applause continued as the cast members separated to find their seats in the theater.

Kaycee searched the dimly lit area in the sea of people in front of her and recognized no one.

"Will you sit with dad and me during the show?"

Kaycee nodded. The introduction music already was playing. Jimmy hurried her up the aisle to where his father sat. There were two empty seats next to him. Derek Zane stood to greet Kaycee. He smiled at her. The resemblance to his son still surprised her.

"Kaycee!" he said in a low voice. "It's so good to see you. I could not imagine spending my evening with a more pleasurable companion." He glanced at Jimmy. "And sorry to say, son, that includes you."

He grinned and Kaycee caught a glimpse of what Jimmy would look like in twenty years.

Jimmy shrugged and smiled. "I agree with you, dad."

Mr. Zane moved to the last seat.

Kaycee sat between the two broad shouldered men and felt small and very feminine.

"If you catch sight of your family, let me know," Jimmy whispered, his mouth close to her. "I'll make arrangements to meet them after."

She nodded.

In the light from the screen, Kaycee searched the rows of people in front of her. Much later, she spotted her mother and father. To think they were sitting in the audience with people they only read about in magazines, and her family fit in beautifully. She felt proud and lucky. Hopefully, the feeling would remain when she heard the opinions of everyone after the show. Kaycee barely watched the movie until the Palisade Head scene. Jimmy reached over and took her cold hand in his. The weight of his arm pressed reassuringly against her leg while she watched the fall. She turned her head to give him a grateful smile and leaned her cheek against the smooth material of his tuxedo.

The cliffhanger ending of the movie ended abruptly, catching them by surprise.

Kaycee sat forward in her seat ready to read the credits. Drake promised to try and have the escort wording changed. Anxiously, her eyes searched the words that rolled slowly down the screen. Kaycee glanced at Jimmy and he smiled and pointed at the audience. Kaycee turned and looked. Most of the other people in the audience were searching the credits for the names. She looked around and saw her family members were doing it, too. When she returned her attention to the screen, she saw she missed her name and Jimmy's name and the description of his duties. She had no idea if the wording had been changed. The music faded and the overhead lights came on signaling it was over.

The audience, amongst the clapping, loudly chanted, "Rick Dawes, Rick Dawes."

Richard Dawes stood and turned around to wave at the

people, who only clapped louder.

Jimmy stood and took Kaycee's hand to help her to her feet.

"Dad, I'm going to dodge over and speak to the Swanson's for Kaycee in case they leave by another door," he explained quickly.

"Do me the honor of taking my arm, Miss Swanson." Mr. Zane said, his eyes twinkling. "Let me be the first tonight to congratulate you on your performance since my son forgot to do so before leaving."

"Thank you, but to Jimmy this is all old news. He watched it all in the cold and wind. He's probably tired of it."

"Not from what he said on the drive down here. He enjoyed all of it."

Jimmy returned several minutes later. He noticed Kaycee's hand around his father's arm and raised his eyebrows at his father.

"Hey, you lost your chance when you took off," Mr. Zane said. "Now you can follow, and I get to be her personal escort."

Kaycee stiffened. Her startled eyes flew to Mr. Zane's face.

"Is that what it said?" she asked in a whisper.

He looked puzzled. "What?"

"In the credits, did it say personal escort?"

"Yes, one of the descriptions was that." He turned to smile at Jimmy. "I had no idea how involved in this production you were until I read those credits. All this time, I thought you were taking time off from work to goof around on the movie set."

Jimmy gave a short laugh. "That isn't the half of what happened up there," he said. His eyes rested on Kaycee's face.

Kaycee was silently struggling with the fact that Drake had not taken care of changing it like he said.

"Are you all right, Kaycee?" Mr. Zane asked her. "I'm

not walking too quickly, am I? I guess I'm not use to walking with a lady anymore."

"No, I'm fine, thank you," she said. A pleasant, warm feeling washed over her at his words. She thought happily, "He called me a lady. Jimmy's father thinks I'm a lady." His opinion meant a lot to her, not as much as his son's, but it was important. Neither Jimmy nor his father found anything strange about the label "personal escort," so she decided to forget it.

When they neared the exit doors leading to the lobby, a wall of bodies slowed their progress to a standstill.

"We're going to meet your parents by the marquis at the front," Jimmy told them. "Then the limo will take us directly to the restaurant."

Mr. Zane released her arm so they could press through the crowd to get out. Kaycee walked around the corner and lost sight of Mr. Zane immediately. She looked behind and found Jimmy had disappeared as well.

Alone she made her way carefully through the crowd. Her heels made her clumsy. A cleared area by the corridor looked welcoming, a place to catch her breath and figure a way out of the crowd. She stopped and looked around catching sight of the front door. With a sigh of relief, she turned then stopped.

That voice…it was that voice again, the heavy Texas drawl of Virginia Mattson. The heiress was standing right across the lobby from Kaycee, and she had her hands on Jimmy. Worse yet, he didn't look like he minded.

Kaycee stepped back. The woman from his past had shown up and was taking over. A beautiful millionaire no less, who adored everything he did and would never run away from him, would never throw temper tantrums, and would never blame him for dating her sister, and could tell the man she loved exactly how she felt.

Kaycee felt small and insignificant watching the parade of people who stopped to talk to the heiress. Virginia Mattson never moved an inch away from Jimmy. He acted perfectly content to have her hanging on his arm. Kaycee could never compete with that.

She needed to get out of there. As Kaycee stalked through the crowd with unseeing eyes, she thought acidly, "I can just hear what she's going to say to him. 'We have so much to catch up on Jimmy, darling. Please, come and stay with me, darling. I'll get my father's private jet and we can go anywhere you want, darling. I'll buy you anything you want. I'll give you anything you want.'"

Kaycee's footsteps hesitated. Wait a minute, where was Mr. Zane? He wasn't with Jimmy. He might be at the meeting place already.

The marquis was under the huge glittering chandelier hanging from the ceiling. A small crowd was clustered near it, looking anxiously around.

"There she is," Cyndy cried out loud as Kaycee hurried toward them, "I knew we hadn't missed her."

Everyone from her family was present and so was Jimmy's dad.

"Is Jimmy coming soon?" Mr. Zane asked Kaycee.

Kaycee shrugged. "I don't know. I didn't talk to him. I lost you in the crowd at the same time."

He turned to Stewart with a frown. "What should we do?"

Stewart glanced at his watch. "I don't think the time we arrive is terribly important. We can wait awhile longer."

Kaycee moved into the group closer to her father.

"Kaycee, what a great movie," Tony said. "I couldn't believe that was actually you up there on the screen. You sure had me convinced, especially on the edge of that cliff. Is it all done with mirrors or what?"

Kaycee laughed. "No, that was really me hanging off that cliff. It was terrifying."

He whistled and shook his head. "I don't know how you did it," he said.

"It was horrible watching you die, Kaycee," Karyn said from behind her. "It all looked so real, but like Tony said, I kept forgetting you weren't the girl you were playing."

Kaycee reached over to hug her little sister. "That is the nicest compliment. Thank you."

Will, who was standing next to Maris said, "We should go to the Palisade Head sometime, and you can tell us where everything happened."

"Sure," she hesitated, "but really Jimmy would probably be a better one to tour guide. He knew all of the technical stuff from the guys working up there." She turned to her father. "Dad, do you remember the family picnics we had on Palisade Head?"

Ellyn broke in. "I was the one who stopped those. It made me so nervous to have my children up on those rocks. Anything could have happened."

Maris said with a shiver, "It doesn't look like it's any safer now."

The family joined in the conversation with memories of the picnics.

Kaycee silently listened while she thought with satisfaction, so far it sounded like they liked the movie, and they believed in my character. I think that's a good enough review.

She glanced at Mr. Zane who, though listening to the conversation, continued to look for his son. He moved away from the group to peer into the lobby.

"I think I'll go back inside to see what's keeping him," he finally said when he walked back to where Stewart was standing. "You go on ahead. We'll follow."

Kaycee wanted to warn Mr. Zane that Jimmy would probably be going to the exclusive reception for the movie in a private helicopter. But she stifled the green-eyed monster eating at her insides and kept quiet.

Stewart hesitated, and then with a glance at his watch, he

nodded in agreement. "It will take us just as long to get situated. You'll probably beat us over there."

Mr. Zane smiled and waved as his long strides took him quickly out of view.

The family, after several moments of mayhem where Stewart calmly explained the situation to them, filed out the door and into the limousine that was waiting.

"Having fun, everybody?" Kaycee asked when she had moved her long skirt over so Will could fit next to her on the seat.

"This is incredible," Kathie cried enthusiastically. She held a disposable camera tightly in her lap. "At the theater, I was even offered a glass of champagne by the cutest waiter." She gave a deep sigh as she leaned back against the plush seat. "I can't wait to develop my film," she muttered dreamily.

"I'm tired," Ellyn said, giving her blond daughter a censorious eye. "Watching that movie was emotionally draining, but you did a wonderful job, Kaycee. You must be so proud. And you, Kathie, remembered to turn that waiter down, didn't you?"

Kathie yawned. "No, but daddy did."

Stewart, who was squeezed into the corner of the seat by the door, across from Kaycee, nodded to his wife. "Kathie and Karyn were with me the entire time, dear."

"Good, I couldn't see a thing in that crowd."

The conversation turned to the upcoming supper, and Kaycee watched the slow moving traffic out the window. The stress from the evening had worn her out. She felt shaky and amazingly very close to tears. She was so upset that Jimmy never reacted to things the way she thought he would. It was obvious that he still must have an attraction for the heiress. She chewed on her lower lip to hold back the tears that threatened to spill.

Too soon for Kaycee, the limousine pulled up in front of the Royale Minneapolis Hotel where the reception was being held. She opened her purse and took out her makeup mirror. She looked pale, but that could be the overhead light in the car. There was nothing to do except pinch some color in her cheeks and add some lipstick. Reluctantly, she slid across the seat. Kaycee reached up to take hold of the hand that was held out to her. She rose slowly and stood up, inhaling a deep breath of cool damp air. The smile on her lips froze when she looked into Jimmy Zane's smiling face.

"Are you okay?" he asked. His dark eyes searched hers. "You look like you've seen a ghost."

Kaycee snatched her hand free and stepped away from him. "I am fine," she said stonily, turning away so fast she slipped.

Jimmy said quickly, "Wait a minute."

Kaycee ignored him to stalk toward the front of the hotel. The members of her family were nowhere to be seen. The two of them were alone on the front sidewalk with half a dozen strangers. Jimmy grabbed her arm. "Hey!"

Kaycee turned her head to give him an icy stare. "Please release me. I have nothing to say to you."

"Kaycee Swanson, I have had enough of this," Jimmy gritted out through clenched teeth. He took a firm hold of her arm and pulled her toward the street. "You are coming with me, and we are going to have a talk, like we should have had ten years ago."

Kaycee didn't struggle. She couldn't on the slippery pavement in her high heels. As soon as he let go of her, oh, she would give him such a slap across his face and take great pleasure doing it. "Let go of me," she hissed. "Why are you here anyway?"

He ignored her and didn't let up until he reached a dark blue Jaguar parked by the curb.

"What are you doing?" she demanded, straining away. "Whose car is this?"

"My father's," he said. He held onto her as he hit the automatic opener and then almost bodily lifted her resisting figure to stuff her inside. "Don't you move," he warned. His face, lean and serious, made Kaycee pause in her plans to jump out but only until he shut the door. Then she jumped to reopen it, but he was faster. He pushed the childproof automatic lock on the keypad. By the time she figured out how to unlock the door manually, he was in the car and pulling away from the curb.

"What did you mean?" he asked. "Why am I here? I always intended to be here. Woman, you are blowing from hot to cold so fast I can't keep up with you. What exactly are you thinking anyway?"

"I'm surprised you could tear yourself away from your…uh…friend," she said, turning to stare with eyes blurred with tears, out the window.

"Friend?" Jimmy repeated puzzled for a moment. "Kaycee, you ran out on me at the movie site without a word, and now, you're going to do the same thing tonight? What in the heck is going on? This can't be back to my dating Cyndy?" He turned to give her a suspicious look. "Or is it?"

Kaycee stuck her nose in the air and turned away from him.

"Are you pouting?" he asked, giving a short laugh. "You know I almost prefer your temper tantrums. At least I knew what you were mad about because you shouted it at the top of your lungs."

Kaycee turned on him. "Good, I'm glad to hear you say that, then I feel free to say exactly what's on my mind," she snapped.

Silence fell between them. Here was her opportunity, and she couldn't think of a word to say.

"I'm waiting," Jimmy's voice sounded subdued in the quiet interior of the car as they sped along.

"Where are we going?" she asked sitting forward to look out the windshield. "This isn't the way to my apartment, you took the wrong exit."

Jimmy continued to drive. "I have no intention of going to your apartment. We are going to stay in this car and drive until everything we have to say to each other is out. This is the only way I can be absolutely sure you won't try to run away from me when you get too close to telling me the truth." He gave her a quick glance. "Understand?"

"How dare you!" Kaycee cried, truly angry. "This is like kidnapping or adultnapping or something like that. I want to go to my party," she wailed. "You turn this car around, Jimmy Zane. This isn't a bit funny."

"Do I really look like I'm planning on having fun?" he asked, impatiently maneuvering through traffic.

She sat back in her seat. What am I going to do? she wondered anxiously. "The others will be looking for us," she declared in a sulky voice.

"Let them look. They will just think we've snuck off to neck someplace."

Kaycee stared at him in surprise. "Us?"

He glanced at her out of the corner of his eye. "It's not out of the question. We've done it once already."

"What would Miss Millionaire say about that?" she retorted, thrown off balance by his remarks.

"Why do you keep asking about some other woman?" he exclaimed in exasperation. "Quit playing games, Kaycee, and come out and say what's bothering you. Who is this millionaire you think I've been with? For claiming to not be a jealous person, this is the second time you've mentioned another woman."

"Oh, all right," Kaycee shrugged. "I heard something in the bathroom tonight."

"About me?" he said, shocked. Then he grinned. "Women are talking about me in the bathroom when I don't even live in this town."

"Yes, about you, and it was a person I know who isn't

even from the state. She's from Texas."

"Texas," he repeated without sounding surprised.

Kaycee stared at his profile waiting for more of a reaction than this.

He turned to look at her. "What?" he said, raising one eyebrow at her. "I'm listening."

"That's all there is, except, well, I think you should know she sounded pretty sure about you."

"What does that imply?"

Kaycee, not wanting to sound as petty and jealous as she was feeling, chose her words carefully. "I don't really know. She just sounded like she knew you really well." Intimately was the word she wanted to throw at him. That should dent this impenetrable calm of his.

Jimmy said nothing. "So you think there's something going on between me and Ginny Mattson. Ginny knew me well?" he said. "That would be past tense, Kaycee."

"Yes, but it didn't sound like she wanted it to stay that way," Kaycee kept her voice deliberately casual. "She mentioned something about before you moved but I can't remember it all."

"Really? How disappointing. I would like to know what women talk about in the ladies' room."

Frustration filled her at having to play this cat and mouse game with him, and he sounded like he was enjoying every minute of it at her expense.

"What makes you think any of what she said referred to me? I hate to admit it, but the odds are pretty slim."

She blurted out, "Because I saw you later in the lobby letting her—"

Jimmy grinned. "Okay, I know Ginny. I haven't seen her in two years. She was a good friend.

"Miss Virginia Mattson," Kaycee supplied with a stab of bitterness in her voice. She caught his look of surprise. "Oh yes, I know of the daughter of George Connor Mattson, of

Austin, Texas. Let me see, her address is…or, wait, do you already know her address? Maybe you know all of her addresses," she declared tartly, hating how she was acting.

"You've heard of her?" Jimmy said sarcastically.

"I've modeled for her on many occasions at their mansion in Austin as well as their chateau in France and, unfortunately, I like her," she added honestly. "She wants you back, Jimmy. I heard her say it. She's a darn good catch." Kaycee fell silent. "You should really turn around. I'm sure she's going to the party."

"She asked me to the party," Jimmy said as he strummed his fingers on the steering wheel. Silence stretched in the luminescent light from the dash of the sports car, as they both stared out the windshield.

"You've left Minneapolis. If you exit on the next curve, we can turn around there."

"You want to meet Miss Mattson, yourself?"

"Don't be ridiculous," Kaycee snapped.

"I'm the one who left Texas, remember. If I had wanted to take Miss Mattson with me, I would have."

"What did you say to her invitation?" Kaycee asked without looking at him.

"I said, no thank you. I have a previous engagement."

She couldn't believe it. He had passed up the woman's great looks, great body, and millions of dollars, twice. Who is this guy? she thought wildly, but her hopes soared for the first time. "With who?"

"Who? Who else? I'm in love with somebody who is extremely dense where her feelings are concerned. I keep hoping that maybe she'll figure out the two of us are made for each other and then we can start working on us."

Kaycee gasped.

"Remember me? I'm not some star-struck guy. I knew you when." He glanced at her. "I know it sounds cliché, but I did, and you may have changed, but I found out you're still the same. For all your flash and poise, you are still the Kaycee Swanson I've known all along. Insecure, impetuous, and, at times, self-centered, but a woman with an unwavering devotion for the people she loves, and I want to be one of those people."

"And you're sure you want me?" Kaycee asked softly. "I'm no prize."

"I let you run away once, and I didn't go after you. Maybe if I had, we would already be ten years into us."

Kaycee felt hot and cold at the same time. Her head was reeling. She closed her eyes. She needed a moment to gather her thoughts.

The movement of the car proved it was not all a dream. Dressed in a gown only suitable for something out of Hollywood and driving in a Jaguar with Jimmy. There were no ghosts of old girlfriends to haunt them, even past differences were to be forgiven. She spoke her voice sounded hollow. "You know me and my flaws. If you still think you want to work on us…"

"The word is 'commitment,' Miss Swanson," he chuckled. "You leave it up to me, the answer is yes! I want to make a commitment with you."

Kaycee sat forward and exclaimed, "Do you see that?"

Jimmy instantly released the accelerator. His eyes searched the dark road in front of the car. "See what?"

"Up ahead." She leaned against the dashboard studying the night sky intently. "It is the aurora, the Northern Lights. Look! Over there above the tree line."

Jimmy stared at the sky so long he almost went off the highway. "Hey," he called, "look at that!" He swerved to straighten the car. "I don't believe it. I haven't seen the Northern Lights since leaving home."

Kaycee smiled slightly, the memory of their conversation on the cliff vivid in her mind. "Neither have I. It's beautiful," she breathed. "Just like I remember."

"It's huge. It must be because we're away from the lights of the city."

Kaycee silently watched the pillars of light vibrate against the blackness of the sky. Sometimes the stars could be seen shining brightly through as it reached its fingers high into the night. "It's like the dancing water fountain they have at theme parks. I can almost hear the strains of classical music accompanying it."

"There's only one place to watch the Northern Lights from," Jimmy stated.

"We're going back, aren't we?" Kaycee asked.

Both of them silently watched the sky as Jimmy continued along the freeway, through Duluth, and onto the highway that led up the North Shore Drive.

The car tires spun on the gravel of the road leading to Palisade Head. When he stopped the car and slowly turned off the ignition, they sat for only a moment before both of them opened their car doors and scrambled out into the night. The sky was immense on top of the cliff. Blackness surrounded them on all sides except up. The Northern Lights danced above the dark water of Lake Superior.

She shivered, and he took off his jacket to engulf her body in the folds of his suit coat.

Kaycee leaned against him, snuggling against his chest. "The children must be happy now," she said in a voice filled with contentment.

"Yes, they must, to be so busy tonight."

"Jimmy, I do love you," she told him at last. "I think I always have, but I never could see it for what it was. I've walked away from you twice, but this time I couldn't put you in the past. Thoughts of you tormented me. Are you sure, quite sure, it's me, Jimmy?"

"You have driven me crazy since the first moment we met," he admitted, and she could hear him smiling. "That was when I first fell in love with you, and I've never stopped since.

Yes, I'm sure it's you, and from now on, it's going to be us."

Shadowed in the light from the stars, he leaned his head toward her, that lock of hair falling down over his forehead. Before he could move, Kaycee reached up and gently brushed her hand across his warm skin. Her fingers tangled in the thickness of his hair like she had wanted to do so many times.

"I asked your father last night for his consent," Jimmy said softly.

"What did he say?" She leaned her head against his chest to feel the rapid pounding of his heart.

Jimmy chuckled. "He told me to put the roses back in your cheeks. He said he'd never seen you look happier than last January when we were working on the movie. He told me he suspected it was because we were together then."

"My dad's a smart guy. He's right. You are the one who makes me laugh. You are the one who makes me happy."

Jimmy lifted her chin gently. "Anything else just isn't living. Are you ready to say you'll marry me so we can go home?"

Kaycee reached up to rest her palm against his cheeks. "I will," she said simply and then kissed him. There were no doubts left between them, only hope about the future they would share together.

The Northern Lights danced merrily above them, decorating the velvet black of the sky.

Other Savage Press Books

OUTDOORS, SPORTS & RECREATION

Cool Fishing for Kids 8-85 by Frankie Paull and "Jackpine" Bob Cary
Curling Superiority! by John Gidley
Dan's Dirty Dozen by Mike Savage
The Duluth Tour Book by Jeff Cornelius
The Final Buzzer by Chris Russell

ESSAY

Battlenotes: Music of the Vietnam War by Lee Andresen
Hint of Frost, Essays on the Earth by Rusty King
Hometown Wisconsin by Marshall J. Cook
Potpourri From Kettle Land by Irene I. Luethge

FICTION

Burn Baby Burn by Mike Savage
Charleston Red by Sarah Galchus
Keeper of the Town by Don Cameron
Lake Effect by Mike Savage
Mindset by Enrico Bostone
Off Season by Marshall J.Cook
Something in the Water by Mike Savage
Summer Storm by Lori J. Glad
The Year of the Buffalo by Marshall J. Cook
Voices From the North Edge by St. Croix Writers
Walkers in the Mist by Hollis D. Normand

REGIONAL HISTORY, HUMOR, MEMOIR

Baloney on Wry by Frank Larson
eyond the Freeway by Peter J. Benzoni
Crocodile Tears and Lipstick Smears by Fran Gabino
Fair Game by Fran Gabino
Some Things You Never Forget by Clem Miller
Stop in the Name of the Law by Alex O'Kash
Superior Catholics by Cheney and Meronek
Widow of the Waves by Bev Jamison

BUSINESS

Dare to Kiss the Frog by vanHauen, Kastberg & Soden
SoundBites Second Edition by Kathy Kerchner

POETRY

Appalachian Mettle by Paul Bennett
Eraser's Edge by Phil Sneve
Gleanings from the Hillsides by E.M. Johnson
In the Heart of the Forest by Diana Randolph
I Was Night by Bekah Bevins
Moments Beautiful Moments Bright by Brett Bartholomaus
Nameless by Charlie Buckley
Pathways by Mary B. Wadzinski
Philosophical Poems by E.M. Johnson
Poems of Faith and Inspiration by E.M. Johnson
The Morning After the Night She Fell Into the Gorge by Heidi Howes
Thicker Than Water by Hazel Sangster
Treasured Thoughts by Sierra
Treasures from the Beginning of the World by Jeff Lewis

SOCIAL JUSTICE

Throwaway People: Danger in Paradise by Peter Opack

SPIRITUALITY

Life's Most Relevant Reality by Rod Kissinger, S.J.
Proverbs for the Family by Lynda Savage, M.S.
The Awakening of the Heart by Jill Downs
The Hillside Story by Pastor Thor Sorenson

OTHER BOOKS AVAILABLE FROM SP

Blueberry Summers by Lawrence Berube
Beyond the Law by Alex O'Kash
Dakota Brave by Howard Johnson
Jackpine Savages by Frank Larson
Spindrift Anthology by The Tarpon Springs Writer's Group
The Brule River, A Guide's Story by Lawrence Berube
Waterfront by Alex O'Kash

To order additional copies of

Northern Lights Magic
or
Summer Storm

visit on-line at:

www.savpress.com
and use PayPal
for immediate shipment

or call
1-800-732-3867
Visa/MasterCard Accepted

E-mail us at:
mail@savpress.com
if you have any questions.

All Savage Press books are available at all chain
and independent bookstores nationwide. Just ask
them to special order if the title is not in stock.